KRIMSON RUN

KRIMSON EMPIRE BOOK 1

JULIA HUNI

KRIMSON RUN
KRIMSON EMPIRE
BOOK 1

JULIA HUNI

Krimson Run Copyright © 2020 by Julia Huni

All rights reserved

All names, settings, characters, and incidents in this book are fictional. Any resemblance to someone you know or have read about, living or dead, is purely coincidental. This is all fiction.

The distribution of this book without permission is a theft of the author's intellectual property. If you would like permission to use material from the book (other than a short excerpt for review purposes), please contact info@juliahuni.com. Thank you for your support of the author's rights.

Cover by Deranged Doctor Designs

Edited by Mia Darien, LKJ Editing

Originally published by Craig Martelle, Inc.

Published by
IPH Media, LLC
PO Box 62
Sisters, Oregon 97759

Second US edition, August, 2023

Dedicated to
our Beta Readers who made sure the story worked, was consistent, and that we published with as few typos as humanly possible:
James Caplan
Kelly O'Donnell
John Ashmore
and especially
Micky Cocker (rest in peace, Micky.)
With special thanks to Craig Martelle, who believed in this story from the beginning.

THE TROPHANY

THE STENCH of fear permeated the shuttle bay, overriding the smell of grease and rover fuel. Hundreds of civilians huddled in clumps like sheep in a snowstorm. Men, women, and children stared at each other, silent except for the babies crying in response to their parents' tension. Even the toddlers stood still, big-eyed and quiet.

The speakers crackled, and a smooth, tenor voice spoke. "Attention, civilians! The Krimson Empire is not attacking. There's no reason for panic. Federation and Empire diplomats have decided the presence of non-combatants in the forward area is hindering negotiations. Therefore, you are being relocated to Federation Base Zauras for now."

Quinn Templeton leaned closer to her friend Tony Bergen and muttered, "Right. And my great-grandmother teaches marksmanship classes at her old-folks home."

Bergen shrugged. "My grandmother *does* teach marksmanship," he said, a hint of a laugh running under his words. "But she's an instructor at the special forces academy."

"At this time, groups one through twenty, proceed to Alpha Shuttle. Follow the blinking lights." Green lights streaked across the shuttle bay floor, creating a meter-wide path to the spacecraft near the huge hangar doors.

Quinn frowned and turned to check on her kids. Ellianne stood silent beside her, one hand gripping a pink duffel, the other clutching the corner of Quinn's jacket. Lucas slouched a few meters away with another preteen, both struggling to maintain cool attitudes. Lucas glanced around, made eye contact with Quinn, and quickly turned away, pretending he hadn't just looked for his mother.

The shuttles loaded quickly. Quinn got Ellianne and Lucas strapped in and their bags stowed. Settling back into the uncomfortable seat, she reached to pull the straps across her body.

"Templeton, Quinn!" a voice barked over the din. "Piruytha, Steve! Front and center."

Quinn jumped, her body responding to the command before her mind caught up. "Don't worry, I'll be right back," she told the kids. Pushing through the sea of people, she worked her way down the aisle to the front door of the shuttle, followed by Piruytha.

"This way." An enlisted man in the familiar gray and black camo uniform jerked his head and started across the shuttle bay, not waiting to see if they followed.

"What's going on?" Quinn asked, but both men ignored her. With a glance back at the shuttle, she trotted after them. In the ready room, she joined a dozen other grumbling passengers.

A tall man stepped to the front of the room and cleared his throat, stilling the muttered conversations. "I am Master Sergeant Kress." The man twitched his sleeve, as if to draw their attention to his rank. "We need to re-balance the load on one of our shuttles. We're moving passengers from that shuttle to the others, and we're going to make a second run to pick up the last of the civilians. You will wait here until the Alpha Shuttle returns from the transport."

"My kids are on that shuttle!" Quinn screamed, pushing back toward the door. Unfortunately, the rest of the group had the same idea. Voices rose in anger and panic, bodies pressing into each other as they all tried to push out of the room.

"Attention!" Kress's parade ground voice cut through the hubbub. The mob settled, people unconsciously stepping back and straightening up. "We know some of you have dependents on the shuttles. We also know you wouldn't want to put those dependents at risk. Many of you are former military or civilian employees—that's why you were selected. You understand the importance of good order and discipline, especially in a situation such as this. We will transport your dependents safely to the cruiser, then the first shuttle will return to retrieve you. Now, Mrs. Andretti would like to say a few words."

Quinn looked around the room, noting the faces. Most she recognized. A few surprised her. Spotting Bergen, she wormed her way through the crowd to his side. "What's the admiral's wife doing here?"

Bergen shrugged, surveying the room. "She's definitely not former military. Unless her recruiter was desperate to make quota."

A tiny, young woman with flowing blond hair, an elegant suit, and extravagant makeup raised a languid hand. "My dear fellow spouses." Her high-pitched voice making more than one listener cringe. "We must all do our duty in this trying time."

Tiffany Andretti, trophy wife of the admiral, had always irritated Quinn. She tuned out the squeaky voice and pulled out her phone to text her son.

Lucas' reply was filled with arcane acronyms and angry emojis. She showed the phone to Bergen. "I don't think Lucas is thrilled."

Bergen reached up and patted her shoulder. "They'll be fine. Melody's on your shuttle, right? She'll take care of them."

"Yeah." Relief washed over her, and she sent a quick message to her friend. Melody's immediate response relieved her further. She put the phone away and leaned closer to Bergen. "What is The Trophany droning on about?"

Bergen rolled his eyes. "Do our duty, support our service members, yada yada yada. I think she's here, so we'll believe they're coming back."

"Doesn't reassure me." Quinn snorted. "Didn't you see that pic of the admiral with the vid starlets last week? Getting rid of this one might be exactly what he's hoping for. So sad, lost in the Krimson surge. Devastating loss. On to wife number four."

Bergen bit his lip, but Quinn could see the smile.

The roar of a shuttle engine drowned out The Trophany's voice. Every head in the room snapped toward the view screen on the wall. A streak of motion, a flare of engines, and the first shuttle took off. Three more followed in quick succession.

"That's it, then," Bergen said, under the angry outburst. "Perfect tactics. Distract us while they finish the deed. Where's that Sergeant Kress?"

Quinn peered around the room. Being taller than average, she could easily see over the group. Even now, most military spouses were female. The few men, like Bergen, stood at the edges of the crowd, making her task easier. "I don't see him."

"Then let's go find him." Bergen moved casually toward the door, stopping when anyone looked in his direction. Quinn followed his lead. The door slid open, and the two made their escape.

The hallway was deserted. Bergen led the way to a door marked Control Center. He tried the handle. "That's odd. This should be locked." The door swung open.

Inside, communication equipment lined the walls, with a large view screen showing the runway. Lights blinked, static buzzed, but no one manned the workstations. "Where is everyone?" Quinn asked.

Leaving the control room, they checked the shuttle bay. Empty. Room by room, they checked the entire facility. "Even if they planned to evacuate the whole base, someone should be here to land the last shuttle," Bergen said. "Let's get back to the Control Center and find out."

Cold sweat rolled down Quinn's back. "You don't think they really left us behind, do you?" She raced down the hall behind Bergen. "I was just kidding about the admiral."

"You might have been kidding, but you might have been right."

Bergen stepped into the Control Center and shut the door behind Quinn. "You were in comm, right? See if you can raise anyone."

Quinn sat and looked over the console. "It's been ten years. A lot of this has probably changed. And I was an officer. I didn't actually work for a living."

Bergen grinned at the old joke. "I'm sure you can figure it out."

She flipped a few switches and got a login command on the screen. "The username is auto filled, but we need a password." Yanking out a drawer, she scrabbled through the contents, turning up the usual office flotsam.

"Check the underside." Bergen yanked another drawer out of the desk, tipping the contents onto the floor as he flipped it over. "Nothing. Try yours." He started rifling through the next desk.

"Bingo!" Quinn ripped a small card off the bottom of the drawer she'd just dumped. She slapped it on the desk and typed the symbols into the console. "Excellent security here."

"Welcome to Sumpter Network" flashed up on the screen. With a grin, she started flicking through the system.

A voice boomed through the speakers. "*Elrond*, this is *Sumpter Delta Shuttle*. We've achieved orbit. Boosting out in five, four, three, two, boost."

Quinn slapped the volume control. "That's Kress!"

"Roger *Sumpter Delta*. We see you. Projected rendezvous in four hours," a different voice responded.

"*Elrond* is the transport cruiser," Quinn told Bergen. "If Kress was telling the truth, the shuttle will return in eight or nine hours."

"But if he wasn't, the transport will be long gone before we know it." Bergen frowned. "Since he's on that shuttle, I doubt he was being honest with us. We need to contact someone."

Quinn scrolled through the interface and hovered over an icon. "What do we tell them? Won't they want to know how we got access to the system?"

Bergen heaved a sigh. "Quinn, there's no one here. No one. They can't get mad at us for calling for help. Besides, it's not like they can court martial you. You're a civilian." He held up a hand. "And don't worry about getting the comm tech in trouble. If they were stupid enough to leave their password on the bottom of the drawer, they deserve to get tagged."

Quinn flicked the switch. "You're right. And besides, my kids are on that shuttle. Momma is coming."

IN THE READY ROOM, the Trophany held court. The group sat in a circle, with the Trophany reigning over a pot of coffee and a tray of snacks. A woman in a pink jumpsuit held a yellow scarf, twisting it between her fingers as she spoke.

"My husband deployed to the front-line last year." Her voice trembled. "He was gone for a week. A full week!" A tear rolled down her cheek.

From the doorway, Quinn took one look and turned to make a run for it. Bergen grabbed her arm.

"Just kidding." She shook her head. "This is why I never attended the spouses' meetings. The Trophany loves to create drama over nothing. That woman is complaining about a *week* of TDY? She should try a real deployment."

Across the room, the Trophany nodded sympathetically. "Being the wife of an admiral's aide is difficult. Not as hard as being the commander's wife, but difficult." She leaned across a stone-faced woman and gripped Pink Jumpsuit's hand. "We're here for you, Marielle. We *feel* your pain. Now pass the talking scarf on."

Obediently, the young woman passed the scarf to the large, bald man on her left. The Trophany smiled, her blue-white teeth flashing. "Tell us your name."

The man rolled his eyes. "I'm Doug, and I'm good." He offered the scarf to the woman on his left.

"No, Doug, you aren't good." The Trophany placed one hand over her heart. "This is a difficult time. Open up to us. We're here for you." She beamed around the circle, and several heads nodded obediently in response.

Quinn shuddered then stepped forward, ripping the yellow scarf from Doug's fingers. "We have a problem."

The Trophany's eyes narrowed. "Quinn Templeton, if you want to join the sharing circle, find a seat." She pointed to an empty chair. "You can't just ram your way into the middle."

"I have the ranting rag, Tiffany." Quinn waved the scarf. "It's my turn to talk, and we're in trouble."

The Trophany leapt to her feet. "It's a *talking scarf*, not a ranting rag. You must honor the process!"

"Look." Quinn held the scarf aloft. "I just talked to the comm guys on the *Elrond*. They know nothing about the shuttle coming back for us. Their orders are to rendezvous with the four shuttles, take them aboard and *immediately* depart for the jump point. No waiting for us."

"Don't be ridiculous," the Trophany snapped. "My husband would never allow us to be stranded."

"Maybe you should call him, then," Quinn replied. "Because the *Elrond* isn't waiting."

THE DOOR to the Control Center opened, and Bergen paused in the entry. "The Trophany requests your presence."

Quinn, seated at the console, ignored his statement. "Tony, check this out." She waved him over, clicking on the panel. "This is a vid from the shuttle bay oversight cams." The view on the screen sped forward then slowed, Quinn narrating as she manipulated the vid. "Here we are, leaving the shuttles. They get everyone out, then they move the passengers from *Delta* to the empty seats in the other three shuttles." The view panned right and zoomed in. "Now they're loading some crates onto *Delta*. We were removed to make room for cargo!" She turned to look at Bergen, arms crossed over her chest. "What do you think they packed in there?"

Bergen's eyes narrowed. "I think we can find out easily enough." He pointed at the screen. "They left some behind."

———

TIFFANY ANDRETTI STALKED across the small office, stopping uncomfortably close to Quinn. The Trophany glared, eyes narrowed to slits, mouth set in an ugly scowl. On the doll-like woman, the effect was less than menacing, and Quinn bit back a grin. Then she sneezed as the trophy wife's perfume smothered her.

"You're telling me those sons of bitches kicked us off the shuttles to bring in a haul of gold?" The Trophany's unusually soft voice cut through the room like a scalpel.

Quinn shivered. Usually, she found the Trophany entertaining, if irritating, but maybe the woman had unexplored depths. "They loaded dozens of crates onto that shuttle, and the three that were left behind contained these, so I think that's a safe assumption." Quinn held up the lump of gold.

The Trophany snatched the heavy rock from her. "How much?"

Quinn shrugged. "I didn't count. Several dozen crates, I guess."

"No, I mean how much is it worth?" The shorter woman licked her lips and caressed the palm-sized lump of unrefined metal. "The whole shipment. How many credits?"

Quinn shook her head. "No idea."

"If I may," a light male voice cut in. The man who had been standing by the door strolled over to them. He held out his hand, and the Trophany reluctantly relinquished the gold. Medium height and weight, with brown hair, brown eyes, and tan skin—the man was completely unremarkable in every way. He took the lump and scanned it with a device he pulled from his pocket. "This piece alone is worth—" He glanced at Quinn and Bergen, then leaned down and whispered in the Trophany's ear.

The small woman's eyes widened. "Holy *chit*! No wonder they dumped us. How much did they leave behind?" She asked, licking her lips again.

"There are three crates," Quinn repeated. "But more importantly, how are we going to get off this rock? I don't care about the gold. I just want to get back to my kids. And don't forget the Krimson Empire is coming our direction."

The Trophany waved that away as a minor inconvenience. "I'll contact my husband's command and have them come get us. Where did they get all this gold?"

"I don't know!" Quinn cried. "Can we focus on getting home?"

The plain man stepped forward, turning slightly so he stood with his back to Quinn. "Rumor has it this asteroid is littered with gold. There are fifteen of us. If we can get a shuttle sent back, there should be room for—" He paused, as if calculating, then continued, "—seven standard-sized crates. More if we—" He broke off, glancing back at Quinn, then guided the Trophany toward the door. "Let's go call the Admiral."

Quinn and Bergen exchanged a glance. "Who the hell is that?" Quinn demanded after the others departed.

Bergen grimaced. "That's Perry Cisneros. Spook. Lieutenant commander, FSF, retired. Barely."

Quinn's eyes left the door through which the couple had hurried and focused on Bergen's face. "What do you mean, 'barely' retired? Recently?"

Taking her elbow, he urged her toward the exit. "A few years ago, he was, er, *encouraged* to retire in exchange for the service dropping charges. He was accused of multiple extramarital affairs with both subordinates and spouses of subordinates. There were rumors of coercion, but they said none of his victims came forward to provide testimony. The JAG let it drop on the condition Cisneros leave the service. He's here because his wife is the new personnel officer." They entered the Command Center as he spoke. "Maybe you should contact the ship again. I'm going to nose around the databases to see what other options we might have."

Quinn waved a distracted hand at him and logged into the comm system. "*Elrond*, this is Sumpter Base, do you read me?" She double-checked the protocols and sent the signal again.

"Unknown caller, identify yourself," a voice replied. The screen remained stubbornly blank.

Giving the cam a puzzled look, she flicked an icon. "This is Sumpter Base. Quinn Templeton speaking. I just talked to someone up there about an hour ago."

"Lieutenant Templeton?" The voice sounded surprised. "Is that you? What are you doing at Sumpter?"

"I was a Lieutenant a long time ago," Quinn replied, cautiously. "Who is this?"

"It's Hoover! Hal Hoover! From Port Lucretia!" The screen flared to life, showing a grinning middle-aged man with thinning hair and an FSF uniform stretched across the beginning of a beer belly. He waved enthusiastically. "I haven't seen you in years! What are you doing on Sumpter, ma'am? I thought everyone there was getting deployed?"

Quinn shook her head. "I'm a dependent now. I separated from the service years ago. We've been left behind. I've got fifteen non-combatants and no active-duty personnel here."

The man's face fell. "Damn. The guys told me someone had contacted us. The brass said everyone had been evacuated, so we thought the Empire was trying to pull something. But that's really you. You haven't been recruited by the KE as a spy, have you?" A grin flashed across his face.

"Don't even joke about that, Hoover. I'm sure this line is being monitored."

Hoover's face fell. "Sorry, ma'am."

"We got left behind. This blasted asteroid is covered in gold nuggets, and our evacuation team decided to take them instead of us.

Can you help us get out of here? The admiral's wife is with us—maybe you can get his XO on the line."

"Admiral Andretti's wife is there?" Hoover gave her an indecipherable look. "Let me see what I can do. Hang tight, L.T."

Quinn opened her mouth to remind him she was no longer an officer, but the screen went dark. She turned to Bergen, but before she could say anything, the door swung open. The Trophany and Cisneros strode in.

"We can't get through to Syed's office," the Trophany announced. "Call the ship for me."

"I just did," Quinn said. "Sergeant Hoover is going to call me back."

Cisneros eyed her. "Get them on the horn. We don't wait on a sergeant."

"He's contacting the XO," Quinn protested.

"Get them on the horn," Cisneros demanded. "They have more than one tech in the comm shack."

Quinn gritted her teeth and turned back to the console. She input the comm keys and waited. "They aren't responding, sir." Bergen grimaced at the title, and Quinn shrugged a little. Even knowing what she did about Cisneros, respect for the rank won out over distaste for the man. Besides, being in this environment took her right back to her active duty days. Old habits were hard to break.

"Then. Try. Again," Cisneros said, as if speaking to a three-year-old. "And keep trying until they respond." He turned to the Trophany and shrugged dramatically. Spotting Bergen, he barked, "You there—who are you and what are you doing?"

Bergen stared him down. "Antonin Bergen, civilian. Fiscal services. I'm looking at options."

"Fine. Anything you find, I want to know ASAP." He turned back to the Trophany. "I think we need to institute SFS protocol four-oh-one immediately."

The Trophany shook her head. "I don't know what that means. Just do whatever you need to do to get us out of here."

Bergen glanced at Quinn and back to the Trophany. "He's telling you he intends to institute martial law and place himself in command. Since he's the ranking retiree." Bergen spit out the words like they tasted bad.

"That sounds like an excellent idea." The Trophany nodded enthusiastically. "Of course, as the admiral's wife, I outrank you. But I will certainly listen to your counsel."

Quinn bit back a laugh. Like the spouses of too many senior officers, the Trophany thought she wore her husband's rank. The two of them could fight it out as far as she was concerned. She just wanted to get back to her kids.

"Sumpter Base, this is the *Elrond*." A voice boomed out of the speakers.

Quinn hit the volume button. Why did it get so loud every time it turned on? "*Elrond*, this is Sumpter. Go ahead."

"Krimson agents, depart Sumpter Base immediately. All Federation personnel have been evacuated. The facility will be purged in twelve hours." The voice sounded automated.

"Hoover!" Quinn slapped the video button, but the screen remained blank. "Hoover! You know I'm not a Krimson agent. Send someone to evacuate us. Please!" She swung her chair around. "Tiffany! Say something so they know it's you. They must have a voice match on file!"

"This is Tiffany Andretti, wife of Admiral Syed Andretti! I demand you send a shuttle to pick me up!" The Trophany's voice ratcheted up an octave as she spoke.

"Krimson agents, depart Sumpter base immediately. All Federation personnel have been evacuated. The facility will be purged in twelve hours," the mechanical voice repeated.

"They've cut reception." Quinn's shoulders drooped in defeat. "They can't hear anything we're saying."

"You're Krimson agents?" Cisneros eyes narrowed. He turned to the Trophany, pointing. "We should lock these two up. We could get a reward for capturing known Krimson agents."

"We aren't agents! Even if we were, you won't get a reward if we're all purged in twelve hours!" Quinn swung back to the console and started activating alternate protocols. "We need to get through to them."

"Step away from that console," Cisneros demanded. "I won't have a Krimson agent using Federation property."

Quinn leapt to her feet. "Are you even listening to me? We aren't agents. And, oh yeah, they're going to dust us!"

Cisneros reached out and yanked Quinn away from the desk, shoving her toward the Trophany. Then he pulled out a weapon. "Hold on to her." He swiveled back to Bergen. "You, Burger, step away from the console."

"Ah, crap." Bergen stood, casually dusting off his pants. "I hate it when this happens."

Cisneros advanced on Bergen. The shorter man waited until the colonel closed in, then with an impossibly fast movement, kicked the weapon from his hand. "Quinn, grab the gun." Another lightning move and Cisneros lay on the floor, Bergen's knee in his back.

Quinn yanked her arm away from the Trophany's limp hold and dove for the weapon. She stood and aimed it at Cisneros, feeling sick to her stomach. "I'm not sure this is a good idea, Tony."

"It's a terrible idea!" the Trophany shrieked.

"We need to act fast, and these two are doing everything in their power to get us killed." Bergen dug through a drawer, unearthing some zip ties. With a swift movement, he secured Cisneros's hands. Then he dragged the protesting colonel up into a chair and secured his feet to the console. He turned to the Trophany. "Ma'am? Are you going to help us, or shall I secure you with the colonel until we are able to obtain transport?"

The Trophany looked back and forth between Bergen and Cisneros. Her mouth opened and closed a couple times. "I just want to get off this rock." She smiled. "And I want to take some gold with me. That's not a problem, is it?"

"I DON'T LIKE THIS," Doug Parra said. "Cisneros is the ranking officer, and y'all tied him up."

While the Trophany attempted to organize her groupies, Quinn and Bergen had pulled aside a couple of retired military members.

"We tied him up because he pulled a gun on us," Quinn said. "We have a plan, but he won't listen."

"I won't be party to a mutiny." The stone-faced woman from the Trophany's sharing circle, a retired shuttle mechanic named Cynthia Horgan, crossed her arms over her chest.

"We're civilians, Cyn, so it's not actually a mutiny," Bergen said.

"I'm not a civilian, I'm retired." Cyn insisted. "So is Cisneros. And Parra. We could be called back to active duty at any time."

Bergen rolled his eyes. "But you *weren't* called to duty. You're here as civilian dependents."

"Could we stop arguing about this and get to work?" Quinn said. "My kids need me."

Cyn nodded in agreement. "Mine, too. OK, if you get us off this rock, we can sort out the mutiny issue later. And if you don't, we'll be dead. What's the plan?"

Quinn looked at Bergen, but he stared back at her. Finally, she shook her head. Obviously, Bergen wanted her to do the talking. "According to information Tony found in the databases, there's a mothballed shuttle at an outpost across the Serpian Crater. If we can get there, can you two get it up and running?"

Doug looked thoughtfully at Cyn. "I've helped recommission shuttles before. What's your background?"

While the two discussed technical details, Quinn pulled Bergen aside. "I'm not comfortable with this. Why are you making me take charge?"

"You're the ranking officer after Cisneros." He held up a hand to stop her disagreement. "Yeah, I know, you aren't an officer anymore.

But these guys are going to respond to your rank even if you don't own up to it."

"That's ridiculous! You take charge." Quinn shoved her fingers through her tangled brown hair. "I just want to get back to my kids."

"You may think it's ridiculous, but you know that's how military folks are wired." Bergen leaned back against the table behind him. "Officers are in charge. If you don't at least pretend to be the boss, you'd undermine any authority I try to exert. No one here trusts Cisneros—his bad behavior is an open secret. They know he'd abandon us in a heartbeat if he could replace us with a crate of gold. They know and trust you, so you're it. You're our best chance for survival."

"Ugh. If I wanted to lead a mission, I would have stayed on active duty." Quinn pulled a tie from her pocket and bundled her hair into a low ponytail. If she was going to have to take charge, she'd better look the part. She squared her shoulders and turned back to the two mechanics. "What do you think?"

Doug shrugged. "If it was mothballed using standard procedures, with the intention of being reactivated in an emergency, we can do it. If it was just abandoned as useless junk, we're screwed."

Quinn nodded. "It's plan C. If we get that far down the list, we're already screwed. The Trophany is supposed to be recording a message to the admiral. We'll launch it in an emergency beacon. And Steve Piruytha is still trying to raise the *Elrond*." She grabbed a piece of paper and a pen. "Tell me what you know about our fellow refugees. We're looking for anyone who could help us get off this rock."

Cyn glanced at Doug. "I've attended a few of—what did you call her? The Trophany?" She smirked. "I've attended a few of the Trophany's spouses' meetings. She seems to attract the most drama-prone among us. Marielle LeBlanc, for example." She laughed as she named the aide's wife. "Did you hear her moaning about her husband's 'deployment'? A whole week at the front!"

Quinn smiled and waved a hand. "Yeah, I heard, but that's not helpful now. Who might be useful? Anyone else with mechanical or tech skills?"

"Cassi Palacios was an EVA Specialist," Doug offered. "She just separated last year, so she's pretty up-to-date. We might need her if this shuttle is across the crater."

"Good thinking. Who else?" Quinn looked from Doug to Cyn and back. "Is that it?"

Bergen made a choking noise from his seat in front of a computer terminal. "You aren't going to believe this."

"What? More bad news?" Quinn rubbed the back of her neck.

"Maybe. We have a security specialist. Black belt in four martial arts and expert marksman in every weapon from slingshot to rocket launcher." Bergen leaned back and laughed. "She worked for the Federation Secret Service."

Quinn whistled. "They only hire the best. That means she's fast, smart, and lethal. Who is it?"

Bergen bit his lip. "Marielle LeBlanc."

"No way!" Doug laughed.

"The moaner? I would never have guessed," Quinn said.

Cyn shook her head, her expression disbelieving. "This is the second time I've been stationed with her, and I had no idea. Do you want me to talk to her?"

Quinn looked at Bergen, but he offered no advice. "Okay, here's the plan. Bergen is going to find as much info as he can on the mothballed shuttle. Parra, you work with him to come up with a launch plan. Horgan, you get Marielle on board. We definitely don't want her siding with Cisneros and taking us out. I'll talk to Cassi about the trip across the crater. We'll meet back here in—" She looked at the chronometer. "Thirty minutes."

Bergen gave Quinn a discrete thumbs up as she and Cyn left the room.

QUINN GROANED in frustration as she watched Cassi Palacios dig through a storeroom. "There are only two EVA suits? And they're both tiny! Child-sized!" She held one of the suits against her long frame. The feet dangled just below her knees.

"Most techs have their own custom suit. I wouldn't trust a station-supplied one if I had a choice." The tall blonde grimaced. "Doesn't matter, since neither of these is going to fit me. We're going to have to depend on the rovers. At least they're all vacuum-tight and fully charged. Normally I wouldn't venture across an asteroid like this without a suit, but this is not normal. I recommend you, Cyn, Doug and I take the rover and find the shuttle. Doug and Cyn can get it up and running—this suit should fit her. Bergen can stay here and organize the wives' club so they're ready to load when we arrive." She wrinkled her nose as she said, "wives' club."

"Not a fan of the Trophany?" Quinn raised a brow as she folded the EVA suit into its bag with the helmet.

"Shh! She hates that name." Cassi looked around the room, then resumed packing the second suit. "And you really don't want her angry at you. She is vicious."

Quinn rolled her eyes. "What's she going to do? Tell her husband on me? Actually, that would be great, because maybe it would get us off this rock." She led the way down a hall toward the massive garage.

Three rovers squatted in the crowded space. They looked like a cross between a deep space shipping container and a spider on roller skates. An open crate lay on the floor next to the farthest rover, and the Trophany and Cisneros stood beside it, scattering packing material as they dug through it.

"Crap!" Quinn grabbed Cassi's arm and dragged her back out of the garage. "She untied Cisneros! I'll bet that crate is full of gold. We need to find Tony. Let's get away from here!"

They ran down the hall, Quinn gabbling into her phone as she stumbled along. "Tony, Cisneros is loose. They're in the rover garage. Where are you?" They scrambled back into the EVA dressing room. "Lock the door!" she told Cassi.

Cassi looked at the panel beside the entry. "There's no lock. What do we do?"

A message pinged on Quinn's phone. "Bergen says he'll come to us, and we should stay away from them."

Cassi gave her a strange look. "You're the L.T. What do *you* think we should do?"

Quinn froze. What *did* she think they should do? "I think we should lock them both up, send the emergency beacon to the *Elrond*, and then get across the Serpian Crater and get that shuttle running. Which is basically what we already had planned, except the locking up part. Let's take those two out. Are there any weapons in here?"

Cassi smiled a little. "There's a vacuum-rated cutter." She brandished a heavy-looking device. "And a couple crowbars."

Quinn laughed and pulled Cisneros' gun from her waistband. "I think this will work better but give me one of those crowbars."

The two women gathered their weapons and headed back toward the garage. Bergen barreled into them from a cross corridor. "Where are you going?"

"We're going to get Cisneros and the Trophany out of our hair and get on with this mission." Quinn raised the gun.

Bergen smiled. "I like it. Do you need help?"

Quinn handed him the crowbar. "Look threatening and back me up."

"Drop the gun," a soft voice said, "or I will fire."

The three froze. "Crap." Bergen shook his head sadly. "Not again."

"Drop the gun and turn around slowly."

"Do it, Quinn," Bergen said. "She's serious."

Quinn carefully placed the weapon on the floor and pivoted, hands held out to her sides. Marielle LeBlanc stood in the hallway, a disrupter aimed squarely at them.

"Crap," Quinn said. "Did Cisneros get to you?"

"He's the ranking officer. Whose orders should I be following? Yours?" Marielle barked a laugh. It sounded like a chihuahua.

"He's a criminal!" Quinn protested.

"Charges were dropped." Marielle shrugged. "He's the ranking officer. Besides, Tiffany trusts him."

Quinn rubbed her forehead. "Tiffany thinks she's going to get rich. She doesn't care about anyone but Tiffany."

Marielle lifted her chin. "She's always taken care of me."

"They're in the rover garage pawing through a crate of gold," Cassi said. "If they get a shuttle down here, what do you think they're going to take with them? You or another crate of shiny metal?"

"Look, I've seen your background. You were FSS." Quinn narrowed her eyes. "You can't possibly be as gullible as you pretend. What is your game?"

The barrel of the disrupter drooped a little. "They're in the rover garage?"

"Where did you think they were?" Quinn asked.

"Tiffany said she was recording the message for the beacon. She told me to come find you and keep you out of the way so she could get her message out." She looked at three of them. "Show me."

Bergen started to move down the hall, but Marielle hollered, "Stop! Show me a surveillance feed. Can you get audio?"

"I can do that," Quinn said. "Let's go to the Control Center."

The four of them moved down the hall, Quinn leading the way with Marielle trailing behind, the weapon still aimed at them. Once inside, Marielle took up a station by the closed door and gestured with the gun. "Dial it up, Quinn."

Quinn sat at the nearest station and picked up a note leaning against the screen. With a humorless laugh, she waved it at Bergen. "Steve went to get lunch." *Civilians. No understanding of urgency.* Dropping the note, she opened the facility surveillance. "They're still in the garage. I'll unmute the audio."

The Trophany's voice grated shrilly through the speakers. "—we get more?"

On the screen, Cisneros fitted the lid back onto the crate. "I don't think it's just lying around on the surface out there, or we'd have heard about it before now. Someone must have found a vein and been mining it."

"Was this whole evacuation just a conspiracy to get the gold off the base?" Quinn whispered.

Onscreen, the Trophany continued to stare at a lump of metal in her hand. "If we could get more, well, I'd be willing to make some *sacrifices* to get it back to civilization. I'm not stupid. I know Syed is done with me—if he wasn't, he wouldn't have left me here. I need to make sure I can provide for myself." Her voice hardened. "But I don't just want to be comfortable. I want to be wealthy. I want to have enough money to *destroy* him."

"What kind of sacrifices are you talking about?" Cisneros asked.

"Why?" the Trophany snapped. "Do you know where there's more gold?"

"How badly do you want it?" Cisneros flipped the switches on the grav cart strapped to the crate. The device hummed and lifted the crate, and he shoved it toward the rover. "If we can get to that shuttle Burger mentioned, we can fill it with gold. I'll fly, you'll co-pilot, and the rest is cargo space. But you'd need to *sacrifice* your little coffee klatch."

The Trophany waved a hand. "There's a new spouses' group at every base. They're all pretty much the same." She laughed as she watched him maneuver the crate through the rover's door. "Lucky for you I don't know how to pilot a shuttle."

A smirk crossed Cisneros' face, but with his back to the Trophany, she didn't see it.

Quinn turned down the volume and looked at Marielle. "Any questions?"

"One," Marielle said. "When do I get to take her down?"

⸻

AN HOUR LATER, the group met in the rover garage. The Trophany and Cisneros had departed before Bergen and Marielle could stop them. While Doug, Cyn, and Cassi checked out the two remaining rovers, Bergen, Quinn, and Marielle brought Steve up to date.

"I have an automated hail going out every five minutes," Steve said, defensively. "I'll get a ping on my phone if anyone answers. I was hungry."

Quinn held up a hand to stem the flow of excuses. "Great. Just keep sending. Make sure the response is monitored at all times. We don't want to miss a chance at rescue because you're in the bathroom. Get one of the ladies to help you. I'm sure you can train them."

Steve stared at her as if she'd grown a second head. "But...they're civilians."

"So are you, Steve." Quinn patted his arm. "At this point, it doesn't really matter. If we don't get off this rock, we'll become the tail of some comet."

Steve blanched.

"Try not to think about it," Bergen said. "But if you get them to send a shuttle, you'll be a hero."

Steve grinned then frowned. "Oh, by the way, you got a message from some guy named Hoover."

"What? Why didn't you say so? What is it?" Quinn clenched her fists trying not to strangle Steve.

"It said—" He patted several pockets, then pulled out a scrap of paper. "L.T. Sorry. XO threatened court martial. I'll try to get a message out."

Quinn closed her eyes. No help from the *Elrond*, then. "Thanks, Steve. Get those ladies trained, will you?" Just in case. Plus, it would keep Steve out of her hair.

Steve squared his shoulders, saluted, and strode away.

Marielle rolled her eyes.

"Bad news," Cassi called as she crossed the garage. "It looks like Cisneros wanted to make sure we didn't follow them."

Quinn's shoulders tightened even more. "What did he do?"

"Come and see." Cassi led them across the room and under the boxy vehicle. She pointed upwards, where Doug and Cyn hung on their backs between open panels on the underside of the rover. Their personal grav lifters whined when they shifted position, as they threaded some kind of tubing into the vehicle.

"He didn't try very hard," Cyn called down as she worked. "He cut the life support connections. But I guess he forgot this is a rover garage. Lots of spare parts waiting to be used. We'll have this one up and running in a few minutes."

"Could this be subterfuge?" Bergen asked. "Very obvious damage so we overlook something more subtle until it's too late? They've made it clear they aren't worried about collateral damage."

"Good thought," Doug said. "I suggest we take the time to run thorough diagnostics before we leave."

"How long will that take?" Quinn asked. "They've already got an hour head-start. Of course, they plan to load all that gold and possibly pick up more along the way. Plus, they'll need to recommission the shuttle. But we need to get there before they can launch it."

Doug and Cyn muttered to each other for a few minutes. Cyn clanged a wrench against the rover's frame and swore. "I wish we knew more about the shuttle's current status. Reactivating it could take minutes or days."

Bergen cleared his throat. "Based on what I found in the files, it's almost ready to launch. It looks like they expected to need it at any time."

"Can you send those files to my profile?" Cyn asked. "I can work up a more accurate estimate."

The short man looked away, twitching his shirt cuffs. Then he turned back to them. "Sure. I'll run back to the Control Center and see if I can send you the link."

Quinn watched him go, wondering what was bothering him. Didn't he trust Cyn and Doug? She'd known him for a decade, and he'd always been upfront and helpful. Something felt off.

With a shrug, she turned to Marielle and Cassi. "Can all six of us go in the rover? Or would it be faster with fewer people?"

Cassi shook her head. "These things aren't fast. They were

designed to carry heavy loads of ore. The military-grade, like these, use that capacity for weapons. It can take one or all six of us."

"Great. Pull anything you think we might need from the third rover—spare parts, extra fuel, suits if there are any. Anything we could possibly require—move it to this one. Just in case Cisneros did something we don't detect." She turned to Marielle. "Get into the armory. Break in if you have to. We need weapons if we're going to take that shuttle away from Cisneros and the Trophany. I hope there are some left. I'm going to talk to the troops."

When Quinn reached the break room, Steve had the remaining refugees gathered in a circle. "If the phone rings, answer it. The only one who can call us is someone on this rock or the Admiral's ship. I've got the signal going to all your phones, so if someone else answers first, that's okay. But whatever you do, don't let it go to voicemail."

A slender man raised his hand. "My phone is set to 'Do not disturb'. Should I change that setting?"

Quinn closed her eyes, and took a deep breath, willing her face to remain passive. *Civilians!* Thank all the stars this lot would be staying on base rather than coming with them across the crater. She rolled her shoulders and tried to consciously relax her neck. With another deep breath, she cleared her throat.

"Thank you all for assisting Steve in this important mission." Quinn made eye contact with each of the men and women gathered around Steve. "I know none of you have been on active duty, and this could be a trying experience for you. But we have a plan in place to get us back to the *Elrond* as quickly as possible."

"Where's Tiffany?" A mousy woman—Kaiden Armitage—stomped forward. "She said the shuttle is coming back for us."

"Yeah, Tiffany said you and that Burger guy were causing trouble." Fabron Mathews tapped a finger to his chin, his eyes narrow.

Dev Singh glowered. "What kind of scheme are you trying to pull?"

"Ladies and gentlemen!" Quinn raised her voice to a parade-ground bellow. "Please, take a seat and allow me to explain our current situation."

The men and women grumbled but pulled chairs from the sharing circle into a small clump.

"Let's hear it," Dev said. "Better be good."

"As you know," Quinn began, feeling her way through the web of truth and fiction. "We were delayed to allow a 're-balancing' of the shuttles. Unfortunately, due to the *Elrond*'s current location and the, er, changing situation on the front, they will not be able to send a shuttle back for us." A shout went up. She held up a hand, waiting for the outburst to end.

"We are working remotely with SFS personnel to reactivate a shuttle that is currently in storage here at Sumpter. We are fortunate to have two retired shuttle mechanics and an EVA specialist at our disposal. I will be taking a small crew across the Serpian Crater to get the shuttle running. We'll land it here to take the rest of you on board and depart for the *Elrond*." She looked around the small group. Less information was probably better in this situation. "Any questions?"

"Where's Tiffany?" Kaiden asked again.

"Yeah, where's Tiffany? And that Cisneros guy?" Fabron demanded. "Tiff said he's in charge because he's the highest ranking."

Quinn held up a hand again to stop the barrage of questions. "One at a time. Tiffany and Colonel Cisneros have already proceeded to the shuttle to begin, uh, initial reactivation tasks. The group I am leading will join them to complete those tasks. Starting up a shuttle is not a fast and easy project. It requires the skills of many technicians. Fortunately, we have people with those skills."

She hoped.

"Who put you in charge?" Dev Singh shouted as he leapt to his feet.

Quinn smiled. "The Federation Space Force did. I was a senior grade Lieutenant before I became a dependent. When Colonel Cisneros left the base, I became the senior ranking officer."

Except she wasn't. She was just a spouse with military experience. But the only people who really knew that were busy following her orders to get the rover working. Sometimes ignorance was bliss. Or at least helpful.

Singh sat down. "Fine. What are we supposed to do?"

"Just stay calm and answer the phone," Quinn replied. "We'll be back to get you in a few hours."

"I HOPE Steve can hold it together back there." Quinn watched the rear camera view as they trundled away from the base.

"They'll be fine," Bergen said. "None of them has the gumption to pull anything, and we'll only be gone a few hours."

"We hope." Marielle fiddled with her weapon.

"If we're gone longer, we're all dead," Bergen said with a fatalistic shrug.

"Hey, Tony." Quinn leaned close to Bergen and lowered her voice. "Who's going to fly the shuttle once we get it up and running? I'm not a pilot, and I don't think any of these good folks has any real stick time, either."

Bergen smiled. "I was wondering when someone would ask that. As it happens, I have twelve hundred hours of flight time, including several hops in this exact model."

"Good." Quinn let out a breath. "I was afraid we'd have to coerce Cisneros into flying it for us. But I thought you were a money guy. When did you do all that flying?"

Bergen shrugged. "I was a transport pilot before I got into finance. Got tired of hauling cargo, so I got my degree and upgraded jobs."

"Huh." Quinn sat back in her seat. "You really are a jack of all trades."

TWO HOURS LATER, they reached the location Bergen gave them for the shuttle. "There's nothing here." Doug set the rover to idle and twisted around in his seat. "We're at the right coordinates, but I don't see anything."

"They wouldn't leave it sitting out in the open, genius." Cyn punched Doug's arm. "It's probably in some kind of underground bunker." She twisted around, too, to look at Bergen. "What do you think?"

"I copied the specs on the hangar, let me send them to you." Bergen scratched his head and poked at his phone. "It's all Krimson to me—maybe you can figure it out."

Marielle gave Bergen a strange look, then turned back to her computer console. She'd volunteered to keep an eye on Cisneros and the Trophany. Fortunately, Cassi had known how to ping the rover's locator without alerting the occupants. Marielle's screen showed a rough map of the asteroid, with the base outlined in blue and their location a pulsing green dot. Another dot, this one red, blinked a short distance away, in the craggy hills to the west of them.

"I think I can run a subterranean scan on this thing." Cassi tapped some controls. Her extensive EVA experience had also given her a working knowledge of most of the equipment in the rover. What she didn't know, Doug and Cyn had figured out.

After a moment, Cassi nodded in satisfaction and pointed to the screen beside her. "This area is hollow. We just need to figure out how to get in." She tried a few more commands and grunted happily when it pinged. "Yup, there's a door right here. Do you have any open scripts in that file?"

Cyn flicked something and grinned. "Got it!"

The forward-facing cams showed a slit opening in the hill off to their left. As they watched, it stretched wider, until it was large enough for the rover to crawl inside.

"Bogies on the move!" Marielle's voice cut through the cheers. "They're headed away from us, though. Must be looking for more loot."

The rover rumbled into the hidden hangar. Cassi did some magic on her console, and the door shut behind them.

"Is there atmo inside this space?" Quinn asked.

"No." Cassi pointed at the front screen. "But it looks like there's an accordion airlock over there. Pull up close to it—might be automated. If it's standard SFS build, it should have recognized our vehicle when we entered and—yes!"

Onscreen, a yellow-green, accordion-folded tube stretched out from the wall. As they moved closer it seemed to home in on them like some kind of alien creature scenting the atmosphere inside their rover. Quinn shuddered. She knew it was standard tech—her imagination was obviously in overdrive.

The airlock latched on to their rover with a muffled clang. Doug climbed out of the driver's seat and squeezed past the passengers to the rear of the boxy vehicle. He opened a panel near the hatch and entered some commands. With a pop and a hiss, the door swung open, cold, stale air flooding into the rover.

"Let me take point." Marielle held up a hand. She checked her disrupter then pulled out a blaster.

"You don't expect anyone to be here, do you?" Quinn asked.

Marielle smiled, grimly. "No, but better safe..."

The rest of the team trooped out of the rover, and Quinn shut the door behind her. "Can you lock that?" she asked Doug.

"I'll put a passphrase on the open sequence." He keyed in a command. "That should keep space pirates from stealing our rover." He grinned and winked.

She smiled faintly and followed him up the airlock.

When the cycle completed, the inner door opened.

"Oh, *chit*," Marielle swore.

Cisneros stood there, smiling. "Drop it." He held a blaster aimed at the Trophany's head.

Marielle laughed, hard and bitter. "I don't think so. Go ahead and shoot her. You'd just save me from having to do it."

"Marielle, how can you say such a thing?" the Trophany cried. "We're friends! Think about how we—"

"Save it, *Trophany*," Marielle sneered. "I heard you plotting with this ass-hat. You were going to leave us behind so you could fill your shuttle with gold. And now that you've realized he's going to dump your sorry butt here, you want my help?"

"What?" The Trophany pulled out of Cisneros' grip. Ignoring the gun pointed at her face, she rounded on him. "You were going to abandon me?! How dare you!?" She kicked him in the shin, the decorative steel tip of her boot cracking into the bone. Then she shoved her knee into his groin.

Cisneros jerked back, hunching over in pain. "You little—!" He slid his finger onto the trigger of his weapon, and his head exploded.

The Trophany screamed as a cloud of disintegrated blood, bone, and flesh showered over her.

Marielle flicked the safety on her blaster and holstered it. She looked at the Trophany, then cocked her fist and drove it into the other woman's face. "You owe me, bitch."

THROUGH THE INNER door of the airlock, they entered a small, rough-walled hall. A door on the left led to a tiny chamber with a cot and a sanitation pod. Three familiar, meter-high crates half-blocked the way. At the other end, another airlock led to the shuttle. Everyone carefully stepped over Cisneros' headless body, leaving it on the floor in a pile of brain dust.

"How'd you get in here?" Marielle poked the Trophany between the shoulders with her blaster. "Your rover wasn't in the garage."

The Trophany stumbled but caught herself. With her arms secured behind her back, she didn't put up much of a fight. "We got into the compound, but Perry couldn't open the shuttle. He sent the rover away on autopilot, and we waited for you." She whimpered and hunched her shoulder up by her bruised jaw.

Cyn stopped tapping on the control panel by the second airlock. "It won't cycle. It's asking for a passphrase, and it's not responding to anything in the file you sent, Tony. You got any ideas, Parra?"

Doug shook his head. "I could try some of the old ones, but they're changed every six months, minimum. We'll probably get locked out if we try too many."

Quinn banged her head softly against the wall. To have come so far and be stopped now! "The old look-under-the-drawer thing won't work here, will it, Tony? Any thoughts?"

Bergen had his phone out and was swiping through it. "I downloaded everything I could. Let me see what I've got." After a few moments of silence, he pushed around the crates. "Let me try."

"I'm already here," Cyn said. "Just read it out to me."

Bergen shook his head. "Too many weird characters. It will be easier for me to just type it in." He squeezed past the others to the hatch. Cyn stepped aside and Bergen typed into the panel, consulting his phone as he did. "Damn. Hang on." He poked the phone a couple more times and tried again. "Ah! Got it!"

With Cassi's help, Cyn donned one of the tiny EVA suits and went outside to do a preflight check while the rest of them entered the shuttle.

Bergen took a quick look at the cockpit then retired to the passenger area. "I'll let Cyn do her thing, then start the warm-up." He grabbed a water pack from the galley and dropped into a seat beside Quinn.

"Quinn," Marielle said. "Move away from Bergen. This thing has a wide range, and I don't want to take you out by accident."

Quinn looked up. Marielle had her small disrupter aimed squarely at Bergen's chest. "What are you doing?!"

"The real question is: what is Bergen doing?" Marielle asked calmly. "He's a Krimson spy."

"What? No!" Quinn stared at Marielle. "Cisneros made that up."

Marielle shook her head, her eyes never leaving Bergen. "He

thought he made it up. Funny, he was actually right, wasn't he, Bergen?"

Bergen looked from Marielle to Quinn, his eyes flicking around the room, evaluating. "You're crazy, Marielle. I'm a finance guy."

"No, you're a Krimson spy." Marielle stood in the aisle, feet apart, weapon pointed, rock-steady, at Bergen. "This isn't an SFS shuttle. It looks like one—they did a good job of mocking up one of ours. But they never expected any SFS personnel to actually get inside. Look at the inside of the door, Quinn. Emergency egress instructions written in Krimson text. The ID numbers on all the fixtures in here—chairs, vid screen, galley cabinets, water packs. Look at any of them, Quinn. They're all Krimson. And only *Bergen* could open the door. I can't believe he thought Doug and Cyn wouldn't notice."

Bergen hesitated, then shrugged. "Our shuttles are built for stealthy insertion. That means using SFS equipment anywhere an SFS technician might look. We frequently land at your bases for fuel and maintenance. But as you said, no one is supposed to come inside. Poor planning on our part, but you know, budget cuts. Getting SFS parts is not cheap."

Quinn gasped, leaping out of her chair. "You're admitting it? But I've known you for years! How can you be a Krimson spy?"

"Deep plant. I've been on the SFS payroll longer than most of their real employees. Of course, my real salary offsets the crappy pay here." Bergen leaned back in his chair, sizing up Marielle. "Here's the thing, though. I'm saving you. Your own chain of command left you here to die, but I risked my mission and my freedom to get you off this rock. I could have left without any of you." He paused, cocking his head. "I could have taken a boat-load of gold back to the Empire, too." He smiled wistfully. Then his face hardened, and he turned away from Marielle, his eyes locking onto Quinn's. "But I didn't. I'm risking it all to save fourteen civilians. Dependents of my government's enemy. Do you want to know why?" He paused.

Quinn nodded, mesmerized.

"I'm saving you because that's what we do in the *Krimson*

Empire. We value loyalty. And family. Children. Friendship. We don't leave civilians to die because it's easier than getting a divorce or because there's a pile of cash." He stood, slowly, ignoring Marielle and her gun, his eyes glued to Quinn's.

"I was sent here to provide information that would help broker peace between our people. I didn't hurt anyone. I didn't provide any information that would endanger anyone, even your military combatants. I told my handlers about the people I met here in the SFS, and that we're all really the same, and that warring with the Federation doesn't help anyone except the fat-cat defense contractors. And I'd like to think my little contribution helped pave a way for peace. I could have gotten on my shuttle, knowing I'd done my part, and flown back to my home. But that's not how we fly in the Empire. So, I'm saving you, and your friends, and your admiral's whiny wife, and even that *fontenk poerken* Cisneros, if Marielle hadn't killed him first. If you'll let me. But you're in command, Quinn. You decide."

Quinn looked from Marielle to Bergen. "He's right. He could have left us. Or killed us. But he didn't. Let's go get the others and find our families."

The Trophany's uncharacteristically meek voice floated over the seatbacks. "Can we take some gold?"

Quinn rolled her eyes. Then she thought better of it and looked a question at Bergen who grinned and nodded. "Yes, we can."

CHAPTER 1

TONY BERGEN HATED the capital city of the United Federation of Planetary Societies, but the weather always raised his spirits. Bright sunshine, but not too hot. A light breeze with a whiff of sea salt, but no trace of dead fish. He wasn't sure how the Federation managed it, but Romara's weather was always perfect.

The same could not be said for the company. Like all Federation cities, the metropolis was overrun with UFPS security. He'd counted forty-three uniformed agents and twelve undercover. None of them had taken a second look at him, so life was good.

He strode down the perfectly fabricated cobblestone street—every square meter included one stone set a half-centimeter higher or lower than the rest. The effect was meant to be charmingly random, but anyone with an eye for patterns could see the careful planning. He shook his head. It would have been cheaper—and easier—to hire humans to install the darn things. But the Federation automated everything.

Halfway down the street, he tripped over a raised stone and stumbled into a wall. That gave him a chance to glance behind without being obvious. Twenty meters back, a well-dressed couple chatted as they strolled. In a nearby alley, two children played a game involving a ball and a stick. A small, furry creature sat on a doorstep—obviously someone's pet. A pretty young blonde carried a bag of groceries toward him.

Tony's eyes narrowed. If Federation Security was watching for him, this was where they'd strike—a narrow street, nowhere to run, and few witnesses. He straightened up and strolled onward, whistling an old tune as he walked. The blonde girl smiled at him and slid her hand into her pocket.

Tony's heart rate increased. Was she reaching for a weapon? The children had disappeared. He sidestepped and glanced back. The couple had stopped talking and increased their speed, closing in with a deceptively smooth gait. Tony picked up the pace.

The girl approaching him pulled her hand out of her pocket. Something metallic glinted in the sun.

Tony flung himself sideways into a shallow doorway. A male voice roared, "Halt! Federation Security!"

With a piercing scream, the young woman dropped her groceries and her silver communications tablet. Round, green fruit bounced out of the bag, scattering across the narrow road. The pet hissed and scrambled up a drainpipe.

The well-dressed couple broke into a run and thundered past both Tony and the girl, shouting incomprehensible code as they ran. The woman's left heel pierced one of the green fruits, but she ran on, oblivious to the new ornament on her bright red shoe.

Tony stepped out of the doorway, smiling sheepishly. "That was terrifying."

"You're telling me," the girl said. "I wonder who they were after."

Tony shrugged, then crouched to help her gather the spilled fruit. "These don't look too bad." He picked up the silver device. "Here's your comtab. Good thing you have a high-density case."

"It's weathered a few drops." She took her comtab with a slight smile. "And the fruit are for a sauce, so it won't matter if they're bruised. Thanks for your help."

She rose and continued up the street. Tony slid the thin, silver chip that had been attached to the comtab into his pocket and strolled in the other direction.

QUINN TEMPLETON SAT in the hard chair, her fingers rubbing the scratches in the arm. She felt a compulsion to smooth them away as if the wood were unfired clay. She closed her eyes and clenched her hands, rubbing her frozen, bare feet together.

"You have been convicted of aiding and abetting a spy for the Krimson Empire," a voice announced.

"I didn't aid him—he rescued us!" Quinn cried. "The Federation abandoned a bunch of civilians on Fort Sumpter, and Tony rescued us. Besides, I didn't know he was an Empire spy until we were on our way home." That wasn't technically true, but she sure as hell hadn't condoned abandoning the only person who'd made any effort to save them. And neither had the rest of her crew.

She'd been arrested and locked up as soon as she'd identified herself at the military base. Tony had dropped them off at the port and flown away. He'd tried to warn them—suggested they come with him—but she was sure he was wrong. The Federation would welcome them back.

They'd welcomed her right into a high-security cell. She wondered what had happened to the rest of the group.

"You will be terminated tomorrow morning," the voice said. "You will be given a final meal this evening, after your visitor departs."

The door opened, and Quinn's head popped up. "Reggie!" She lunged toward her husband, but the chains held her in the chair.

"Quinn, what happened?" He stopped just inside the door.

"Reggie!" She stretched her hands out as far as the chains would allow. "The *Elrond* left us behind, and now they've convicted me of treason!"

"I've read the file." Reggie put his own behind his back. "And Admiral Andretti confirmed it. You worked with an enemy agent to steal equipment from a Federation base. How long have you been a Krimson spy? Did Tony recruit you? Were you a sleeper agent?"

Quinn stared at him. "We didn't steal equipment! We used it to rescue ourselves!"

"They must have planted you when you were very young." Reggie ignored her interjection. "Or maybe they killed the real Quinn Templeton, and you took her place."

"Are you insane?" Quinn demanded. "I went to the academy! You've worked with some of my classmates!"

"I've heard the Krimson Empire has some excellent plastic surgeons." Reggie shook his head. "And everyone knows they have top-rate spy training. They use hypnosis, sometimes. You probably believe you're actually Quinn Templeton."

"Yeah, that's it." Anger at his betrayal burned in her chest. "When I—I mean the real Quinn—was in the hospital giving birth to Lucas, I killed her and took her place. I can't believe you didn't notice the switch. But spying on a second-rate public affairs officer up close and personal was worth the risk."

Reggie's pale face went red, then purple. "Obviously, it was," he snarled, pounding on the door. "Did you hear that? She confessed."

"The prisoner has already been convicted," the robotic voice said. "No further evidence is required."

Quinn glared. "Why are you here, Reggie, if you think I'm a spy?"

His shoulders twitched. "I don't know. I guess I needed some closure." He shuffled his feet. "Do you need anything?"

"If you've got a pardon in your back pocket, I could use one of those."

He sighed. "If you aren't going to take this seriously, I'll go. I didn't really have time for this today, but I made time—for you."

"Gee, thanks for fitting my execution into your busy schedule." She glared at him. "I want to see the kids."

He stared back, aghast. "You want me to bring my children to death row to visit a traitor?"

"They're my kids, too!"

"Hah! Proof you're a spy! The real Quinn would never ask that," Reggie said. "Bringing them here would be politically unwise."

"Politically unwise? Is that all you care about?" Quinn's hands clenched against the chair arms. "How it will look for you? I'm so sorry. Trying to figure out how to spin this must be difficult."

"It's not doing my career any favors, that's for sure. You might have considered that before consorting with the enemy."

"For the last time, I wasn't consorting with the enemy!" Quinn screamed. "I was abandoned by your chain of command and left behind to die! And I want to see my children."

Reggie waved at the camera in the corner of the room, then pounded on the door again. "I'm done here! Let me out!"

"Please," Quinn begged. "Let me see them. Please." Her voice dropped to a whisper.

The door opened, and without another word, Reggie walked out.

Quinn whimpered, tears running down her cheeks. "I just want to say good-bye."

As soon as the door slammed shut, another behind her opened. Quinn didn't bother turning to look—only prison staff used that door.

"Time to go back to your cell," a kind voice said. "We'll get you cleaned up and order your last supper. What do you want?" An elderly woman in a starched white uniform, with "Shirley" embroidered on the chest, unlocked the manacles that held her arms and legs in place.

"I want a divorce," Quinn muttered.

"We can do that." Shirley patted her arm.

Quinn choked out a laugh and swiped her hand across her eyes. "They sent you in here alone? Aren't you worried I'll try something?"

The woman smiled. "You could try, dear, but I'm not worried." She patted Quinn's arm again. "The people I tend don't have much fight left in them."

Quinn snorted. "Really? They aren't desperate, with nothing to lose?"

"By the time they get here, they know there's no way out," Shirley said. "You saw the security when you came down. Even if you managed to kill me, there's nowhere to go. Every door requires ten-digit passcodes and retina scans. And before you suggest gouging out my eyes—the retina scanners can detect that. Come along."

The crone led Quinn around the chair to the back door. She tapped a code into the touchpad and peered into the scanner. The door slid open. The two of them stepped into a bare metal box. The doors closed, and the box descended.

"If you were really a Krimson spy, I might be worried." Shirley rocked a little on her heels. "But innocents rarely put up a fight. They can't believe this has happened to them, and they expect some kind of last-minute reprieve." She shrugged. "Of course, it never happens."

"You know I'm innocent?" Quinn cried.

"They're all innocent." Shirley chuckled. "Let's face it, real Krimson spies are much harder to catch. But the Federation needs scapegoats to parade for the public."

"If you know, why do you let it happen? How can you live with yourself?"

The woman's cheery voice turned cold. "I serve the Federation. It's not my job to question."

Quinn shivered. If she really were a Krimson spy, she'd choke Shirley out and... Her imagination ran dry. The woman was right—there was nowhere to go. Even if she escaped this prison, where would she go? What would she do? The Krimson Empire didn't have a clue she existed, so they'd be unlikely to provide sanctuary. Besides, she'd never see her kids again if she ran. Of course, she'd never see them again anyway. Her eyes burned, and tears rolled down her cheeks.

The door slid open.

"After you, dear," Shirley said. "First corridor on the—" Shirley hissed and slumped to the floor.

Someone hoisted the woman up, dragged her out of the elevator, and held her face in front of the scanner. Quinn blinked, trying to clear her eyes. The device hummed and beeped. Dragging Shirley back into the elevator, the man dumped her on the floor as the doors slid shut. The elevator began to rise. Quinn swiped the tears out of her eyes.

"Good to see you, Quinn," Tony Bergen said.

CHAPTER 2

"TONY!" Quinn threw her arms around him. "How— What—"

"In the immortal words of George Lucas, 'I'm here to rescue you,'" he quipped.

"Who?"

"Never mind." Tony crouched and pulled a miniature blaster and three knives off Shirley's body.

"Is she dead?"

"No, stunned." He gestured to her eyes, blinking angrily up at them. "She can see, hear, and breathe but is incapable of voluntary movements. Perfect for retinal scanners. You didn't happen to see her passcode, did you?"

"Yeah," Quinn said. "She didn't try to hide it."

Tony rolled Shirley over onto her stomach and zip-tied her arms behind her back. "Shirley, Shirley, Shirley. Just because they're all innocent doesn't mean you should let your guard down."

Quinn's jaw dropped. "Did you hear us talking?"

"I planted a bug on her." Tony peeled a dark hair off the back of Shirley's crisp, white uniform. He held it up. "Almost undetectable." He rolled the woman onto her back again.

Faster than Quinn's eyes could follow, Shirley's legs snapped up in a scissor movement. They locked around Tony's waist, pulling him down.

Tony slapped a hand against Shirley's leg. Sparks sizzled, and her legs thunked to the floor. He pushed himself up, shaking his head. "Nice try, Shirley." He showed Quinn a flat device in his hand. "Takes out cybernetics. Hers were programmed to take down potential escapees. They activate if the user has been incapacitated." He slid off his jacket and handed it to Quinn.

"That's why she wasn't worried about being alone with me." Quinn slid her arms into Tony's coat. "What else has she got?"

"I'm not certain, but I'd bet on tracking software, definitely a duress beacon." He rubbed his chin, glancing at Quinn. "Zip it up. Hide your filthy shirt. She's not important enough to have direct-connect comms."

"Direct-connect?" Quinn repeated. "You mean, she could call for help with her mind? That was far in the future when I was at DRiP."

Tony snorted a laugh. "I forgot you worked for the Defense Research Program. No, direct-to-the-mind connections are still science fiction. But some of the bigwigs have a comm chip installed in their jaw. It's wired into the eardrum and allows communications without an external device. You still have to talk aloud, though. It's stolen Krimson tech. But it's not cheap, so lower-level employees don't rate the upgrade. Not sure you'd want it—I've heard the Federation's post-retirement repo program is brutal."

Shirley's eyes widened.

Tony grinned at the woman on the floor. "That's right, Shirley, they take all the tech back. If you want to keep those fancy legs, you're going to have to work until you die."

The elevator slid to a halt. Quinn looked at Tony. "Now what?"

"Now we improvise." Tony hoisted Shirley to her feet.

The doors slid open. Tony staggered into the lobby, dragging Shirley with him. "Someone help me! This woman collapsed!"

Two guards rushed forward, hands on their weapons. Tony flung Shirley at them, taking them to the ground. The matron's heavy cybernetic legs held them down. "Head for the stairs!" Tony pointed across the lobby.

Two more guards stood on the far side of the security screening post, staring, dumbfounded. Tony fired two fast shots, dropping them both. They raced across the lobby to an unmarked door. "Punch in Shirley's code."

"But the retina scan—" Quinn chanced a quick look over her shoulder at the downed guards. They started to rise.

"Don't need it to go up." Tony spun and fired a shot over the guards' heads. They ducked behind Shirley's inert body.

Quinn typed the code into the system. i L 0 v E m Y J 0 b. "I hope that was sarcasm, Shirley." Blaster fire hit the wall and she ducked. The lock popped. Grabbing the handle, Quinn yanked the door open and dove through.

Tony followed, peeking around the doorjamb. "Come on, boys, give me one more chance. Yes." He fired twice and dragged the door shut behind them. Jumping to his feet, he fired a long burst at the doorknob, melting it to slag.

"That'll slow any pursuers. Go!" He pushed Quinn up the stairs.

"Are they following us?" Quinn gasped.

"Not those two."

They raced up three flights, but as Quinn rounded the corner to start up the next one, Tony grabbed her arm. "This way." Putting his weapon back into his holster, he opened the door marked with a huge "4" and strolled in.

A maze of cubicles spread out before them, set on stained beige carpet and butting against smudged tan walls. The low muttering of busy employees competed with the click-clack of keyboards. The smell of stale coffee and burnt popcorn tickled Quinn's nose.

"Where are we?" Quinn whispered.

"My old stomping grounds: Federation Accounting." Tony slipped into the nearest cubicle and grabbed a sweater. "Here, put this on."

Returning Tony's jacket, she slid on the puce polyester knit. It reminded her of Reggie's great Aunt Edna. A retired government lawyer, she still wore sweater sets and high heels at all times. Quinn wrinkled her nose at the rose perfume wafting from the sweater. It draped sloppily over her stained green top and patterned leggings.

Tony looked her over. "A little brighter than most accountants, but it should work for any brief encounters." He zipped his jacket over his shoulder holster and smiled, handing her a pile of papers. "Keep your eyes on the paper and pretend I'm fascinating. If anyone bothers us, drop the stack. But try to scatter the pages—we don't want them noticing your bare feet."

They strolled through the room, keeping their heads down. "We're going to walk across this— Numbers are in the toilet." His voice rose a little as a head popped over the nearest cubicle. "We need a complete analysis of the tax invoices for the last three quarters." He glanced at the curious man and raised his voice. "You! How are you with baseline estimates of large microdata files?"

"Uh, not— What? Sorry, I'm— There's my comm." The head disappeared.

Tony smirked. "Keep walking. There's another stairwell in the far corner."

"Tony! Tony Bergen!" A large woman sailed up a side-aisle like an interstellar cargo ship heading for the jump point. "What are you doing here? I heard you were out at Fort Sumpter! Is it true they evacuated?"

"Go," Tony muttered. "Head for the roof. I'll meet you there." He yanked half the files from Quinn's hands and pushed her onward, turning away. "Evelyn Seraseek! How long has it been?"

The woman hugged Tony. Over her shoulder, he mouthed "GO!" at Quinn.

Quinn clutched the papers to her chest and stumbled down the aisle. As she went, more and more people popped out of their cubes. The words "It's Tony—Tony Bergen!" rushed ahead of her like an unstoppable wind. Clearly, news of Tony's Krimson spy status had not reached his old friends.

When she got to the stairwell door, she turned to look. A crowd had gathered around Tony, hiding his short form. The rumble of his deep voice reached her ears, but she couldn't hear the words. A shout of laughter erupted from the crowd.

Quinn dumped the remaining papers on a table and punched in Shirley's code. She pulled the door ajar, peering around the edge. The stairwell looked and sounded deserted. With a last glance at the crowd around Tony, she slipped through the door into the silence.

She'd barely reached the sixth floor when an alarm blared. Breathing hard, Quinn redoubled her efforts and charged up the remaining steps. Pain radiated from her side, but she clutched it and staggered on. Above the ninth floor, she reached a door labeled: "Alarm! Access to roof and mechanical." Shrugging, she shoved it open. No new alarm sounded.

The door swung wide, slamming into something. A grunt followed by a thud told Quinn she'd accidentally taken out someone. One down. She peeked around the open door. "Sorry," she whispered to the unconscious man crumpled on the gravel-topped roof.

Two more men stared at her as they raced toward the stairwell, weapons drawn. They wore Federation Aviation uniforms. Quinn opened her mouth, but nothing came out.

"What's happening?" the first man demanded. The second raced to his prone companion.

"There's an escaped prisoner! I chased her up the stairs. Have you seen her?" Quinn gasped.

"She didn't come out here," the first man said. "She must be on one of the floors below. Petrovian, leave him. Let's find the escapee."

"I'll take care of your friend." Quinn put a hand to her heaving chest. "I can't believe I lost her. I need to get in shape."

"Leave this to us, ma'am," the second guard said. "You take care of Stephan."

They thundered down the stairs, and Quinn bit back a laugh. She didn't know if they discounted her because she was female, or because she looked like a middle-aged accountant, but she'd take it.

She pulled Stephan's blaster from his holster and stuck it into the back of her waistband. Then she ripped a packet of zip ties from his belt pouch and secured his arms. Pulling an embroidered handkerchief from the sweater pocket, she took a second to wipe the blood off his face before stuffing it into the guard's mouth. "Sorry about this," she whispered, dragging him around the corner of the mechanical room.

"Crap!" On the far side of the stairs, a helicopter sat, blade idling. The pilot stared through the bubble at her. His hand reached down—whether for a weapon or a radio, Quinn didn't know. "Help!" she yelled. "Guard down! Can you help me?"

The man froze, then pointed to his chest.

"Yes, you! I need help! This man is unconscious," She pulled off her borrowed sweater and draped it over the guard to hide his bound hands.

The pilot climbed out of the helicopter. "I'm not supposed to leave the helo. But I have a first aid kit here somewhere." He turned and rummaged under the seat.

Pushing down her exhaustion, Quinn padded across the roof, the gravel biting into her bare feet. She pulled the blaster out of her waistband and had it aimed squarely at the pilot when he turned around. "Set the first aid kit on the seat and step away from the copter." Desperation added steel to her voice.

The man's eyes darted from the gun to her face and back to the gun. "You— Who are you?"

"Let's chat later. I'm a little busy right now. Lie down on your stomach, with your hands on your head."

He hesitated.

She waved the blaster at him. "I haven't fired one of these lately, so if I have to shoot you, I'll probably have to do it multiple times. Just to make sure I hit you. You don't want that. Have you seen what blaster fire does to your internal organs?"

The man dove to the ground. "Please, I'm just a pilot. I don't care who you are. Leave me out of whatever this is!"

Quinn placed her knee in the middle of the man's back and grabbed his arm, wrenching it around. She pulled another zip tie from her pocket and bound his arms. Then she leaned down and whispered in his ear, "You don't care who I am? Well, I'll tell you anyway. I'm one of the innocents that the Federation convicted because the real traitors are too hard to catch." She let her weight settle on his back before getting to her feet.

The door of the stairwell slammed open, and Quinn whirled, blaster ready. When Tony's head peeked around the edge of the mechanical building, she sagged in relief. "Over here!"

Tony leapt over the unconscious guard—she hoped she hadn't permanently injured him—and trotted across the roof. "Who's your friend?"

"Pilot. Do we need him?" She jerked her head at the helo.

Tony smiled. "I can't believe you even asked."

CHAPTER 3

THE HELICOPTER SHOT UPWARD THEN RACED away from the justice building, angling across the city toward the coast. "Where are we going?" Quinn asked, gripping a handle on the dash with white-knuckled hands.

"You might not want to yank on that." Tony nodded at the handle. "It's the ejection handle."

"What?!" Quinn yanked her hands away and tucked them under her legs.

"Kidding." Tony laughed.

Quinn growled. "I have had a really crappy day. I'm about this close to hysteria." She squeezed her thumb and forefinger together and waved her hand in front of his face.

"I thought you had a pretty good day," Tony said. "You got rescued from a high-security prison by a charming and handsome man."

Quinn's hand dropped into her lap. "You're right. Thank you for getting me out. But now what? They'll probably have our faces plastered all over the six-o'clock news. Escaped Krimson spies are big ratings boosters. There's nowhere to hide."

"We aren't hiding. We're fleeing. I have a ship waiting to take us back to the Commonwealth."

"Where?" Quinn asked.

"The Commonwealth. It's what the rest of the galaxy calls us. Only you Federation types call us the Krimson Empire."

"I can't go to the Empire!" Quinn waved both hands. "My kids are here."

"We'll take them with us. Your husband sounds like a real douche. You don't want to leave them with him."

Quinn shuddered. "No. And his mother is worse. But I don't know where they are."

"During the evacuation, dependents were taken to Zauras," Tony tapped her knee, the gesture strangely calming. "After the cease-fire, they returned home with their sponsors. Reggie took them back to his mother on Hadriana."

"How did you know he's from Hadriana?"

Tony smiled. "I do my research. That's why I didn't bust you out sooner. Had to get my ducks lined up."

"What's a duck?" Quinn asked. "No, never mind. Let's go get the kids."

THE HELICOPTER LANDED on the roof of a warehouse near the port. A huge faded symbol identified the landing zone, but it obviously hadn't been used in many years. Tony shut the machine down and stowed the keys in the glovebox.

"Since I stole it, I'm not too worried about it wandering away. But as a pilot, I hate to leave it unsecured." He shook his head in mock concern. "Of course, only a trained pilot can fly one of these without crashing, so..."

"Won't they find us?" Quinn asked as Tony pulled the stairwell access door open.

"I'm sure the helo is tracked. But since there aren't legions of FPS guards closing in on us, they can't have realized we took it. Yet." He let the door shut behind them and automatic lights flashed on. After a few seconds, the strobing effect stopped and they were able to see again. "Come on."

They trotted down five flights of stairs to a door marked "Basement Access." Tony flashed a card at the reader beside the door and it popped open. He pulled it wide for Quinn, then followed her through. They entered a concrete hallway lit by red emergency lights. Dozens of conduits hung above their heads, and thick metal doors with grates in the top stood on either side.

"I'm kind of surprised you aren't being tracked." He slipped past her and led the way down a dimly lit hall.

"How do you know I'm not?" she asked in alarm.

"I scanned you in the elevator." He held out his arm, displaying a large watch-like device on his left wrist. When he rotated his arm, the screen lit up, showing a pristine mountain lake. As they walked, he tapped the device. "Scanner, comm, alerts. It even plays music."

"I had one of those," Quinn said. "But it didn't scan for bugs."

"Special app for Krimson spies." Tony nodded wisely. "That alone should have been proof you weren't one of us."

"Yeah, well, lack of enemy technology is not considered proof of innocence," Quinn muttered as she glanced at a small, dark dome mounted above the door. "Aren't you worried about cams?"

Tony shook his head. "Already taken care of. This is one of my regular bolt-holes. I don't need the Federation watching me. This cam is always glitchy." He winked.

At the end of the hallway, Tony waved his card again and unlocked another door. This one led to an underground parking garage. He led Quinn up the ramp to the back of the facility and beeped open a sleek, black car.

"Your spy-mobile?" Quinn propped a fist on one hip. "Isn't it a little on the nose?"

"It's a nice little car." He opened the passenger door for her. "But there are thousands of these on the road. We're basically invisible."

They strapped in, and Tony revved the engine.

"It sounds like a spy's car," Quinn said.

"Relax." Tony guided the car out of the garage. "No one knows we're here." He zipped into the crowded street and around the corner.

Sirens wailed and lights flashed behind them.

Quinn turned a panicked face to Tony. "How did they find us?"

"They can't have." Tony pulled the car onto the shoulder. "Stay calm. There's a sweatshirt in the back seat. That shirt is a mess."

"I can't imagine why." Quinn twisted around to snag the garment from the seat. "I've only been wearing it for three weeks."

The police car zoomed past and pulled over another black sports car right ahead of them.

Tony pulled back into traffic. "I have clean clothes for you in the safehouse. In hindsight, I guess I should have put them in the car. But I wasn't sure we'd be taking this route."

"How much of this rescue followed your plan?" Quinn asked.

Tony waved a hand. "There were many plans. But 'steal a helicopter' was not one of them. That was excellent improvisation. For a non-spy, you've got some moves."

"I don't want moves. I want my life back." Quinn bit her lip. "I'm sorry. I'm not at my best today."

"Don't worry about it. A couple weeks in prison could make a saint cranky. A saint is a holy person," he said in response to her questioning look. "Besides, I bet you're hungry. Let's get some food."

Tony swerved into the exit lane and merged onto the ramp. At the bottom, he turned right and stopped at an intersection bright with neon fast-food signs. "What'll it be? *Crispy Bucket? Monty Oh's? Burger Lord?*"

Quinn barked a humorless laugh. "I've been away from civilization for so long, I don't have a clue. I want fries and a milkshake. Other than that, I don't care."

"*Zippie Sammie* it is." He cut across all three lanes of traffic to turn left. Horns blared, but they emerged unscathed.

"*Burger Lord* would have been fine!" Quinn's fingers clamped onto the handle above the door. "You don't need to prove to me that you're a secret agent! I already believe you! Drive like a normal person!"

"I drive like an accountant." Tony pulled into the busy drive-through.

"An accountant with a death wish." Quinn glanced down at herself, making sure she wasn't obviously a fugitive. No bright orange FPS coverall or name tag that said: "hi, my spy name is...."

Tony noticed her look. "You're fine. That sweatshirt really helps. Your hair could use a brush. Or maybe just shave it off. It's really terrible. Here, take this." He reached behind her and pulled a ball cap from the seat pocket.

While Tony ordered enough food for an invasion, Quinn stared out the window, fighting off tears. A few short weeks ago, she'd been a normal military spouse. She walked her kids to school, joined the PTA, attended spouses' club meetings. Of course, the walk to school had been down three underground corridors on an asteroid outpost, and the PTA and spouses' clubs were basically the same twenty members. But it had been normal, for a military dependent.

Now she was on the run—convicted of treason and sentenced to death. All because she hadn't lain down and died on that asteroid. If she didn't have kids to protect, she'd spend the rest of her life hunting down Master Sergeant Kress and his greedy, amoral confederates.

"Here's your shake," Tony said, shaking her out of her reverie. "Strawberry, right?" He smiled and handed her a cup and a bag. "Eat that, you'll feel better."

I'll feel better when I get my kids back, Quinn thought, but she took the food and smiled her thanks at Tony.

CHAPTER 4

WITH AN ULTRA-LARGE STRAWBERRY shake and a MegaPile of fries in her stomach, Quinn fell asleep before they left the city. When the car slowed to leave the highway, she woke.

Darkness pressed against the windows, the beams of their headlights the only illumination. Something darted across the brightness, and Quinn gasped.

"Good morning." Tony shot a grin her direction. "Don't worry about the bats. They're too fast to hit."

"I lived here in Romara for three years. I'm familiar with the bats. But I haven't been this far from the city since my first assignment, and it surprised me. What time is it? And where are we?"

"It's oh-dark-twenty." Tony smothered a yawn. "We'll be at our destination soon."

"But you aren't going to tell me where that is." Quinn made it a statement.

"Never reveal the location of your safehouse," Tony replied. "Spy rule number one."

"Isn't your cover pretty much blown? Time to retire, maybe."

Tony hitched a shoulder up. "My cover is blown. But other agents might need this safehouse."

"Sure, sure." Quinn peered out the side window. The faintest hint of light glimmered in the distance. "If that's sunrise, we're in the Churia Hills."

"Impressive. I didn't know you were a geography buff. There's water in the back, if you're thirsty." He jerked a thumb over his shoulder.

She twisted around to grab a water pack from a box on the floor behind his seat. Twisting the spout, she popped it open and gulped. "I'm not a geography buff. Spent a weekend here back in the day. Eight junior officers, ten catered meals, and two bottles of Sergeant Sinister's Spiced Rum. Good times."

"That must have been before Reggie," Tony said casually.

Quinn laughed. "Oh yeah. Reggie doesn't do spiced rum. Or weekends with friends." She looked up and shrugged. "Or friends at all, really. Reggie has colleagues."

"I... *overheard* your conversation with him," Tony said after a few minutes of silence. "I always thought he was an ass, but I didn't expect him to buy into the party line."

"I thought you bugged Shirley." Quinn ignored the second comment. "She wasn't in the room."

"No, but she was listening in the next room. You don't think anything said in the justice center is private, do you?"

"I guess not." Quinn sighed. "Nothing in the Federation is private."

He pointed at the dashboard. "This car is. Full-spectrum signal blocker running at all times. The Federation doesn't even know this car exists. Well, they know it exists, but they think it's still parked in my garage in New Berlin."

"Wouldn't they have searched your garage in New Berlin?" Quinn asked. "Considering you're a known Krimson spy?"

"If they knew that garage belonged to Tony Bergen, I'm sure they would have." He smirked. "This car was purchased by Dale Engstrom, and he only drives it twice a month to visit his mother in Srandron Village."

"Of course." She laughed and shook her head. "Even with the rescue from Sumpter and the prison break here, I can't get used to the idea that you're actually a spy. I mean, we've been friends for over a decade! You've been to my kids' soccer games. How did you hide it so long? Is Tony even your real name?"

He looked at her for a few seconds, his eyes somber. "Yes, Tony is my real name. I'm trusting you with that."

"I will take it to the grave." Quinn pressed a hand to her heart. "Which, if it weren't for you, I'd be reaching in a few hours."

"Lots of Tonys in the universe." He shook off the serious mood with a laugh. "It's not like I gave you the password to my encrypted email account. Time to head up into the mountains." He spun the wheel, and the car skidded off the highway and onto a narrow road.

"We're already in the mountains."

"These are the tourist mountains. We're headed deep into the wild."

The road grew rough, and Tony focused on driving. After a short distance, they turned off onto another, narrower road. This one twisted and turned, and the growing light of dawn disappeared behind a steep slope. A few klicks later, they pulled onto a smooth paved road. It turned two more times, crawling up a hill. The car crested the top, and a beautiful villa came into view.

"That house is amazing!" Quinn gaped at the building. "How did it get built out here in the middle of nowhere?" With the sunrise, a faint glow brightened the hilltop. Trees and hills stretched for kilometers in every direction. The tile roof of the house sparkled, held up by rough stucco walls with graceful arches. A square tower stood at the back of the house, somehow looking like an interesting architectural choice rather than the security feature Quinn assumed it was.

"The Marconi family built it." Tony pulled the car into the empty carport. "Back before the cultural revolution. Everything was dropped directly from orbit. The road was added afterward."

"The Marconis?" Quinn scoffed. "They're fictional."

He laughed. "No, they're Commonwealth. They built the house

before the Federation locked down. The Marconis have been sneaking people in and out of Romara for generations." He opened the door and climbed out. "Come on."

Quinn pulled herself out of the car, her joints and muscles screaming. The race to the roof, combined with weeks of little activity, left her stiff and sore. "Are there any Marconis living here?"

"No, it's for agents transitioning in and out." Tony moved to the trunk. "It's possible another Commonwealth agent is here, but since no one is pointing a gun at us, we're probably alone." He popped the trunk and pulled out a duffle. "My go bag."

"You said you didn't expect to use this car?" Quinn's eyes narrowed. "How come you're all packed and ready to go?"

"I keep a go bag in every car." He swung it over his shoulder and led the way to an arched doorway. "And a lot of other places." He unlocked the wrought iron gate and held it open for her. After beeping the car locked, he shut the gate behind them. "Straight up this hall."

"What if you lost that key?" Quinn asked.

"If I told you that, I'd have to shoot you."

The short hallway ended in a heavy steel door painted to look like wood. Tony pressed his palm against an access-plate, then punched in a code. The door clicked. He turned the knob and eased the door open.

Lights sprang on, illuminating a short, tiled hallway with open doors on both sides. As they walked through, Quinn peeked into the rooms: laundry, bathroom, storage. At the far end, a glass door led to a luxurious kitchen.

Tony set his bag on a thick wood table and gestured to Quinn to stay put. Then he pulled his blaster and cleared the rest of the house.

At least, that was what Quinn assumed he did. She raced back to the bathroom and used the facilities. Then she stood there for a moment, wondering if she should flush.

"Quinn?" Tony called.

She flushed. After washing her hands, she headed back to the kitchen. "Sorry, couldn't wait any longer."

He shook his head, a little grin quirking his lips. "Clearly, we need to do some remedial training. You don't tinkle until the building is cleared."

She leveled a look at him. "If I'm not allowed to tinkle first thing, don't feed me an ultra-large milkshake then take me on a drive into the hinterlands. I've had two kids. My bladder ain't what it used to be."

Tony pinched the bridge of his nose. "Noted. Come on. There's a shower and clean clothes upstairs."

The second floor held two bedrooms, each with an en suite bathroom. "This closet has women's clothing." Tony ushered her into the room on the left. "The other has men's. Help yourself to whatever fits. When you're dressed, pack a bag. We want to travel light, so pick stuff that's functional."

"What else would be stashed in a spy safehouse?" Quinn asked, but Tony had already shut the door. With a shrug, she pulled open the closet door. She had assumed it would be a walk-in closet, but this? Wow.

A large room filled with rows of racks stretched out before her. The far wall was covered with drawers from floor to shoulder height. Above that, shoes filled the wall. Sports shoes, high heels, and everything in between. She wandered along the racks, her fingers trailing over the fabric. Dresses, shirts, pants, even ballgowns, all arranged by size. The drawers contained underwear—grannie panties to lacy lingerie—socks, silky stockings, workout clothes, comfy pajamas. Grabbing a bag from the shelf near the door, she located her size and stuffed in quick-dry undies and bras. Socks, in a variety of colors and yarns, soft shirts, leggings, jeans. She ignored the dress clothes, although her eyes snagged on a dramatic red number each time she passed. "Maybe someday," she whispered to the dress.

After a shower that felt like heaven, she managed to get a comb through her tangled hair. Then she padded back to the magic closet to pick out something for the day. Stretchy black jeans and a slim-fit t-shirt, topped with a funky leather jacket and mid-calf boots. She gave the red dress one last, covetous look, then grabbed her bag and carried it downstairs.

"Spies dress well," Quinn said as she descended the stairs into the living room. Huge windows looked out at the mountains, offering a gorgeous view. An enormous deck, enclosed by the house on three sides, seemed to stretch out into empty space. "Isn't this house super visible from down there?" She pointed at the distant highway.

Tony looked up from his comtab and shook his head. "Nope. This place is well camouflaged. Even if you know where to look, you can't see it. I've tried." He narrowed his eyes at her bag. "How much does that weigh?"

She shrugged. "I dunno."

"Would you be able to carry it through a crowded spaceport without stopping to rest?"

She hefted the bag. "Yeah. My shoulder might get tired. I'd prefer a wheeled bag, but there weren't any in the closet."

He laughed. "I told you to pack light. Stick it over there by the door." He nodded to the glass door leading out to the deck.

"What now?" She dropped onto the overstuffed couch.

"Now, we wait." He held up his comtab. "I've signaled for pickup, but it could be as long as a week before they get here."

"A week?" Quinn gulped. "What kind of spy network leaves you hanging for a week with the bad guys on your tail?"

"The bad guys aren't on our tail," he said. "They have no idea where we are. I've been monitoring the news, as well as some, er, *other* channels. They're watching the ports for you, and they aren't sure who your accomplice is."

"Seriously?" She stared at him. "What about your girlfriend? Evelyn Parasite, or whatever her name was. Tons of people saw you in accounting."

"Yeah, but they don't believe the rumors about me." He shrugged. "They know me as a careful, methodical man. It would never cross their minds to mention they'd seen me because they don't believe they're supposed to be looking for me. Evelyn said as much. They'll protect me. For a while."

She glared at him. "No one has any trouble believing I'm a treacherous spy."

"Well, look at you." He flipped a hand at her. "You look pretty bad-ass."

"Thanks." She rolled her eyes. "Do you know what happened to everyone else? It sounds like the Trophany testified against me, but what about the rest of the gang from Fort Sumpter? Cassi, Doug, Cyn?"

"From what I've been able to dig up, you were the scapegoat. Tiffany and the rest were let go. I'm sure the Feds are watching all of them, but no one else got arrested."

"But Marielle *killed* Cisneros!" She gestured wildly. "I didn't hurt anyone."

"I guess that narrative doesn't serve their purpose. No one has even mentioned Cisneros. It's like he never existed. His wife hasn't even mentioned him."

"She's probably glad he's gone," Quinn said. "I never did know why she married hi— Hey, how do you know what his wife's doing?"

"Quinn, Quinn, Quinn." Tony shook his head with a rueful grin. "Krimson spy, remember? I know everything that happens in the Federation."

Quinn rose and wandered around the room picking up and setting down the knickknacks laying on the tables and shelves. "What do we do now? How are we going to get to Hadriana? How will we find the kids? Where will we go once we've got them?"

"Take a deep breath, Quinn. We don't have to have everything figured out right now. We'll take this one step at a time."

As he spoke, a faint buzzing intruded on the conversation. It seemed to be coming straight toward their hideout. She spun around to face the windows and saw something high in the sky. The buzzing increased, and a small ship descended, landing on the deck. A cylindrical body hung from four struts that were connected in a square above. At each corner, a set of blades, like the helicopter, whirred. She swung back to Tony.

"What's that?"

"That's our ride." Tony jumped up. "Grab your bag." He opened the door and let her out onto the vast deck.

"You're kidding, right?" Quinn demanded. "That's a drone. Like they use to deliver groceries. That thing can't hold people!"

"It isn't, and it can." Tony locked the house behind him. He strode across the wooden deck, fiddling with his comtab. As he approached, a door popped on the side of the drone. He slung his bag into the capsule and reached for Quinn's.

"When does the real transport get here?" Quinn clutched her bag.

"I wasn't kidding." Tony stopped trying to pull the bag from her grip and climbed into the capsule. "This is our transportation. Unless you want to stay in Romara." He held out a hand.

Quinn started to reply, then shut her mouth. She'd trusted Tony this far, and he'd proven a better bet than her husband or the Federation. She handed him the bag, then climbed into the capsule. It sagged a little with her weight, then recovered. Tony pulled the door down and latched it, then he tapped his comtab.

The capsule lurched, and the rotors whined. Quinn held her breath, but they didn't plummet to their deaths. Yet.

CHAPTER 5

THE DRONE ROSE into the air, the rotors whining under the weight of two occupants and their luggage.

"We weigh a lot more than a load of groceries," Quinn said. "Are you sure this thing won't give up and fall out of the sky?"

Tony lay back on the padded mat, arms crossed under his head. "I travel this way all the time. These things are made to look—and sound—just like the package haulers, but they're specially built for transporting agents. They go as high as the rotors will take 'em, then we rendezvous with a low-orbit scoop."

"A what now?" Quinn's stomach lurched and her ears popped.

"Low-orbit scoop. We launch them from a ship. They swoop down and scoop up whatever needs scooping. In this case, us."

Quinn stared at him in horror.

"What did I do to deserve this? I keep thinking nothing could be more insane than what has already happened. And then life proves me wrong." Quinn curled up on her side, pulling her knees to her chest. "I'm going to lie here and pretend I'm back at Fort Sumpter, before the evacuation. In a few minutes, I'll wake up. I'll make lunches. I'll walk Ellianne to school, maybe argue with the Trophany.

I'll help my kids with their homework. And I'll treasure the monotony for the rest of my life."

Tony patted her shoulder. "Feel free to take a nap if you want. Drone transport is sneaky, but it isn't fast."

A GENTLE SHAKE woke Quinn before she realized she'd fallen asleep.

"Scoop in thirty seconds," Tony said. "It can be a bit jarring, so I thought I should warn you."

She rubbed her eyes and looked around the capsule. "I can't decide if I wish there were windows or if I'm grateful there aren't."

"That feeling will increase over the next few minutes." His lips twisted. "Twenty seconds."

"Shouldn't we strap in or something?" She looked around the pod but saw nothing resembling a seatbelt.

Tony gestured to the curved side of the capsule. "If you put your back to the sidewall, you can brace your feet, but it's not really necessary. It's a fairly smooth process. The unnerving part is the noise."

Quinn scrambled around and braced her feet. "Why? What does it sound—"

A harsh whistling pierced their ears, rising quickly in volume and pitch. Then a scraping and a deafening *ka-thunk!* followed by multiple loud snaps, bongs, and cracks. The whir of the rotors cut out. At the same moment, a shudder went through the capsule, as if they were a flying disk caught by a dog.

Then silence. The rising sensation resumed.

Quinn laughed shakily. "I don't know what you were worried about. That wasn't terrifying at all."

Something popped softly, and four masks drifted from the ceiling. He handed her one. "We're heading into orbit. You'll need this."

Quinn's eyes grew wide over the top of the mask as she pulled the straps tight enough to cut into her cheeks. "I don't like this."

"You've made that clear. Not much we can do about it now. Relax. Get some sleep, if you can. This takes a while."

Her ears popped several more times, and the pod grew chilly. Quinn closed her eyes, but who could sleep while being carried into orbit like a long-distance package? Her mind raced, running in circles. Every time she opened her eyes, Tony glanced up from his comtab and smiled. She managed a sickly grin and clamped her eyes shut.

"Quinn." Tony shook her shoulder. When she opened her eyes, her hair drifted away from her head, tangling in front of her.

"Almost there," Tony said.

The capsule shook and rang like a gong. Quinn clapped her hands over her ears as more thunks and bangs echoed through the tiny space. "Are we crashing?"

Without warning, the capsule door popped open. Quinn squeaked and twisted around so fast she flew up off the mat and bounced off the ceiling. Tony grabbed her arm and hauled her back down. "You can remove your mask."

A smiling young woman peeked in through the hatch. "Hey, Tony! You must be Quinn. I'm Dareen. Come on out."

"Hi." Quinn looped her arm through her duffle bag strap and pushed off the wall of the capsule. Sailing slowly through the hatch, she tucked, twisted, and rolled, ending upright near a vertical beam. She grabbed a handle and looked back at the capsule.

The drone hung within a framework—presumably the scooping device. Bare beams and struts formed a cage around the drone, with rockets attached to all four corners and a huge tank overhead. The whole thing hung from an arm attached to the roof of the cargo bay. Quinn swallowed, grateful she hadn't seen this contraption in action.

"Nice low-G moves," Dareen said as Tony followed Quinn out of the pod. "I thought Tony said you were a stay-at-home mom."

Quinn nodded. "My kids love the low-G gym. Plus, I logged a few hours in military transports." She made a mental note to ask Tony what else he'd told this woman.

Dareen nodded. "Right, former military. Come on, the captain is eager to get moving." She put a foot against the side of the capsule and pushed off. Quinn followed, matching direction and velocity easily, with Tony bringing up the rear. They sailed into an open airlock and grabbed handles.

Dareen closed the hatch behind them. "Ready?"

Quinn swung her legs until they were under her body and pushed her bag to the deck. Across the lock, Tony did the same. "Ready," they replied in unison.

"Gravity in three…two…one…engage." Dareen hit a button.

Weight pulled on Quinn's body, growing with each passing second. She bent her knees, letting her legs absorb the change.

"We run at three-quarters standard G most of the time," Dareen said. "Makes moving stuff easier. This way to the bridge." She opened the other hatch and bounded into a corridor.

Tony waved a hand. "After you."

"Do you know the captain?" she whispered.

"Yeah, we go way back." He smiled, but there was something in his tone that made Quinn nervous.

Three long strides took them to another hatch. Dareen pressed her thumb to a plate, and the door popped open. She pushed it inward. With a glance at Tony, she stepped in.

The shuttle's bridge was cramped. Two bulky seats faced the forward viewscreen with two narrow jump seats tucked in behind. A steel-haired woman turned to look over her shoulder at them. "Tony, how nice to see you again. Finally."

Tony grinned. "Nice to see you too, Gramma."

"Grandma?" Quinn whispered.

"Didn't Tony warn you?" Dareen asked. "This is kind of a family affair. We're cousins." She gestured to Tony and herself. "Gramma is the captain. Uncle Kert is maintenance and load master. My brother End takes care of communications."

Quinn leaned closer to Tony, lowering her voice. "I thought you were a Krimson agent. I was expecting a military ship."

"He *was* an agent." The older woman turned back to her controls. "But this isn't official business."

"It isn't?" Quinn's eyes darted from one woman to the other.

"No, Tony tried to go official," Dareen said. "The agency wouldn't agree to extract you. Too much political fallout if it went wrong. And no upside for the Commonwealth even if it went perfectly. So he quit and roped us into helping. Not that it took much convincing. This is where he belongs. Back with the family."

"You quit?" Quinn turned to Tony. "To rescue me?"

"Technically, I retired," Tony said. "Twenty-two years of service. You heard Dareen. The family has been after me to come back for years. You provided a face-saving excuse."

Dareen rolled her eyes. "Whatever. You're back where you belong."

Quinn looked at the younger woman. "Thank you. You took a big risk for me, and I am grateful."

Dareen waved her off. "Not a big deal. We do lots of extractions. We have an understanding with the agency. We bring out an agent when they ask, they ignore certain other activities. Like this one, for example."

Tony coughed.

Dareen laughed. "If she's going to ride with us, it's only fair she knows what she got into." She patted Quinn's arm. "Cousin Tony's ultra-patriotic and law-abiding, but that's not necessarily true for the rest of the clan."

Quinn stared at Tony, her eyes big. "I have no response to that."

Tony shook his head slowly, a grin quivering around the edges of his mouth. "I was a big disappointment, joining the Commonwealth Investigative Service. They practically disowned me as the sole white sheep of the family."

"But you've come around now, in a big way!" Darren flung her arms wide. "Prison break? Right on, Tony!"

"Don't forget stealing the helicopter," Quinn muttered, trying to hide a grin and failing.

"That was your idea." Tony ducked his head in mock humility. "I was ready to parachute to the next building."

"You mean jump off?!" Quinn's voice cracked. "I don't think so!"

"Children, time to strap in. We're *ronday-voodooing* with the ship," the older woman said. "Tony, you want to ride shotgun?"

Dareen pouted.

"Thanks, I'll stay back here and help Quinn get strapped in." He winked at his young cousin. She grinned back and climbed into the right-hand seat.

Quinn stowed her bag in a small cargo net behind Dareen's chair and folded down the jump seat. Following Tony's example, she crossed the straps over her chest and lap, latching them to a short strap between her legs. "This looks just like military transport."

Tony nodded. "There's a reason for that." He looked at the ceiling.

Quinn followed his gaze and stared. Across the roof of the shuttle, stenciled letters proclaimed: "Property of the United Federation of Planetary Societies."

"You stole this ship from the Federation?" Quinn whispered.

"No, not stole," Tony said. "The family purchased it at an auction. And added a few upgrades."

"What kind of family does extractions for the Krimson Empire, but buys equipment from the Federation?" Quinn demanded.

"The kind of family that rescued you." Tony crossed his arms, giving her a pointed look.

"Sorry, I didn't mean—"

"Docking in five…four…" Dareen called out. "…three…two…one…dock. And locked. Nice work, Gramma!"

"Thanks, sweetie, your praise is heartwarming." The old woman unlatched her restraints. "Run the shutdown. I'm going to take our guest aboard." She climbed out of the chair, moving quickly and easily. "Tony, help your cousin."

"But—"

The old woman cut him off with a look. "Help your cousin, *please*." The last word was sweetness infused with steel.

"Yes, ma'am." Tony flipped a jaunty salute.

"Come on, Quinn." The old woman reached down to grab Quinn's bag. She led the way to the airlock at the rear of the shuttle. A couple quick swipes and flicks, and the door popped open. "Welcome to the *Millennium Peregrine*."

"Peregrine?" Quinn stepped past her into the larger ship.

"Falcon has trademark issues."

"Oh. Well, thank you." Quinn swung around. "Uh, I don't know what to call you."

The woman grinned at Quinn. A gold tooth glinted. "You could call me Gramma, like this lot does. But if that's not comfortable, how about Lou?" She held out a hand to shake. "Louisa Marconi."

CHAPTER 6

"MARCONI?" Quinn gave the offered hand a quick grip. "Like the legendary, but apparently-not-fictional crime family?" She stared at the older woman. Lou was short, like Tony, but built on broad lines, giving the impression of a human steamroller. Her short, gray hair stuck out at odd angles, and her eyes had faded to a watery blue.

Lou winked. "Probably best if you don't say it like that. Some of the family are sensitive."

"*Futz*," Quinn swore.

Lou's face hardened. "We don't use language like that."

"I'm so sorry." She slapped her hand over her mouth. "You— I wasn't expecting—"

"Naw, I'm just *futzin* you!" Lou roared with laughter. She slapped Quinn on the shoulder, hard, knocking the taller woman into a bulkhead. "Come on, I'll show you where you'll stay."

The shuttle airlock connected to a narrow corridor. On the right, thick windows allowed Quinn to see the cargo hold. Stacks of boxes, barrels, and crates filled the huge space. At the end of the hall, they took a stairway up to the second level.

"Crew's quarters are above the cargo bay." Lou pointed down the hall that seemed to stretch the length of the ship. "Not very quiet, if we're loading. But if we are, everyone should be down there helping, so it's not a problem. Mess hall is down that way as well. Engine rooms beyond that."

She turned the opposite direction. "You're a passenger, so your room is up here. We have two staterooms, but no guests right now, except you. Most of the time, they're used by our 'evacuees.' The bridge is up front, of course. Couple office spaces between here and there." She opened a narrow door on the right. "This is yours for the duration."

The stateroom featured a bed, desk, chair, and small lavatory. "Showers are sonic, of course, not water. Dinner at the bell—probably about three hours from now, if Liz remembers to fix it." Lou dumped Quinn's bag on the bed.

"Liz?" Quinn asked faintly.

"My daughter, Dareen's mom. Tony's aunt. She books jobs for us. Liz's ex-husband, Maerk, is our engine guy. Dareen helps him keep this boat running."

"Did you say ex-husband'?" Quinn asked, bemused.

"Yeah, they get along better now that they ain't married." Lou checked her watch. "We got a slot in the Hadriana jump queue, so we gotta get moving. Get yourself settled in. Tony'll be in the back, I'm sure, if you need company."

Lou slapped her shoulder one more time and stomped away.

Quinn carefully shut the door, then sat down on the bed, hard. The last forty-eight hours had contained more change than she believed possible. She'd been convicted of treason, sentenced to death, abandoned by her husband, broken out of jail, and flown like cargo to a Krimson spacecraft run by a crime syndicate. She burst into tears.

THE LOUDSPEAKER CRACKLED. Quinn yawned and stretched, woken by the noise.

Lou's voice rumbled out of the speakers, static dancing along with her words. "Attention, everyone! We're next in the jump queue. Please put your tray tables in their upright and locked position! Jump commences in thirty minutes on my mark." There was a long pause. "Mark."

Quinn automatically hit the timer on her watch. Jump was typically a non-event—technology had made the process smooth as silk—but every ship Quinn had ever sailed on used the same protocols: announcing a jump in advance, securing anything that could move, including passengers, and counting down to the event. On the other side, they'd do a full-system review, verbal check-in with every section on board, and official signoff.

She located the intercom in her room, so she could report when needed. She secured her bag, straightened her bed, and looked around the room. There was nowhere to strap in, so maybe she'd better find the crew lounge.

Closing the door behind her, she headed toward the back of the ship. When she passed the stairwell, she thought she heard sounds echoing up from below. Maybe someone securing cargo. She continued down the hall, peeking through doors—and closing them—as she went. Crew lav, with multiple stalls and three sonic showers. Galley, all drawers and cabinets latched and stowed. Crew berths, she guessed, although most of those doors were already shut. The last room, a compact riot of pink paint and boy band posters, had to be Dareen's. With a grin, she slid the door shut.

At the back, near a stairway that must lead down to engineering, there was a larger room on either side of the passageway. One had a table and chairs, the other couches and video screens: the mess hall and crew lounge.

Tony waved to her from the lounge. "Come on in. There's beer in the fridge if you want one." He lifted a bottle in her direction and pointed with the other hand.

"I thought you were working?" Quinn crouched to peer inside

the small fridge. She pulled out a Romara hard cider and popped the top.

"They don't need me for jump. Besides, I've earned a rest." He patted the couch. "Come sit down."

"Shouldn't we strap in?"

Tony laughed. "No one in the real world bothers with that. It's not like we get bounced down a wormhole or shot through a—" He paused for a moment, thinking. "—a wormhole. Have you ever noticed how fictional FTL travel always involves wormholes?"

"Whereas real FTL involves wormholes." Quinn raised a brow.

"Yeah, but not those bouncy-jouncy wormholes like on the vids." He waved his hand vigorously up and down. "Real wormholeses are smooth an' quick." He tried to snap on "quick," but his fingers slid sloppily past each other. He peered at them, as if perplexed at their lack of dexterity.

"How many beers have you had?" Quinn settled down on the far end of the couch.

"Three." He tipped the bottle back and chugged the rest. "No, four." Staggering up from the couch, he dropped the bottle into a recycler and headed to the fridge.

"Maybe you should stop at four."

"No, I need these." Tony pulled another bottle from the cooler. "I don't do well with jump. Gotta cushion the system."

"Are you pulling my leg again?"

"Nope." He popped the "p" sound. Then he laughed and did it again. "*Futzy* thing for someone who travels as much as I do, but if I'm not well buzzed by the time we jump, I'll be sick for days."

"Four beers should be plenty buzzed." Quinn sipped her cider.

Dareen popped her head through the door. "Ten minutes, Tony. You good?"

Tony waved his bottle as he staggered back to the couch.

"He says he needs to drink more beer," Quinn said. "He's had four."

The girl nodded. "For a jump like this, five should be good enough. He's kind of a lightweight."

"Are you serious?"

"Deadly." Dareen nodded again. "If Tony isn't plastered, he's incapacitated for days after a jump. But if he gets drunk, he's fine. Something about the alcohol cushions his system. Gotta run." She disappeared down the corridor.

Quinn turned narrowed eyes on Tony. "My mom-radar is screaming. I think you just invented a convenient reason to drink."

"Good thing you aren't my mom." He tipped the bottle back and chugged again. "That'll do it." He smiled at Quinn, eyes half-closed, and his head fell back against the sofa.

Grabbing the nearly empty bottle from his lax fingers, Quinn carried it to the recycler and dumped it. She took a trashcan from the corner of the room and tucked it next to Tony. Then she settled back into the far end of the couch, watching her friend.

She'd known Tony for years. They met on her last assignment, about a year after Lucas was born. She'd worked in the IT department for Headquarters Strategic, stationed in the Gamma Sector. Tony had managed all their purchase orders for everything from comm pads to paperclips. At the time, he'd seemed like any other finance guy—smart, detail-oriented, not particularly adventurous. They'd connected over a shared love of ridiculous comedy, swapping notes on favorite shows whenever they met.

After Quinn left the service, they'd stayed in touch via annual holiday greetings and the occasional social media post. Then, when Reggie had been assigned to Fort Sumpter, there he was again. Still counting beans and laughing at Mr. Bean.

The revelation that he was a Krimson spy had hit Quinn out of the blue. Mild-mannered, number-loving Tony Bergen, a spy? Impossible.

She was wrong.

And not just a spy, but a member of a crime family as well. What had she gotten herself into? It wasn't like she had a choice, though.

He hadn't said, "Come with me if you want to live," but it was the solid truth. Without Tony and his terrifying family, she'd be facing a firing squad right now.

Instead, they were on their way to Hadriana to liberate her children. She wondered, briefly, what the Marconi family would expect from her in return. The mafia didn't do extractions out of the goodness of their hearts. Not only had they saved her from death row, but now they were helping her kidnap her children. What kind of favors would she owe?

She took a deep breath, forcing the air out of her lungs. It didn't matter. She would do anything to protect her children. Leaving them with Reggie was out of the question. He'd proven he would abandon her at the first sign of trouble—could she expect any less for their kids? And she wouldn't leave them with his mother in any circumstances. She'd been protecting them from Gretmar LaRaine for their entire lives. A little thing like a death sentence wasn't going to stop her now.

CHAPTER 7

LOU'S VOICE crackled through the comm. "Jump in ten seconds. Nine...eight..."

Quinn settled her butt deeper into the soft couch. Jumping without any restraints made her nervous. She gripped a fold of the armrest fabric. At the other end, Tony snored gently, his head lolling on his shoulder. After the jump, she'd lay him down so he didn't get a crick in his neck. She closed her eyes.

"...two...one...jump."

They said jump felt different for everyone. For Quinn, it felt like an electric buzz zapping every cell in her body. Afterward, her skin felt sensitive, as if she'd gotten sunburned all over. It wasn't exactly pleasant, but the effects were short-lived. And better than the debilitating response some people experienced.

"Jump complete," Lou announced. "Navigation shows us in the Hadriana system, as plotted. Sections, report."

"Weapons systems nominal," a female voice reported through the intercom. That must be Liz.

"Engineering is green," Dareen said.

One by one, the rest of the crew reported in: Kert in maintenance,

End in comms, Stene in cargo. At least they took this part of the jump seriously.

"This is the lounge. We're green," Tony said, his voice even and clipped.

Quinn's eyes flew open. The other end of the couch was empty.

"Over here," he said from behind her.

She spun around. He stood near the door, his finger still hovering near the comm panel.

"You sound sober," Quinn said slowly. "You didn't really drink five beers, did you?"

Tony shrugged. "I think it was five. I sometimes lose count after the third or fourth one, to be honest."

"But— What the heck?" Quinn spluttered.

He shrugged again. "Jump sobers me up. Strange but true. Not even a hangover. It's basically the only time I drink."

"Now the mom-meter is seriously pegged."

"I am the last one to question the mom-meter," Tony said. "But this is absolutely true. If I don't drink, I'm out for days. If I get drunk, I'm fine, and the jump dries me out. Chalk it up to the mysteries of the universe."

She pondered him for a few minutes. No sign of the little quirk at the corner of his mouth that indicated he was yanking her chain.

"Seriously. Look it up online. It's a known preventative for some forms of jump sickness."

"Still seems like a pretty convenient way to get out of work." Quinn shook her head. "But I suppose it's possible. My sister gets migraines from jump. Maybe she should try that."

"Couldn't hurt." Tony slid the door open. "Well, I suppose it could. But it's still worth a try. Come on, let's go talk to Lou."

"Tony." Quinn followed him toward the bridge. "What's all this going to cost me?"

"What? The trip to Hadriana?" Tony glanced over his shoulder but continued down the corridor. "There's no charge."

"Tony," she repeated his name, more urgently.

He stopped, turning to look at her.

"Your family are the Marconis." She glanced around, knowing someone must be listening. There were undoubtedly microphones all over this boat. "The Marconis aren't exactly known for, uh, charity work."

He laughed. "You watch too many movies." He leaned in closer. "Don't tell Lou I told you this, but 'the Marconis' aren't what you've heard. That name gets the blame for everything bad that happens in the Federation. In reality, there are many other families and ships doing the same kind of work. Kind of an underground network. For some reason, it all gets attributed to 'the Marconis.' Easy scapegoat, I guess. We know the Federation is good at that."

"But I don't want to owe 'unspecified future favors' to—" Quinn started.

"This one's on me. I spread around some of that Sumpter gold and called in a few favors. Lou was happy to help—you brought the prodigal son back to the bosom of his family. A couple extractions are a small price to pay for that." He turned and walked away, whistling a cheerful tune.

Quinn swallowed her words, and her uneasiness, and followed him to the bridge.

The bridge of the *Millennium Peregrine* was spacious for a ship this size. Two chairs faced the forward viewscreens, with panels of controls laid out before them. Another station took up the back of the room, with enough space to hold a small dance in between.

Lou spun the left chair around as they entered. "Hadriana, as requested." She gestured at the screens. A blue-green world lay before them, with traffic patterns plotted in bright-colored lines.

"Three days ago, your kids were on the family estate." Tony flicked the screen. A bright green star bloomed and faded to a pulsing dot. "We'll check the net to see if they've moved."

"It's racing season," Quinn said. "Gretmar will stay in the country until that's over."

"Gretmar?" Lou asked.

"Quinn's mother-in-law," Tony answered when it was clear Quinn wouldn't. "Wealthy socialite. Lives on the family estate during racing season, then moves into town for the social whirl. Travels the rest of the time, although she stays on the planet."

"Fortunately for me, she doesn't do well with jump, either," Quinn said. "I will not be sharing your secret with her."

Tony cracked a smile. "It only works for the pure of heart."

Lou snorted.

"I'll check with my contacts," Tony said. "I want to make sure she hasn't altered her usual schedule."

"You clearly don't know Gretmar." Quinn propped a fist on one hip. "She alters her schedule for no one."

"Not even for her treasonous, prison-escapee daughter-in-law?" Lou jerked her head at Quinn.

"Especially not for me," Quinn said. "I have no doubt she's beefed up security on the estate. But there's no way she'd let me disrupt her life more than that."

"I've got someone on-site." Tony sat in the chair at the back of the compartment. "I'll check in with them." He pulled on a pair of old-fashioned earphones.

"Have a seat." Lou pointed to the co-pilot's chair.

Quinn sat, eyeing the old woman nervously.

"Don't tell the others—" Lou leaned closer, lowering her voice. "But Tony is my favorite. I'd do anything for him." She sat back, giving Quinn a hard-eyed stare. "He wants to help you, so I'll help you. But don't think for a second that I'm doing *you* any favors. It's all for him. And if I have to choose his welfare over yours, you know who's going to win."

Quinn watched the woman warily. "Understood. Family first is a sentiment I can get behind."

Lou's lips twitched. "That kinda talk usually scares the crap out of people."

"There is no crap left to be scared out of me," Quinn said. "And leaving my kids with Gretmar frightens me more than you do. I will do whatever it takes to get them out."

"I like you," Lou said with a nod. "Smart, strong, determined. I think we'll work well together."

Before Quinn could think of a reply, Tony slid his chair back on its rails and pulled off his headphones. "Confirmed. The kids are still at LaRaine Estates. Security has been doubled, but they're just rent-a-cops. Your husband is there, too."

"Ex-husband," Quinn said. "At least, you should be granted an automatic divorce if your spouse abandons you on death row."

"I will not argue that," Lou said. "Of course, they can't take your house and your ship if they're dead."

Quinn blinked at Lou. Was she saying Quinn should kill Reggie? Or that she sympathized with Reggie's decision? Or maybe that Lou had bumped off her own spouse? Who was this woman?

Did Quinn really want to know?

Lou smiled sweetly. "Let's go get those kids."

DAREEN TOOK THEM DIRTSIDE. She piloted the shuttle with expert flair, showing Quinn the basics as they went. "If you're going to be with us for very long, you need to learn to fly a shuttle. Mandatory family requirement. Of course, these things almost fly themselves—if you don't try anything fancy."

"I had basic pilot training in the academy." Quinn watched the girl's fingers fly over the dash. "But that was a long time ago. And we used a T-98 simulator. No real stick time."

Dareen grinned and hit the auto-land icon. "We'll get you up to speed in a few weeks." She landed the shuttle on a small runway at LaRaine Station. The town had been started by Gretmar's ancestors, and many of the local businesses still bore the family name. If rumors were to be believed, the town paid a hefty annual fee for the privilege, but no one would dare change the name and anger the matriarch.

"Go back to the ship," Tony told the girl as he and Quinn gathered their things. "We'll call when we're ready to leave. I don't want you sitting here attracting attention."

Dareen looked pointedly around the small, empty landing strip. A single building at the side contained maintenance and operational offices. An opaque force-fence surrounded the entire field, hiding the surrounding town from view and making the building the only exit point. "More attention than I've already drawn, you mean?"

"Exactly." Tony picked up his small bag and jerked his head at Quinn. "Let's go check in at customs."

"Tell me again why we didn't land on the front lawn?" Quinn followed the short man across the apron. "Grab the kids and run. Or since we're sneaking in, why didn't we land at the larger port? That's where Reggie and I always landed."

"That would have attracted too much attention. Those were commercial flights. Small shuttles land here. It doesn't look like it, but this is actually a busy little place."

"But surely she has people watching for me," Quinn said. "She must know I'd come to get my kids."

"Exactly. We probably can't land anywhere on this mudball without attracting her attention, so why bother trying?"

CHAPTER 8

IGNORING QUINN'S OUTRAGED GASP, Tony stepped up onto the narrow porch.

She grabbed his arm. "What are you talking about?"

"Later." He pulled open the door and led the way inside.

Polished wood floors stretched out before them, shining and bare. There was no furniture, just a big empty space with a frosted window and a door in the far wall. Amateur-looking paintings hung on the walls, illuminated by carefully placed spotlights. Quinn didn't need to look at the gold plates to know they were Gretmar's mother's work—the woman had been as prolific as she was untalented, and her *art* graced every public building in the town. The overall effect was more cut-rate museum than customs hall. Quinn's boot heels clicked against the floor as she walked, echoing through the massive room. Tony moved silently at her side.

When they reached the window, it slid open. A thin man with a pinched face and bushy eyebrows peered at them over his half-moon glasses. "Welcome to Hadriana. This is LaRaine Station. Anything to declare?"

"Some sales samples." Tony swung his bag up onto the counter. "We're selling Cartesian Caviar."

The thin man looked at the rows of tiny jars snugged into the special case. He looked up at Tony, then over at Quinn. His eyes widened, just a fraction, then dropped to the case again.

Quinn's breath caught in her throat. This man had recognized her. She was sure of it. Her heart started pounding. She tried to suck in some air, knowing biometrics were monitored in all customs stations. Even if he hadn't recognized her, the clerk must know she was hiding something.

"These are all samples?" The man reached out and picked one a jar at random.

"They are," Tony replied. "We don't do same-day sales. Our caviar is good enough to wait for. That's our tagline. Catchy, isn't it?" He grinned and winked, then pointed upward. "Deliveries are cleared and taxed at Hadriana Prime. That way, I don't have to deal with all the money. I'm not great at bean-counting."

Quinn stared at Tony, the man she'd known for years as an accountant. She dropped her eyes. He was good at this, but she was going to get them caught. Her heart pounded faster.

The clerk swiped the jar of caviar across the scanner built into his counter. It beeped twice. He replaced it in the case.

"Would you like to try the product?" Tony pulled the jar out again. "I'd be happy to leave a sample with you."

The man smiled, his face creasing. Instead of looking pleasant, it sent a chill down Quinn's spine. "Thank you, but no." He pointed to a sign behind his head. It read, "Gratuities will not be accepted."

The door to their right popped open, and the clerk gestured. "Welcome to LaRaine." The frosted window slid shut with a click.

Quinn looked at Tony. "What—"

He cut her off, ushering her through the door. "Let's get going. We have an appointment at ten."

A short hallway with one door on either side led to a heavier external door. It slid open at their approach and they stepped onto a wide porch. Two steps down left them on a sidewalk beside a quiet street. A couple of kids on bikes rode by, talking and laughing.

Tony stopped by a bench and pulled his comtab out of his pocket. "We have a ride coming to pick us up."

"You called QuickRide?" Quinn stared at the bright icon on the screen.

"Yes."

"Really?" Quinn couldn't believe he'd do something so risky.

"We're here on business. It's exactly what we'd be expected to do." Tony sat on the bench and fiddled with his shoelace.

She dropped beside him. "That man recognized me," she whispered.

"Of course he did," Tony said. "You're part of the LaRaine family. Lots of people are likely to recognize you. That's why we changed your hair." He gestured to her blonde updo. "It should help. Some."

"He'll report me!" Quinn's voice cranked up a few notches. "He'll tell Gretmar, and she'll—"

"No, he won't. We took care of it."

"You mean he's with you?" Quinn said. "Part of the family?"

"Oh, no, not part of the family. He's a well-paid business associate. That caviar he scanned? Deposited a payment into his bank account."

"Doesn't that leave a trail?"

"Yes, of sorts." He glanced at his comtab and tapped the screen. "The Federation runs on bribes. It would be suspicious if we *didn't* bribe him. Standard business procedure. But in this case, the small bribe hides a much larger bribe that went into a separate account and will keep him from reporting your arrival."

Quinn's mind whirled. "But I've traveled through here before. We never bribed anyone."

"You arrived here with the heir to the LaRaine empire," Tony said. "When you fly with the crown prince, no one's going to demand a bribe."

"So, you've come here before, too?" Quinn tried to still the nervous tapping of her foot.

"I was here last week, setting up this little excursion. I met a few family connections and greased a few palms."

"You met him?" She jerked her head at the building behind them.

Tony chuckled. "No, he's a tiny cog in the system. My contacts here set up the—let's call it the 'hassle-free entry.' But Lou has people coming to Hadriana on a semi-regular basis. Since this is primarily an agricultural planet, Federation security is low here. Plus, LaRaine has a deal with them. They leave her alone, and she keeps the peace here. Made this operation easy to set up."

"Don't you think they'll send more?" Quinn asked. "I mean, they know my kids are here, so I'm probably going to come here."

"People on the run don't usually hide with family." Tony shrugged. "Besides, you're another tiny cog in the system. No offense."

She shook her head to indicate she wasn't offended.

"You were a convenient scapegoat for their blunder on Fort Sumpter, but hardly worth an expensive hunt. If someone reports you to the Feds, they'll give LaRaine a heads up and expect her to do the takedown. They aren't going to send in a battalion. Just between you and me—" He looked up and down the empty street. "—I think LaRaine must have dirt on someone high up in the Federation. They aren't usually this hands-off. But unless she demands help, *and* there's a compelling reason for them to recapture you, we probably only have local talent to deal with."

A small car with a bright pink sticker on the windshield pulled up. "QuickRide for Cartesian Caviar?" a voice robotic asked. "Two passengers?"

"That's us." Tony jumped up. He grabbed both bags in one hand and waved his comtab at the car with the other. The door swung open, and he leaned down to peek inside, then stepped back to allow Quinn access. "After you."

She slid across the seat and fastened her belt. Tony followed her in, closing the door. He flicked his comtab again.

"Destination: LaRaine Hotel," the car said. "Estimated travel time: ten minutes. Fare: fourteen credits. Please confirm."

"Confirmed." Tony swiped his comtab, and a faint humming emanated from it. He held his finger to his lips, then settled back into his seat.

The ride to the hotel took only seven minutes. They traveled along quiet streets between hedges that blocked their line of sight. After a few miles, they moved into a residential section. A few blocks later, the cab stopped in front of a wide plaza. "LaRaine Hotel," it said. "Enjoy your stay."

A large building rose four stories above the far side of the plaza. Small cafes lay on the sides, their tables spilling into the square. Cars and buses jockeyed along the busy street opposite the hotel. Pedestrians ambled across the space, and pigeons scattered at their approach, circling around to land behind.

Quinn and Tony grabbed their belongings and climbed out of the cab. Tony set off across the plaza toward a huge bronze statue of a man and a woman each holding a small lumpy sphere. Several bronze bags lay at their feet, one spilling open to reveal more lumpy balls.

Quinn's lips twitched. "The famous LaRaine potatoes. And Philpert and Reginalda LaRaine, Saviors of the Colony."

"Those are potatoes?" Tony stopped to look at the statue. "I wondered."

"According to the history books, the LaRaine family ended a famine by developing a strain of potato that could grow here." Quinn looked around the square and lowered her voice. "Rumors among the locals say they waited until everyone who could afford to flee did so. That left them in control of not only the settlement, but anyone who couldn't get off this rock. They essentially used slave labor to run their plantations."

Tony glanced at the statue again, shook his head, then continued across the square. Quinn followed him through the wide doors of the hotel. The entrance opened into the two-story lobby, with marble floors, crystal chandeliers, and tasteful, plush furniture grouped around large stone fireplaces. Tony strode through, ignoring the massive piano played by a metal-skinned android. They turned in front of a discreet gift shop, and strolled along a narrow hallway with wood wainscoting and hand-printed floral wallcovering. At the end, they turned again and pushed through a pair of swinging doors.

Beyond the doors, the plush atmosphere disappeared. Thick carpeting and fabric-covered walls gave way to plain beige paint and scratched vinyl flooring. The rumble of machinery filled the space. A rank of metal carts stood against the wall, piled high with towels, sheets, and sundries. A couple of women dressed in hotel uniforms chatted as they loaded their carts. They didn't even glance up as Quinn and Tony crossed the room. Further on, mops and brooms stood ready. Steam oozed around the edges of a door marked "laundry."

They turned down another hallway and around a corner. Tony stopped, looking both directions. He waved his comtab at a side door and pulled it open. Harsh lights shone on steps leading down. Quinn slipped inside, and he followed, closing the door carefully behind them. The loud rumble cut off when the thick door latched.

"Downstairs," Tony said, unnecessarily since there was nowhere else to go. "All the way."

They descended a flight of steps to a landing with a door marked "Wine." The stairs turned and continued down, so Quinn followed. The lights grew dimmer—fewer fixtures hung overhead. At the bottom of two more flights, they reached a small cement-lined space and a heavy wooden door.

At Tony's nod, Quinn pulled on the ring set in the door. It swung open easily on well-balanced hinges. Behind the door, there was a room dug into the living planet. Dust and musty vegetables assaulted her nose. "Is this a root cellar?"

"It's a cellar." Tony followed her in. He pulled the door shut, then shone his comtab up at the roof. "And I see some roots up there, so I'm gonna say yes."

"A root cellar is a place to store vegetables for the winter. They used to store potatoes in these, back in the bad old days. What?" she asked in response to his look. "I had to learn all that crap when I married Reggie."

"You realize normal families don't require you to study their history when you marry into them?" As he spoke, he worked his way around the barrels and boxes stacked in the cellar.

"Normal families like yours?"

He snorted. "Here it is." The squeal of hinges drowned out whatever else he said. A few seconds later, Quinn heard a soft click, and light streamed into the cellar. "The way out."

She wove around the neatly stored items and reached the door. It opened on a clean, white space with soft lights and a spiral staircase corkscrewing up. "What are we doing down here? We walked right into town like we own the place, and now we're sneaking around the basement?"

"It's a little overdramatic," Tony agreed, "but the hotel surveillance is tight. If we aren't seen walking out one of the known exits, then as far as anyone watching is concerned, we're inside. If Gretmar, or her security, got wind that we've landed, they'll look for us here. I paid a lot of credits to keep that information quiet, but there are always leaks."

"Why didn't we take the drone in? Then you wouldn't have to pay anyone." Quinn's heart sank when she thought about how much money Tony—and his family—must have spent on this venture. How would she ever pay it back? The idea of being in debt to the Marconis terrified her.

"That method of travel is very secret. We use it only in tightly controlled locations, like the house outside Romara. Or if we're absolutely out of options." He sat on the lowest step and set his bag on the floor between his feet. "Here, we're relying on older methods to stay under the radar. My family wields some clout on Hadriana, but it's all under the table. We've worked hard to keep our network hidden from the LaRaines. The detour through the hotel was in case we had an accidental sighting along the way."

She sat next to him. The metal grating of the step bit into her butt, but she was too tired to care. "Now what?"

"We wait for our contact. I don't think it will take long."

CHAPTER 9

DAREEN PULLED on the throttle and the shuttle raced down the runway. She reached launch speed and adjusted the pitch. The ship lifted, and the ride smoothed. Once she cleared air traffic, she'd take the time to look around. It wasn't often she got to fly solo, so she'd make the most of it.

"I see you clear above ten thousand," a voice said through the radio. "Safe travels."

"Thanks, tower," Dareen replied. "Shuttle *michael tango ex-ray four niner one* out." She pulled the throttle, and the ship swooped upward. Slamming the joystick to the right, she spiraled the shuttle into the sky.

"You aren't doin' acrobatics in my shuttle, are you?" Lou's voice came over the speaker.

Dareen yanked the joystick back to center. "No, ma'am." *Not any more.*

How had Lou known? The rotation should have been tight enough to be invisible to the *Peregrine's* cameras at this distance. Dareen chuckled. Gramma had probably guessed. Or she had a tracker on the shuttle. Either way, she'd better keep it on the straight and level.

"Dareen, I'm sending you back down," Lou said. "Yer ma has a pickup. Coordinates sent."

"Roger, Lou. I'm going back down." She loaded the new location into the system and tipped the nose down again. The computer spit out a list of three landing fields near the coordinates. The closest was only two klicks from the pickup location. She tapped the screen and locked in the flight plan. "Destination set. How big a rig?"

"The bike will work," Lou said. "It's a small package."

"I'll give you a shout when I take possession. Dareen out." As the shuttle curved around to the far side of the planet, she considered trying a barrel-roll. Her hand hovered over the joystick but knowing Lou might be monitoring stayed her hand. She'd only been doing solo missions for a short time—no point in pushing her luck.

The landing was uneventful, and she taxied the shuttle to the temporary parking. A swipe to the payment screen, authorizing the fees, secured her space for a couple of hours, with the option to extend later. It didn't look like she had to worry about capacity; with no other parked shuttles, and an automated tower, she could probably stay here indefinitely without anyone noticing.

She shut down the engines and walked to the cargo bay in the back. The empty drone scoop hung above her head, nestled in the overhead struts. A cupboard against the internal wall unlocked with her handprint, and the hidden latches snapped open. She rolled the bike out of its storages space and hit the ship's tailgate release.

The back door rotated open, squealing loudly at the halfway point. Dareen gritted her teeth and made a mental note to oil the hinges when she returned. With a grin, she rolled the bike down the ramp formed by the now-open door. She'd made that same mental note every time they'd opened the cargo door in the last six weeks. One of these days, she'd remember.

Hot, dry air assaulted her, bringing a whiff of a sharp, papery scent. Serge brush, Tony had called it when they'd landed on this continent last week. She slapped the green door button on her comtab, and the ramp creaked upward, squealing again before shutting and locking. She slid the comtab into the slot on the front of the bike and pulled a helmet from the basket on the back, fastening it over her curly hair.

Smack! "Ow!" Dareen rubbed her arm. An oblong pod rolled away from her feet. She picked it up, then looked around. Flat, scrubby desert stretched in all directions. There were no trees in sight—where could it have fallen from?

A shriek from high above brought her head up. High above her, a creature soared effortlessly on wide wings. Across the flight line, another movement caught her eye. A second bird circled there. As she watched, it dropped something.

"Did you drop this on me?" she yelled up at the first bird, shaking the seedpod.

It didn't answer.

"Stupid bird."

A ping brought her attention back to her comtab. A map popped up, so she climbed on the bike. With a quick check of the status bars, she was off, into adventure. Her lips twisted. Who was she kidding? They only gave her the most boring errands. Maybe she'd hit a pothole—that would be exciting. She waited for the automated gate to open but didn't pause to see if it closed behind her.

Feeling rebellious, she ignored the speed limits and tore along the empty road at top speed. Clouds of dirt boiled up behind her, and the hot wind blew away the sweat. By the time she reached the programmed pickup point, a fine layer of dust covered her bare arms and legs.

She slowed the bike, staring around. The map showed she'd reached the correct coordinates, but it was just a wide spot in the road. She coasted the bike off the road and stopped, putting down a foot for balance. Rolling desert stretched away in all directions. Back the way she had come, she could see the shimmering force-fence that protected the shuttle landing strip, tiny in the distance.

What was she supposed to pick up? Family protocol dictated she not contact the ship except in dire need. Even encrypted signals might put off a contact. So she waited.

Thunk!

A pod bounced off her helmet and rolled across the dirt. She glared up at the brilliant sky, squinting against the sun. "What the hell! Are you following me?"

The bird sailed on, impervious to her yelling.

The sun rose higher, baking her bare skin. Shorts had seemed like a good idea when she landed. She climbed off the bike and pulled a coverall from the storage bin in the back. It was made of thin, breathable, smart fabric that would provide sun coverage in the heat, or insulation in the cold. She stepped into the dark blue clothing and zipped it shut.

"Don't turn around," a voice said behind her.

"Seriously?" she replied, spinning.

"I said don't!" A skinny boy stood before her, his own body covered in a similar coverall, but his was beige. It blended into the desert behind him.

"How long have you been standing there?" Dareen demanded, her heart pounding with what she told herself was righteous indignation. "Did you seriously watch me get dressed?"

"You already had clothes on. I liked the shorts better."

Dareen's eyes narrowed. "Do you think I care what you like? I'm here to get a package."

"I'll need some ID." The boy made a gimme motion.

Dareen stared him down. "Like what? My shuttle license? I don't think so."

The boy's eyes widened. "Gawd, no. I don't want to know your real name! That's crazy. Use the authenticator."

Dareen's face heated, and she ducked to look at her comtab, hoping her hair covered the blush. He must think she'd never done a pickup before. She flicked through the screens and clicked an icon. "Good enough?"

The boy looked at his own device and nodded. He held up a finger and took a couple steps back.

And disappeared.

Dareen stared. "Hey, where'd you go?"

"I'm still here." The desert before her flickered, and the boy reappeared. "Do you agree that the device was in working order when you collected it? Tap the yes button."

Dareen looked at her screen again. A blue button labeled "yes" and a red button labeled "no" filled the screen. Nothing else. She clicked the blue one. The words "deal accepted" appeared, then the screen went blank.

She eyed the boy and held out her hand.

He stared at her for a few seconds, then stepped forward and placed a small box in her hand, his warm fingers brushing her cold palm. He smiled, and her heart skipped a beat. He might be scrawny, but that smile!

"Thank you," she said with dignity. Too bad it came out an octave too high and breathy. Her face warmed again.

"Maybe we'll do a pickup again some time." His warm eyes roamed over her face.

Dareen's breath caught in her throat. There was something about those eyes and smile that made her want to melt. "Maybe," she replied, still breathless. Trying to regain control, she busied herself with stowing the small box in the cargo pod. Then she swung her leg over the bike and pressed the starter. "If you're lucky." She grinned and sped away.

The comtab chirped. "Crap." She slowed the bike. In her haste to get the last word in, she'd driven off in the wrong direction. She glanced behind her but couldn't make out the boy through the heat haze. According to the map, the only way back to the landing strip was right past the meeting point. If he followed protocol, he'd be long gone by now. At least, that was her family's protocol. Who knows what his family did?

She pulled to a stop by a large bush. It didn't provide much cover, since it was dry and lacy, but it was the best she could find. She could wait here, then drive past fast, hoping he was long gone. Or she could drive by slowly, as if she'd meant to do it.

Or she could use the device.

Heart pounding, she climbed off the bike. Messing with a delivery was totally against family protocol. But the boy had demonstrated the device. Surely using it one more time wouldn't hurt? And if it really made her invisible, she could get back to the shuttle without embarrassing herself. She opened the cargo pod and pulled out the box. The smooth, cold metal box felt heavy in her hand. The lid hinged open from the top. Once open, the screen inside lit up.

Dareen stared down at the screen. It read, "Activate?" Her finger hovered over the button, hesitating. Should she? She thought about the boy. Squinting, she peered across the desert. She still couldn't see him, but that didn't mean he was gone. Maybe he had another of these things?

Who was she kidding? She wasn't the rebellious type. She was a rule-follower. She reached for the lid.

Bang!

A seedpod hit her hand, slamming her palm against the screen. "Crap!"

Buzzing rattled her jaw—not quite a sound, but more than a feeling. She glanced up, and everything seemed blurred, as if she had been crying. Or had ointment in her eyes. She shuddered and looked down at the box. The screen read, "Active."

That stupid bird had turned on the device!

CHAPTER 10

A DOOR OPENED at the top of the stairwell, spilling light and shadows across the spiral above Quinn's head. She reached for her bag, but Tony held up a finger. Someone knocked on the wall.

Five raps, in a rhythm everyone in the galaxy would recognize. *Shave and a haircut...*

Quinn gave Tony an incredulous look. He grinned and knocked *three* times. Their contact knocked once.

"That's them. Let's go." Tony grabbed both bags and started up the steps.

"You picked the most well-known rhythm in the universe as your secret knock?" Quinn spluttered as she followed.

He grinned over his shoulder at her. "Easy to remember, and an unexpected response. If our contact used that knock and someone replied with the expected two knocks, they'd know it wasn't us."

"You're the expert." She trudged up the steps behind him.

At the top, an ancient woman with steely blue eyes in a deeply wrinkled face and carefully rolled curls stared at them. "About time. I've got things to do."

"Mrs. Ricardi?!" Quinn stared.

"Close your mouth girl," the crone said. "You'll catch flies."

Quinn snapped her jaws shut and turned to Tony. "Your contact is Gretmar's housekeeper?" She clenched her teeth. "Are you insane? She's been with the LaRaine family since she was—probably before she was born."

"That's why she's an excellent contact," Tony said. "No one would ever suspect her."

"But—" Quinn could think of a million reasons why that made her a terrible contact.

Before she could articulate any of them, Mrs. Ricardi cut her off. "The LaRaines have treated my family like indentured servants since the dawn of time. My great-grandfather developed that damn potato for Philpert and Reginalda. What thanks did he get? Generational servitude."

"But why don't you leave?" Quinn asked.

"With what credits?" Mrs. Ricardi slapped a hand on the stair railing. "All my life, I've earned barely enough to put clothes on my children's backs. Housing and food are provided by the estate as part of my compensation." She spat the last word like a curse. "Every estate on the planet runs the same way. So we supplement our income any way we can. I do it by working for the Marconis. They've allowed me to send all my children to off-planet universities. It's the only way off this rock."

"If you have proof your ancestor developed the potatoes, couldn't you take them to court?" Quinn asked.

"Weren't you listening? We have no money. And lawyers aren't cheap." The woman shook her gray curls. "Every penny I earn goes to my children. And grandchildren. And the children of other LaRaine staff."

"Shouldn't they be sending you money by now? Then you could retire."

Mrs. Ricardi looked away.

Tony put a hand on Quinn's arm. "Money doesn't flow easily this direction. The government keeps a tight grip on incoming funds. If you aren't paying off the right people, you get nada."

"Then instead of sending your kids off-planet, stage a revolution," Quinn said.

"Stay out of it, girl," Ricardi growled. "You didn't give a crap about us when you visited before, you can keep your nose out of our business now."

"I didn't know—" Quinn started, but Ricardi spun around and yanked open the door.

"Quinn, you can't fix their problems for them," Tony said in a low voice. "We can only help them finance their own solution."

"And this little operation will provide enough to do that," Ricardi said. "So, pipe down, and let's get on with it."

They followed the old woman up another flight of stairs, her cane clunking heavily with each step. At the top, another door led to a kitchen with old but functional appliances and a weathered table. A big bowl covered with a cloth sat on a shelf above the stove. Steam drifted lazily from a pot below it. Scents of warm fruit and spices wafted around them. A mug and spoon lay on the counter.

Ricardi led them across the kitchen, dropping something into an open canister as she went. Quinn peeked inside and saw a ten-credit note.

"Spreading the wealth," Tony whispered.

The door opened onto a fenced yard. Rows of plants filled the open area, with a short, gravel path leading to a gate at the back. This led to an alley lined by tall wood fences. The desire for privacy definitely made skulking around easier. Ricardi pointed to a small, green truck. "In the back." She stomped to the driver's door and climbed in.

Quinn and Tony crawled over the low tailgate and ducked under the cloth canopy. Boxes of fruits and vegetables lined the sides, with a pile of dirt filling the rest. Quinn helped Tony move the boxes to the rear of the truck, giving them a narrow space to sit. He slapped a hand on the back of the cab, and the vehicle hummed.

As they coasted almost silently down the alley, Tony draped a tarp from the back of the produce boxes. "Stay behind this tarp. We don't want anyone to see us. When we get closer to the estate, we'll cover ourselves completely."

"After the fancy drone pickup, this all seems ridiculously old-fashioned."

Tony shrugged. "It's the KISS method: keep it simple, stupid. The higher-tech we get, the more opportunity for failure."

"I suppose. Maybe you can tell me the plan, now."

"Sorry, I didn't mean to keep you in the dark," Tony said. "I tend to work on a need-to-know basis. That way, if something goes wrong, you can't—" he broke off.

"Spill the beans?" Quinn gave him a hard look. "If something goes wrong, I am dead. Literally. I sincerely doubt they'd give me a chance to spill any beans. And these are my kids. I need to know what your plan is for rescuing them!"

He held up a hand. "You're right. Now that you know about Mrs. Ricardi, you should know the rest. She'll take us up to the estate. We'll grab your kids and be extracted."

"The drone thing again?" Quinn's stomach lurched. "At least Lucas should like that."

Tony grinned but shook his head. "No, no drone today. We'll take the train down to New Astorian, and Dareen will pick us up at the shuttle port. Your mother-in-law is out all day—one of her many charity boards or clubs. By the time anyone realizes we've taken the kids, we'll be back on the *Millennium Peregrine* and headed out of the system."

"That does seem simple," Quinn said. "What about school? Shouldn't the kids be in school?"

Tony shook his head. "They aren't going to school. LaRaine hired a tutor."

Quinn groaned. "My poor children. All Gretmar, all day."

"She's not around that much. According to our sources." He nodded at the front of the truck. "But they're probably lonely."

"Good thing we're getting them out." Quinn peeked over the boxes. They'd left the residential area behind. Traffic on the country road was light, and soon they turned onto a private drive with massive metal gates between high hedges.

"Time to cover up." Tony grabbed the edge of the tarp. They pulled it up over their heads and anchored it into the pile of dirt.

Quinn squirmed down onto her back, her legs tucked into an awkward angle against the dirt. "I hope the tarp is clean. Otherwise, we'll be filthy by the time we get there."

Tony tapped her leg and shushed her.

The truck drove along for a while, then stopped. Ricardi shut down the vehicle and slapped the side near their heads. Her cane thumped loudly as she walked away.

"That's our all-clear." Tony pulled the tarp back. He dragged a couple of crates away from the tailgate so they could climb out.

The truck sat inside a huge, sparkling clean garage. A shining red Citralus XL sports car stood in the farthest stall, with empty spaces between it and the truck. On the other side, steps led to a simple wooden door.

Tony handed their bags to Quinn and grabbed a crate of produce. "Let's make ourselves useful."

As Quinn opened the door and held it for Tony, she looked around. She'd stayed in this house a dozen or more times over the last fifteen years but hadn't been to this wing since the kids were young. "This leads to the kitchen." She pointed down a dark hallway. "The kids and I used to sneak down for a snack when they were little, but Gretmar didn't approve. Storage and maintenance are that way." She pointed to a side hall.

"Let's go." Tony strode toward the kitchen. At the end of the hall, he pushed the door open with his shoulder and stepped into a well-lit room.

Where four men aimed blasters at them.

CHAPTER 11

THE BUZZING in Dareen's jaw spread into her ears. She looked at the box and then her hands. Was she invisible? She could still see herself. The bike looked normal. But everything else—everything more than a meter away—was blurry, as if she was looking through old, thick glass. Should she turn off the device? She looked back to the rendezvous spot again. Even though she couldn't see the boy, she *felt* he was there.

The device was active. Best to make the most of it. She slammed the cargo pod closed, carefully set the device in the small basket on the front of the bike and climbed on. She gunned the engine, or at least tried. The electric bike didn't make a satisfying vroom noise like her shuttle. With a shrug, she spun the bike around and zipped back the way she came.

She zoomed past the meeting point, slowing as she approached, but there was no sign of the boy. He must have another of these devices. The desert was barren—no place to hide. She turned the throttle and hurried back to the shuttle field.

When she reached the gate, it didn't open. She waved her arms, but nothing happened. Then it clicked. She really was invisible!

Glancing around to make sure no one was in view, she snagged the device from her basket. The screen read "Active." She tapped it. Nothing happened. She swiped.

Nothing.

She closed the box.

Nothing.

Opened it again. "Active."

Panic started to wrap its tendrils around her throat.

"Calm down, Dareen," she whispered. "The boy turned it off, so there must be a way." She closed her eyes and tried to remember what he'd done.

Nothing—because he'd been invisible when he did it!

"Aarrgh!" She yanked off her helmet and threw it. It bounced in the dirt, then rolled away, *through* the distortion. Maybe that was the key! She flicked the kickstand down and balanced the bike. Setting the device back in the basket, she climbed off and walked to her helmet. The gate opened.

"Perfect," she grumbled. But at least it was open. She turned, and the bike was gone.

She caught her breath and then laughed. It wasn't gone, it was invisible. Dareen picked up the helmet and walked forward four steps. The bike reappeared.

Before the gate could lock her out again, she tossed her helmet into the basket, leapt onto the seat, and urged the vehicle through the gap. The old gate started rattling closed before she was all the way through, but a little goose to the accelerator got her in. She buzzed back to the shuttle and flicked the unlock sequence.

Once she'd stowed the bike, she grabbed the device and set it in the middle of the cargo bay. Standing a meter away, she stared at it. Then she backed away from the box. One step back, and it disappeared. She stepped forward and it returned. Maybe the boy hadn't turned it off. Maybe he'd stepped out of range of a *different* device and given her this one?

Either way, she was in deep trouble. Gramma was expecting the delivery. But no one had told her to test it. In fact, how did she know this was even the item she was supposed to get? They hadn't told her squat. Now that she thought about it, Gramma had set her up.

Time to hand the problem back to its maker.

Leaving the box in the middle of cargo, she strode to the cockpit. As she stepped through the door, the buzzing in her jaw ceased. She hadn't realized how loud it had been until it was gone. She rubbed the back of her neck and sat in the pilot's seat.

The comm system pinged.

She slapped the screen. "Dareen here."

"What took so long?" Lou stared out at her. "Was there a problem?"

"Yes and no," Dareen said. "I'll explain when I get back."

"Did you get the package?"

Dareen grinned, but the grin faded quickly. "Yeah, I got it. Why didn't you tell me what I was picking up?"

Lou's eyes narrowed. "You didn't need to know. You didn't open it, did you?"

"The boy—I mean contact—demonstrated it for me." She rubbed her neck again. "I had to confirm that I saw it in action."

"That was not in the contract," Lou said. "Get back up here, and we'll sort it out."

"Roger." Dareen tapped the control panel and started the shuttle engine. "On my way. Out."

THE SHUTTLE LATCHED into place beneath the cargo bay, and the shuttle bay door closed. Dareen shut down the engines and unstrapped. Opened the hatch at the back of the cockpit and eyed the entry to the cargo bay. Should she get the device, or leave it where it stood?

With a grin, she slapped the controls and opened the hatch to the hold. It looked empty, of course, but she remembered where she'd left the box. She crossed to the center of the space and stopped.

Crap. Where was it? She'd left it right here, in the middle of the room! Blood rushed through her ears and her breath hitched. Gramma would toss her out the airlock if she had lost the delivery! She stumbled forward.

The box lay on the floor, exactly where she'd left it. She just hadn't been inside its field. She picked it up, frowning. Was the field smaller than it had been? She popped the lid open and glanced at the screen. It still said "Active" with no obvious way to turn it off. It probably ran until the power died. Great, a one-time device. And she'd started the clock. Gramma *would* toss her out the airlock.

Head hanging, Dareen went back to the airlock and let herself into the ship. She pulled out her comtab and called Lou. "Where are you, Gramma?"

"I'm right here." Lou stepped around the corner ahead. "Where are you?"

Dareen slid the comtab back into her pocket. "This was the little problem I was telling you about." She set the box on the floor and took a few steps away.

"*Futz.*" Lou rubbed her temple as if a headache was building. "Tell me you didn't turn that thing on."

"Not on purpose." Dareen hung her head. "The boy showed me how it worked—I told you, he made me confirm it was working. Then I took it and opened the lid. A stupid bird dropped a pod on my hand, and…" Her voice trailed off. "I'm really sorry."

"Why didn't you turn it off?" Lou walked slowly toward the invisible box.

"I couldn't!" Dareen flung herself against the bulkhead. "It had an on button, but no off!"

Lou disappeared. For a moment, there was nothing, then Lou reappeared.

"How'd you do that?" Dareen cried.

"Look." Lou held up the box. With a smirk, she pointed to the underside of the lid.

In small, black letters, it read, "To deactivate, press and hold the screen for five seconds."

CHAPTER 12

"WELL, CRAP." Tony set the crate on the counter and scrutinized each of the four men.

"Did she betray us?" Quinn whispered.

Tony raised his eyebrows. "Did she?" he asked more loudly, his eyes boring into Mrs. Ricardi where she lurked in the shadows.

"Did she what?" Ricardi planted her hands on her hips. "Accept a huge pile of money in exchange for turning you over to her employer? Yes, she did."

"Mary." Tony shook his head sadly. "Why?"

Ricardi glared at him.

"You don't really believe LaRaine will come through, do you? When has this ever worked?" He pinpointed each man with his gaze. "Oriell tried to cut a deal with LaRaine fifteen years ago. Remember what happened to him? He got framed and thrown in prison for accounting violations. He was a gardener, not a book cooker, but they made the charges stick. Pariena tried to sell out the rest of you. He ended up broke and on the streets after he betrayed half the staff. LaRaine doesn't play fair. She's too cheap and short-sighted to reward people who try to help her."

"He's right," one of the men muttered, the muzzle of his weapon dropping a bit. "None of those *crepic* ever got rich. Most of them landed in jail."

"Or dead," a second man said.

Tony nodded, focusing on Ricardi. "If you turn us over to LaRaine, she'll put off paying you for a week or two—claiming some kind of financial red tape—and then she'll find a way to get rid of you. She'll frame you, or fire you. You can't afford to be out on your ear. Who's going to take you in?"

"My staff will take care of me." She waved at the men between them.

The men looked at the floor, some of them muttering.

"I'm sorry, Mary, but you aren't that special." Tony shook his head. "They won't dare. LaRaine will get rid of anyone who tries to help you. You've seen it happen. Why do you think you'll be any different?"

Ricardi's chin went up and she sneered. After a moment, she closed her eyes and shook her head. She must have been desperate for credits to convince herself this would work. Then she stomped forward. "You're right. LaRaine is a worse criminal than you Marconis. But I want you to be clear on something. These men work for me. They will do what I tell them. So, if you think of double-crossing me, or try to do something I don't agree with, we *will* turn you in."

"Let *me* be clear." Tony's tone was cold and clipped, and his smile didn't reach his eyes. "The Marconis have done business with you for years. If you try to double-cross me again—or attempt to coerce me in any way—that relationship will end, and they *will* extract retribution. You know how they work. Is that something you want?"

The two locked eyes. A shiver went through the old-woman's frame, and her gaze dropped. "I understand. But I won't be taken advantage of."

"You won't be. You know we treat our partners well." Tony glanced around at the armed men. "Do you?"

"Put your guns away." Ricardi made a shooing motion. "Get back to your patrols." The men muttered among themselves but lowered their weapons and filtered out of the kitchen. The last one tried to take a cookie from a tray on the side table, but Ricardi slapped his hand. "Those are not for you!"

"Thank you." Tony pulled a stool away from the counter and sat. "How much does LaRaine know?"

Ricardi turned on the electric kettle and yanked some mugs from a cupboard. They rattled together as she shoved them onto the tray with the cookies. "She knows nothing. She suspects Quinn will show up at some point, and she told us to keep an eye out. She said we'd be well rewarded if Quinn was detained." She tucked some napkins under the cookie plate. "I'm sure she didn't expect the Marconis to be involved."

"No one expects the Spanish Inquisition," Tony muttered to himself. "Is she here?"

"Where are my kids?" Quinn interrupted. "Are these cookies for them?"

"Madam LaRaine is in town. Today is her mahjong day. She'll be back at four to change, then has a dinner engagement." She glared at Quinn. "Your children and your husband are here."

"Why is Reggie still here?" Quinn asked.

Ricardi shrugged. "He expects you to show up in the next few weeks."

"But he's— Didn't he have to go back to Zauras?" Quinn asked. "He didn't have much leave saved up."

Ricardi looked at her from under her thinning eyebrows. "He was asked to retire. The Federation doesn't want officers whose wives are traitors. Apparently, it's considered a conflict of interest. Once you've been executed, he can request a return to active duty."

A shiver went down Quinn's spine at this casual mention of her death sentence, followed by a spike of hot fury. "So, if I was dead, it would be okay to dump his kids with his mother for months at a time? That—" Her jaw clenched over the swear words threatening to spill from her mouth.

Tony lifted a finger to stem the tide. "Where are they?"

"Ellianne is upstairs with her tutor." Ricardi picked up the tray. "I'm taking this to them now. Master Reggie took Lucas horseback riding this morning. They took a lunch, so I don't expect them back until later. And he isn't going to dump them here for months at a time. Madam wouldn't stand for that." She turned her back on them and stomped out of the kitchen.

"I need—" Quinn leapt up from her stool.

Tony put a hand on her arm. "Wait. What we *need* is a solid plan before we approach them. Last week, I asked Ricardi to pack a travel bag for each of them, so when we're ready to snatch them, it will be quick. But we can't do it while Lucas is out with his father."

"Maybe we should." Quinn twisted her hands together. "We can take a couple horses and follow them. Grab Lucas, take Reggie out, come back, grab Ellianne, and go."

"Take Reggie out?" Tony pinched his lips together as if fighting a smile. "How are you planning to do that?"

Quinn's face hardened, and her hands closed into fists. She mimed a perfect roundhouse to Tony's temple. "Stop laughing. I could do it."

Tony's smile broadened. "I believe you. But I can't ride a horse. We're better off to wait. My other sources told me Reggie has an appointment in town this evening. After he leaves, we'll grab the kids and go."

"An appointment?" Quinn's eyes narrowed. Something about the way Tony said the words pricked her interest. "What kind of appointment?"

Tony shrugged. "Doesn't matter. He'll be gone."

"What other sources?" Quinn asked. "How do you know he'll be gone?"

Tony looked away. He tapped on the counter, then turned back to her. "He's meeting a woman in town. Old girlfriend. He's been seen there every night since he returned to Hadriana."

"But he was in Romara—he can't have gotten here much faster than us," she protested.

"He brought the kids here as soon as you were arrested. He was here for three weeks before going to visit you. I'm sorry."

She laughed without humor. "Sorry for what? Sorry that my spineless, opportunistic husband is also a cheating scumbag? I'm sorry, too. But not as sorry as I'm going to make him."

Tony raised his eyebrows.

"I know." She deflated with a sigh. "I'm not the vengeful type. But a girl can dream." She straightened her spine. "My mission is to get my kids and get out. So, what's the plan?"

Tony held out a ring of keys. "Here's the escape plan."

Quinn took the keys. Her eyes grew wide when she identified the fob. "We're stealing Reggie's Citralus?" She laughed. "I thought you said we didn't have time for vengeance?"

His lips quirked. "We don't have time for vengeance for vengeance's sake. We definitely have time to make the most of our opportunities."

"Won't he take that to visit his *friend*?" Quinn asked, the spark leaving her eyes.

"Unfortunately, he won't be able to find the keys." He plucked the ring from her fingers and jumped off his stool. "And even if he has a spare set, there might be a minor mechanical problem. The car will be mysteriously inoperative when he tries to start it." He looked at her as if sizing her up, then nodded. "Do you know where the video surveillance room is?"

Quinn nodded with a smirk. "We were here when they installed it. Reggie insisted Gretmar put one in. I think he mainly wanted it to watch the staff. He doesn't trust anyone."

Tony nodded and pulled something out of his pocket. "They have cams all over this place." He held out a small device. "If you plug this into the back of the main computer, we'll be able to see what they see."

Quinn took the thing he held out. It was the size and shape of a standard memory module—the connecting plug was bigger than the electronics inside. She'd used these before, extensively, when she was on active duty. They allowed remote monitoring of a computer system. Some of the more sophisticated devices allowed the user to take control of the computer.

This would allow Tony—and potentially the Marconi family—to monitor Gretmar's security system. The Gretmar who had made her life miserable whenever she visited the LaRaine Estate, and whose son had abandoned Quinn to her fate. She smiled. "My pleasure."

"I'll meet you back here." He tapped the kitchen counter

She nodded, and he ghosted out of the room.

Quinn listened at the door Mrs. Ricardi had used, then cracked it open. No one in sight. She slipped into the butler's pantry. For formal dinner parties, dishes were staged here for the wait staff to carry into the dining room. Mrs. Ricardi would return through the door on the right that led to the servant's hall. Quinn hurried across the room and pushed the dining room door ajar.

The vast room stood dark and empty. An enormous table filled the space, with tall chairs standing sentinel along the sides. Throne-like seats on either end cast long shadows in the faint light sneaking in around the curtained windows. A whiff of roses and lilies made her queasy. Holding her breath, she slid between the chairs and the sideboard, pausing at the far end of the room.

Huge double doors led to the entrance hall. The house had been built with servants' hallways in the back, ensuring the staff was seen only when convenient to the owners. But the security office stood alone near the front door. Quinn wasn't sure if this was because the LaRaines didn't trust their staff, or because security had been added at a later date. Probably both.

She cracked the doors and peered out into the massive entry. Everything about this house was larger than life: ridiculously tall ceilings, vast rooms, enormous ornamental fireplaces. Huge antique furniture lurked around the edges of the rooms, emphasizing the size of the cold empty spaces. The entrance hall was no exception. A massive, handwoven carpet stretched across the empty hall. Two-meter high hammered metal urns stood on either side of the door in front of frosted sidelights, and at the other end wide marble stairs with ornate wooden banisters curved up on either side, leading to a gallery on the floor above.

Quinn's footfalls echoed through the vast room. She tiptoed across the space, darting into the coat room near the front entrance. A plain wooden door at the rear of the closet led to the security room, but it was locked. Quinn stretched up and ran her hand along the top of the door lintel. Her fingers slid across the smooth wood, then stopped. With a smirk, she grabbed the key and unlocked the door. So much for security.

Shutting it quickly behind her, she crossed to the desk and turned on the monitors. The screens flickered to life, resolving to a rotation of cameras: entry hall, living room, dining room, upstairs hallway, garage, front walk, back garden, stables—on and on.

First things first. She dropped to the floor and crawled under the table. The computer sat on a shelf beneath the desk. She pulled it a few centimeters from the wall and slid her fingers up the back. After years in IT, she'd learned to identify ports by touch. There, that one was the one she wanted. She held the device Tony had given her in the tips of her fingers and stretched her arm behind the computer again. A fumble, a save, and then victory. The device was installed. No one would notice it unless they pulled the machine away from the wall. With a grin, she crawled out and looked at the monitor.

She touched the screen, activating a menu. Clicking a red triangular icon brought up the security recording menu. The system flipped through the "public" areas of the house, recording only when motion was detected. One by one, she opened the recordings and quickly deleted each frame showing her and Tony. If anyone had been watching in real time, they'd have been caught, but now the evidence was gone.

Then she opened the list of cameras. Scrolling down, she noticed each guest room was on the list. Feeling sick, she scrolled farther.

There was a camera *outside* Reggie's room, but none inside. Relief washed over her. The idea of someone watching them—ew.

She clicked on the library and caught a glimpse of two people at a table. The next cam gave her a closer view. Ellianne and a young woman sat at a table, working on a math problem.

Quinn smiled, tears pricking her eyes. Her beautiful child: dark curls falling across her cheek, hand scrubbing an eraser across the paper. The woman reached over and pointed at something. Ellianne glanced up at her, then scribbled some figures. For long moments, Quinn sat and watched her daughter work.

The tray of cookies and tea across the table finally registered in her mind. Ricardi had already been there and left. Leaving Ellianne up on one screen, Quinn scrolled through the cams, looking for the housekeeper. She didn't trust the woman.

She finally caught sight of the old woman leaving Gretmar's suite. The matriarch had a sitting room, office, bedroom and home gym on the second floor, isolated from the guest rooms by the library. None of those rooms had cameras—at least not on this system. As Quinn watched, Ricardi carefully locked the door behind her and made her way to the servants' stairs at the far end of the hallway.

At least, that was where Quinn assumed she was heading. If so, *she* needed to get back to the kitchen. She took one more look at Ellianne, then shut down the monitors. She crossed to the door and peeked into the coatroom. It was dark and still. After carefully locking the door, she returned the key to the doorframe hiding spot. With a grin, she crossed to the entry hall. Easing the door open, she peeked through the space between the door and jamb. The hall was empty.

Quinn slipped into the entry and froze.

Voices filtered into the house, and shadows moved on the frosted sidelights. Someone was on the front porch.

Quinn sprinted across the room and dove into the dining room as the front door opened. She dashed around the huge table and darted into the butler's pantry. Turning as she swung the door shut, she realized she'd left the dining room doors open. Nothing she could do about it now.

A heavy sigh filtered through the room: Gretmar's well-used signal of disapproval. Quinn's blood ran cold.

"Those children must have been playing down here again," her mother-in-law said in a long-suffering tone. "I will be so relieved when they finally return to Zauras with their father."

Reggie was planning to take the kids back to Zauras? He must be sure his request to return to active duty would be approved. Of course, he'd been in league with Admiral Andretti, the commanding officer who had left them behind on Sumpter. He probably had enough dirt on the admiral to get a promotion out of the deal.

Remembering what Tony had said, Quinn smiled as she tiptoed through the butler's pantry. Reggie's return to active duty depended on her execution. And that wasn't going to happen. Now, or ever.

CHAPTER 13

QUINN SLIPPED into the kitchen and met Tony's eyes. "The old bat is home."

His eyes widened. "Let's move, just in case." He jogged to the door and held it open for Quinn.

"Wait," Quinn said. "I don't trust Ricardi. The garage is the first place she'll look. Let's go down here." She led the way to the mechanical rooms that ran along the back of the house. They ducked around the hot water tank and climbed over some boxes. "There's a bolt-hole back here." Quinn tapped a small cupboard in the internal wall. "Lucas and I discovered it when he was little. We think the original indentured servants had a kind of escape route for runaways, and they hid here. We have to be really quiet—there's a peephole into the kitchen."

She pulled, and the cupboard rotated silently away from the wall. Tony glanced inside, then made a horrified face. She took in the cobwebs and hid a smile. Holding up a finger, she turned to survey the room. Like the rest of the house, the mechanical room was spotless, even though it was used for storage. Finally, she nodded and climbed over the boxes again.

When she returned, she held an old-fashioned string mop.

Elbowing Tony aside, she slid the mop into the hidey-hole and swept up the cobwebs. "Clean enough for you, Mr. Squeaky-Clean?" She stashed the mop behind the water heater and ducked down the four steps into the hidden space.

Tony followed her and pulled the cupboard shut behind him. Then he showed her his comtab. The screen said, "I was more concerned about the venomous jumping spitters than the webs."

"They live on the northern continent," she typed into the device. After handing it back to him, she slid open a small panel in the wall.

They leaned in close and peeked through the ornate grate. From the kitchen, this opening looked like an old-fashioned heating duct set a few centimeters above the floor. The steps down into the hidey-hole allowed them to sit on the floor and peer across the kitchen floor at eye level.

After an interminable wait, a door opened. Only feet and legs were visible through the grate, but Quinn would recognize those high-heeled, viper-skinned shoes anywhere.

"Where is she?" Gretmar demanded.

"They were here." Ricardi's voice was low and angry. "They have to be in the house. She wouldn't leave without the kids."

"Keep that *crepiva* away from my grandchildren," Gretmar said. "Put the security team on alert. We have intruders in the house."

"Security to the house," Ricardi said, apparently into her comtab. "Alert in the house. The target is in the library. Send extra security there."

"You will be rewarded for your loyalty, Mary," Gretmar said. "I take care of my people."

Yeah, by knifing them in the back. Quinn glanced at Tony.

He raised an eyebrow and mimed shutting the door.

With the grate covered, they moved to the back of the hidden space.

"We aren't going to get them out now," Tony whispered.

"You heard her—they're pulling guards into the house," Quinn replied. "This is the perfect time to get to Lucas."

"If we knew where they rode, we might be able to reach them," Tony said. "This is a big estate."

"How about this. We can hide out in the barn and grab him when they come back."

"They won't leave him unguarded. Your ex will be with him. I'm sure the battle-ax will tell him what's going on."

"You think?" Quinn's lips quirked. "She doesn't share her cards with anyone. I bet she won't even contact him."

"We have no way of knowing if she did, so we have to assume the worst," Tony said. "But we *know* she's going to search the house, so unless you're positive they won't find this bolt-hole, we need to leave."

"Agreed." Quinn slid open another panel near the steps and listened intently. "No one in the mechanical room. Let's go."

Leaning against the back of the shelf, she pushed the hidden door open. They crept up the stairs and into the mechanical room. Tony pushed the shelf back into place and followed Quinn deeper into the room. A large metal box filled the back wall. It hummed slightly, providing a little cover noise.

"Heater," Quinn whispered. "There's a hidden passage this way." She flattened herself against the wall and slid into the narrow gap between it and the heater. Her upper body fit with room to spare, but her hips were another matter. With her butt jammed against the wall, her stomach still pressed against the warm metal box. Her nose brushed the heater as she turned her head back to Tony. "Not much room for the mom bod here."

Tony made a show of sucking in his stomach and followed her in.

The wall pressed tight against her back. She shuffled on, hoping the hidden path still went somewhere. If not, getting back out might be a challenge. She squeezed around the corner of the heater, and a dark space opened up. A second later, Tony grunted as he emerged, and his comtab flared to life.

The light revealed a narrow, wooden door in a recessed area. Cobwebs festooned the corners of the doorframe. Dust lay thick on the floor. Clearly, no one had been back here in years. Hesitantly, Tony reached out and pulled on the metal ring set in the door.

It didn't budge.

"Twist the ring," Quinn whispered.

The mechanism creaked and groaned as he turned the ring. Then the door jerked open in his hand. Quinn squeezed back into the corner so he could pull it past her. She squinted, but the light from Tony's comtab made it hard to see anything but the door. Cold, musty air wafted over them.

After pulling the door wide, he edged around it and aimed the light through the opening. Narrow steps descended into thick darkness. More cobwebs hung across the cramped space, clinging to dry stone walls.

They exchanged a look.

"You're sure there aren't any venomous jumping spitters here?" Tony whispered.

"Not the venomous ones," Quinn replied with a grin. "But plenty of non-venomous creepy-crawlers. I should have brought the mop."

He pulled a handkerchief out of his pocket and wrapped it around his hand. Reaching up, he swept his arm through the webs across the steps, clearing the way. "This will have to do. Can you take the comtab?"

Quinn grabbed the device and followed him down the first step. "Wait a sec while I shut the door." It grated and groaned behind her, shutting with a satisfying thunk.

They crept down the steps, Quinn shining the light over Tony's shoulder while he cleared the dusty webs. As they descended, the musty smell grew stronger, and the darkness pressed against the back of Quinn's neck. She shivered, nearly dropping the comtab.

"Here's the bottom." Tony's voice sounded muffled. "Dirt. And a tunnel. It probably leads into the woods behind the house. Have you been through here?"

"No," Quinn said. "I've opened the door at the top of the stairs, but Lucas was only four—he was too scared to go down. I never came back."

"I guess we'll find out. I hope it hasn't caved in or been blocked. The good news is there aren't many webs in the tunnel."

The heavy darkness pressed down, emphasized by the small bright pool cast by Tony's comtab. Roots poked through the ceiling above them. Their shuffling feet raised clouds of dust from the floor, and the musty smell increased as they walked. Gradually, the dirt disappeared, replaced by rough rock. Moisture beaded on the walls.

"When you said the house was a stop on the underground railroad, I didn't think you meant literally," Tony said.

"I never said underground railroad." Quinn's nose wrinkled. "There are no trains."

"Historical reference." Tony shook his head. "You said it's an escape tunnel for runaway servants. Watch your footing, there's some loose rock here."

"That's what we thought," Quinn said. "I suppose it could have been for smugglers. After the LaRaines took over and built up their empire, the locals started smuggling goods to avoid the exorbitant taxes."

"That's probably when the Marconis got involved. The family has had connections here for generations. I think the tunnel is going up. Shine the light on the ceiling."

Quinn tipped the comtab. The circle of light illuminated the sharply slanting ground and a wooden hatch in the roof. "I guess we're here."

Tony grabbed a metal ring and twisted. Metal shrieked as the ring rotated. "Hope no one is listening for us." He climbed higher up the slant and pressed his shoulder against the wood. With another ear-shattering squeal, the door hinged upward.

A faint breeze carried a whiff of fresh air to Quinn's nose. The absolute darkness of the tunnel gave way to gloomy gray.

"I think we're in a cave." Tony climbed out and reached a hand down to help Quinn, keeping his voice low. "It's definitely lighter that way."

"Should we shut it?"

"Yeah. We don't want anyone sneaking up behind us."

Quinn shut the lid. It moved more easily, barely squeaking. She dusted her hands on her pants and followed him across the cave. A low tunnel let in dim light.

They ducked to peer out. The passage burrowed through the rock, angling up a short distance. Tony crawled up, then gestured for Quinn to follow. The rocks ground against her palms and knees as she climbed the short slope. At the top, she banged her head against the upper lip. Biting back a curse, she blinked tears out of her eyes.

The sloping ground flattened out, and the cave wall curved upward, allowing them to stand. A huge tumble of boulders blocked their way, but brighter light shone around the pile. Tony climbed on one of the meter-high rocks and peeked over the top.

Quinn put a foot on the rough stone, but Tony's upflung hand stopped her. Voices murmured, freezing her in place. Who could be out there?

Tony jumped down. He leaned in and whispered, "It's Reggie and Lucas."

CHAPTER 14

QUINN'S EYES widened and her heart stuttered into double-time. Lucas was here! She lunged toward the boulder, but Tony gripped her arm.

"We need to make sure they're alone," he whispered. "And find out why they're in this cave. They're supposed to be riding." He stepped back up onto the boulder and held out a hand.

Quinn grabbed his fingers and let him pull her up onto the rock. She leaned against the boulder, the cold stone contrasting with the heat rolling off Tony's body. She glanced at him, but his attention was focused on something beyond the pile of boulders.

Their perch allowed them to peek over the rockfall into an outer cave. Quinn's breath caught when she spotted Lucas slouched against the stone wall, comtab in hand. Reggie stood beside him, peering out the mouth of the cave.

Beyond the two, she could see a glimpse of green foliage and grass, but the angle prevented her from seeing more.

"How much longer do we have to stay here?" Lucas grumbled. "I got no service." He shoved his comtab into his pocket.

"Just until they catch the intruders." Reggie's voice was tight.

Quinn recognized that tone. That was Reggie's "these kids are driving me crazy, take them away before I explode" voice. It was her signal to swoop in and distract the children so their father wouldn't be bothered. She mentally shook her head. How could she have been such a doormat for all those years?

She leaned close to Tony. "They're alone. I'm going to talk to them."

"Wait," he hissed, but she'd already climbed onto the next boulder so she could slither down the other side.

"Who's there?" Reggie demanded, swinging around.

"It's me," Quinn said. "Your worst nightmare."

"Quinn?" Reggie's voice cracked. "What are you doing here?"

"Lucas!" Quinn ignored her husband and rushed across the cave, stumbling over the rough floor. She flung her arms around her son, pulling him tight against her chest. He stiffened, then relaxed and squeezed her back.

Tears pricked her eyes. She bit her lip, trying to hold them in, then gave up and let them roll down her cheeks. After a moment, she leaned back. "Are you taller? How could you have grown in three weeks."

Lucas rolled his eyes and groaned. "Mom!"

Reggie grabbed Quinn's shoulder and ripped her away from Lucas. "Get your hands off my son, traitor!"

"That's how you're going to play this?" Quinn's glare could have frozen molten lava. She maneuvered slowly, never taking her eyes off Reggie.

"Lucas, your mother is an enemy of the state and a convicted traitor to her people." Reggie pushed Lucas behind him.

"*The state* left me behind to die," Quinn said. "*The people* convicted me for daring to rescue myself."

"I assume that's why they left you behind in the first place," Reggie said sanctimoniously.

"Yeah, that's what happened," Quinn said. "They decided a bunch of us were Krimson spies and left us to be purged. No trial, no jury. Oh, and that included the admiral's wife, his XO's wife, and a bunch of civilian employees. It had nothing to do with the piles of gold they took in our place."

It was hard to tell in the dim light, but Reggie's face seemed to flush. Quinn continued to stare at him while slowly easing around him. Her fingernails dug into her palms as she clenched her fists so tightly.

"Did they buy you off?" she demanded. "Was it 'trade your spouse for cash day' on Fort Sumpter?"

Reggie drew himself up, throwing his rounded shoulders back. "How dare you say such a thing! I am an honorable man."

"So honorable you leave your wife on death row so you can hang out with an old girlfriend?" Quinn demanded. "That's right, I know about her."

"Stop it!" Lucas yelled. "Stop fighting!" He ran out of the cave.

"Damn it, Quinn, now look what you've done!" Reggie howled.

Quinn shoved past him, knocking him off his feet and running after Lucas. She ducked out of the cave, pushing through a veil of vines and leaves. Sunlight filled a small, grassy field. A dirt path meandered across it, leading into the trees. Lucas ran into the woods, his long legs covering ground quickly.

"Lucas!" She raced after him.

The woods here were well-manicured—the underbrush carefully mown and the trees thinned. Lucas's bright red shirt flashed between the trees as he ran toward the back of the house. Quinn reached the edge of the wood, her lungs heaving and a stitch pulling at her side. She stopped, but Lucas raced across the field.

She couldn't follow him—returning to the house would ensure her capture. And if Gretmar caught her, she had no doubt she'd end up back on death row in Romara. But she ached to pull Lucas back into her arms. Her eyes burned, and she bit her lip.

A meaty hand grabbed her arm and yanked her around. Reggie's pale blue eyes bored into hers. "Leave my children alone." He gasped, his breath short and ragged.

"*Your* children?!" Quinn whispered, her tone harsh and cold. "They're my children! I bore them. I raised them. You showed up once in a while. I should have left you years ago."

Quinn's anger flared higher, but the threat of getting caught started to tamp down the flames. Time to make a fast exit. She had to get back to Tony.

"You're a Krimson spy. You belong on death row," Reggie said.

Quinn looked up at the trees above them, grasping at patience. "Are we on that again? I *am* Quinn Templeton, not some replacement agent."

Reggie snorted. "Did you know the Empire has lifelike androids? Of course you do. You probably are one."

She stared at him. "Have you completely lost your mind?"

"They probably made one to look just like my Quinn and replaced her." He nodded as if this made perfect sense. "When did they plant you? When we moved to Sumpter? And who's your controller? Probably that Tony Bergen."

Over Reggie's shoulder, Quinn caught a flutter of movement. While Reggie raved on, Tony crept closer. He pointed at his wrist in the ancient signal to hurry up.

Quinn glanced at Reggie, but he was so wrapped up in his theory, he didn't notice she'd stopped listening. Tony made "let's go" movements with his hands. Then he mimed swacking Reggie on the head and collapsing to the ground.

Quinn smothered a snicker.

Reggie's tirade stopped mid-word. "Did I say something funny?"

"You said a lot of funny things," Quinn said, shaking her head. "But I need to go. I'm not going to wait for Gretmar's security to grab me and hand me over to the Federation."

"You aren't going anywhere, android." Reggie took a tighter grip on her wrist. "Let's get back to the house. I have things to do."

"*Things* to do?" Quinn repeated, anger bubbling up in her chest. "Don't you mean *your old girlfriend* to do? I'm not going anywhere with you." She twisted her hand, forcing his thumb back.

He yelped and let go. "Be reasonable—"

"Reasonable?!" Quinn snarled. "I'm facing execution, and you left me to come home to your girlfriend. What about that is reasonable?" She surged forward.

Reggie stumbled away, holding his hands up. "Quinn, I meant—"

"I don't care what you meant!" She stormed closer, crowding him against a thick tree. "Here's reasonable!" Pulling her elbow up and back, she rammed her fist into his face. Pain exploded in her fingers, spiking up her wrist and arm.

Reggie's head slammed into the tree behind him with a solid thunk. His eyes rolled back, and he slid bonelessly to the ground.

"Damn, that felt good."

Tony crouched beside the prone man. He thrust his fingers against Reggie's neck for a moment, then surged to his feet. "He's alive. Searchers will be coming. Soon. We need to hide." Taking Quinn's hand, he pulled her into the trees.

As they ran along the manicured path, Tony dropped her hand and pulled out his comtab. Focused on the device, he lurched off the path. Quinn grabbed his shoulder, pushing him in the right direction. "Put that thing away," she hissed. "What are you, twelve?"

"I'm arranging a pickup.'

"We can't go back to the ship without the kids!"

"We aren't." He tucked the comtab away and increased his pace. "But we need to regroup. We have a safehouse. Just need a ride."

They ran on, following the path deeper into the woods. It wandered past a creek and through a couple more meadows before straightening out along a fence. Quinn ran, her side aching and lungs burning. Tony pulled away as her pace slowed. He glanced back and matched his stride to hers, urging her along.

Ahead, a narrow, paved road appeared. Before the path intersected it, Tony pulled Quinn behind a thick stand of brush. "We'll wait here until our ride comes."

Quinn leaned over, hands on her knees, lungs heaving. "Who?" she gasped.

"Robo-car."

"Taxi?" She stared at him incredulously. "Tracking!"

He shook his head with a smile. "I've been doing this for a while. I'm not going to get us caught. Here it comes."

A small, gray car with dark windows pulled up. Quinn squinted at the windshield but couldn't see inside. The rear door popped open, and Tony peered inside. "All clear. Let's go." He ushered her inside and climbed in behind her.

"This is the family's car," Tony said. "We keep it in the safehouse. We have them on every planet where we do business. The call is encrypted and untraceable. The car is off the grid."

"You don't know much about communications if you believe this is all untraceable," Quinn said.

Tony conceded with a nod. "Theoretically, anything that emits a signal is traceable. I guess it's more accurate to say this car is a tiny fish in a big pond, and the risk of being traced is negligible. We work hard to stay under the radar."

"I'm an escapee from death row." Quinn stabbed a finger at her chest then waved it in a circle encompassing everything. "Come to my husband's home planet—the planet where his family is undeniably part of the ruling class—to kidnap my children from their father. Do you really think I'm a small fish?"

"You aren't." Tony pointed a thumb at himself. "But Tony Bergen isn't a known member of the Marconi family. Connecting you to them is not an easy jump. Unless Ricardi has utterly betrayed us, there's no reason for Gretmar to track the Marconis."

Quinn looked out the window, not bothering to argue. The sunset painted brilliant red and orange stripes across the western sky.

"It's winter here," she said in surprise. "I'd forgotten how mild the winter weather is. Sunset must be, what, about five-thirty?"

"Almost six," Tony replied. "Do you think your mother-in-law will still go out tonight?"

"I told you, she doesn't rearrange her schedule for anyone," Quinn said. "Canceling now would require her to explain why, and she doesn't want to remind her friends of her son's unfortunate choice of spouse. But Reggie will probably stay home to watch for me. I blew it by letting him know we're here."

"You did, but there's nothing we can do about that now," Tony said. "Time to move on to plan B."

CHAPTER 15

DAREEN POINTED AT THE SMALL, metal box in her grandmother's hand. "What *is* that thing?"

"Obviously, it's an invisibility cloak." Lou shut the lid and slid the device into her pocket.

"But that's not possible," Dareen argued. "No one has developed that technology."

"You're right." Lou nodded amicably. "It doesn't exist."

"But it does!"

"Make up your mind." Lou turned and stomped away.

Dareen hurried along behind. "Where did it come from? How did we get it? Why did we get it?"

"Haven't you learned not to ask those questions yet?" Lou grumbled. "Ever since you were a baby, we've been telling you don't ask. But still you ask."

Dareen grinned at Lou's familiar response. "You know I'm going to keep asking."

"One of these days, my girl, I will drop you off at the Commonwealth Military Academy and just keep flying."

Dareen's grin widened. "No, you won't. I'm your favorite grandchild."

"Tony's my favorite," Lou said. "You're a distant third."

They stopped at the hatch to the bridge. Lou turned, her hand resting on the access-panel. "We got it to help Tony. He might need it."

Dareen whistled. "It must have cost a fortune. Tony really is your favorite."

"And don't you forget it." Lou punched Dareen's shoulder lightly then slapped the hatch release. "Get back to work."

DAREEN BANGED her wrench against the thick metal casing of the jump drive.

"Don't do that!" her father said. "That thing cost more than you can earn in a year. And that's counting the under-the-table jobs you do for Lou."

"I didn't hit it hard, Dad," Dareen said. "If that tap broke something, we already needed a new one."

Shaking his head, Maerk turned back to the computer. He tweaked the fuel levels for the in-system drives and ran another diagnostic. Behind him, Dareen clanged her wrench against something else. "If you want to pound things, go to the gym," he said without looking her direction.

"I'm just so— Urgh!" Dareen tossed the wrench into the toolbox. "Gramma sent me on a pickup and she won't tell me—" She broke off and stomped across the room.

"She won't tell you anything?" He swung the stool around to face her. "Why does that surprise you? Lou has always played everything close to the vest. Ask your mother. When we were dating… Why would Lou be any different with you?"

"I don't know!" Dareen stomped the other way. "She didn't tell me what I was picking up! She didn't tell me who I was meeting! She didn't tell me what I'd have to do!"

Maerk's head came up. "What did you have to do?" he asked with deadly calm.

"Oh, Dad, nothing like that." Dareen flopped onto the stained chair tucked into the corner of the engine room. The flowers had long ago lost their brilliant color, although hints remained near the straining seams. "I waited out in the desert, and then this boy showed up."

"Oh ho!" Maerk said. "Now we're getting somewhere!"

"Dad! It wasn't like that. He made me confirm the device was working. There was a button on my comtab. It freaked me out."

"Having a button on your comtab freaked you out?" Maerk scratched his chin. It wasn't like Dareen to be so illogical. Or so emotional.

"Nooooo!" She jerked forward. "I didn't know for sure what I was agreeing to. You've always taught me to read the fine print, but there wasn't any! Just a yes or no."

"Did the boy demonstrate the device?"

"He demonstrated *a* device. I don't know if it was the device I brought up here." She thought a moment. "Although that one worked, too."

"So, what's the problem?" Her dad turned back to the computer.

"I don't know! I want Gramma to trust me!" She flung herself back on the chair, her head thunking the wall above the low back. "OW!" She rubbed her head. "Then that damn bird dropped his stupid seedpod on me."

"I have no idea what bird you're talking about," Maerk said sympathetically. He set down his tool and looked at his daughter. "But there isn't much you can do about Gramma. It's the way she is."

"I could leave," Dareen said. "I could go to college, or the academy like Tony did."

"You could," Maerk agreed. They'd had this discussion many times—usually when Lou treated Dareen like a child. Dareen always came around. She was mature for her age, current demonstration notwithstanding. "But you'd hate it there."

"That's what you always say." Dareen struggled out of the low seat. "Maybe I'll try it out myself."

"You think Lou treats you like a child? The academy is worse!" Maerk called after his daughter's retreating back, but he doubted she'd heard him. "Saint Aloysius, protect me from teens," he muttered before going back to his calculations. She wouldn't leave. She never did.

DAREEN STOMPED THROUGH THE SHIP, her steps echoing through the corridor. She hated feeling this way. Like she didn't matter—that no one understood her feelings. Being the only nineteen-year-old girl on a spaceship full of family sucked. Sometimes.

Of course, none of the other teens she'd met could pilot a shuttle. Most of them had never been off their home planet. But still! She was legally an adult! Gramma should treat her like one.

She treats the adults the same way, a little voice in her head whispered. *They're all children to her.*

That was probably true, but she didn't feel like being logical right now. She felt like doing something bold. Something no one could ignore or dismiss.

Something daring.

Something risky.

Something amazing.

With a nod to herself, she hurried to the bridge. End was standing watch, dozing in the command chair. When she opened the door, he jerked and sat up. "What?"

"I came to get the device, sleepyhead," Dareen told her brother. End was her elder by eleven months, but he behaved like he was years younger most of the time. Why Gramma trusted him to stand watch, even when they were in orbit, was beyond Dareen.

"What device?" End rubbed his eyes. He didn't even pretend

he'd been awake. "The mystery box? Does Gramma need it?" He looked at the locked cabinet where some of the weapons were stored.

"Yeah." Dareen's chest tightened. She never lied—not to her brother. Surely End would realize this was a complete fabrication. "She wants me to take it down to Tony. Covert." She put her finger to her lips.

End nodded. "Go for it. Good luck." He slumped back in the chair, eyes sliding closed.

Dareen stared at him. He really couldn't tell. She'd always felt they had an almost twin-like connection, but clearly that didn't work both ways. She set her palm against the access-plate to the weapons locker. It beeped and she typed in the passphrase. It asked for a reason. She could use the emergency override, but that would sound a ship-wide alarm. So, she typed in "delivery" and the door slid open. Easy.

As her hand touched the smooth, metal box, doubts assailed her. Taking the device was wrong. Even though she planned to deliver it to Tony. What if Gramma had another use for it? Could she be screwing up a complex plan? Everything Gramma planned was complex. Too complex, sometimes. Keep it simple, stupid. That was what Tony always said. And Gramma had said she got the device for Tony. Therefore, it made perfect sense for her to deliver it to Tony.

She grabbed the box and slapped the access-panel to close it. Then she hurried to the door.

"Safe flying," End mumbled.

"Thanks," she whispered. Then she ran for the shuttle bay.

CHAPTER 16

THE SAFEHOUSE SAT about ten miles away on the outskirts of LaRaine City. The car pulled into an ordinary suburban neighborhood and wove through the streets. They passed churches, a community center, a small grocery, and several apartment blocks before angling into another residential area. Mid-sized houses sat on wide, shallow lots. A tiny strip of green fronted each house, and identical fenced-in yards ran behind.

The car drove up to the third house on the block and stopped in front of the garage. The door rolled open, and the car slid inside without input from Tony. They waited in the dark until the garage had closed behind them, and the overhead lights sprang on.

"Let's go get something to eat and work on our next move." Tony opened his car door.

Quinn followed him out of the garage into a short hallway. "Bathroom on the left." Tony pointed as he passed the closed door. "I'm going to see if there's anything in the fridge."

When she walked into the kitchen a few minutes later, Tony had laid out vacuum-packed sandwich fixings on the counter. He'd built himself a huge sandwich.

"He'p oo'self," he said around a bite.

"I'm not really hungry." Quinn played with a package of plant-based sandwich slices. "What are we going to do?"

"We have a couple options." Tony opened a cupboard and pulled out two glasses. He filled them with tap water and handed her one. "We can wait a few days for things to settle down, make them think we've left, and then hit hard. Or we can strike again tonight. Hopefully, they won't be expecting us to regroup this quickly."

She rubbed her forehead. "If I were Reggie, I'd be expecting me to try again tonight. He knows I'm not going to wait around and get caught."

"So, we wait." Tony nodded and took another bite.

"We can't wait!" Quinn thunked her glass on the counter. "You may think this house is completely off the grid, but I'm not buying it. We need to get in, grab the kids, and get off this mudball. Now."

"But you said he'll be expecting us—"

"I know," Quinn said. "But the longer we wait, the better prepared they'll be. I say we go back. Now."

"I was hoping you'd say that." Tony fished his comtab out of his pocket and typed something into it.

"What are you doing?"

"When we're ready, I'll send this text. Reggie will get a frantic message from his girlfriend saying someone has broken into her home." Tony slapped together another sandwich and handed it to Quinn. He gathered up the rest of the food and shoved it back into the fridge. "While he goes to help her, we grab the kids."

THE CAR DROPPED them off on the opposite side of the estate from where they'd exited. "If Reggie has a brain in his head, he'll have people swarming over that area." Tony gestured vaguely across the estate. "We might be able to get back into that cave, but I suspect they'll have discovered the smugglers' tunnel by now."

They crept into the trees outside the estate wall and followed it for a few hundred meters.

"I'm going over the wall," he whispered. "There's got to be someone guarding the back entrance—" He pointed in the direction they'd been traveling. "I'll take him out, and let you in."

"If you take him out, it will tip our hand," Quinn said. "I can go over the wall."

"No offense—" Tony looked Quinn up and down. "But you aren't really in wall-climbing shape."

"Are you dissing the mom-bod? I can do this."

Tony shrugged and pulled a few items from his pack. Motioning Quinn to step back, he swung a grappling hook up over the wall. "There's a blip in their external cams here. Every ninety-five seconds, this stretch of wall is out of view for fifteen." He grinned as he showed her a grainy vid on his comtab. "They think it's not long enough to be a problem. Thanks to your little installation, we know when it happens so we're golden. Get ready to climb. When you get over, there's a bush about three meters that way. You need to get to it before the cams swing back."

Quinn wiped her sweaty palms on her pants and grabbed the rope. The wall stretched about a meter above her head. It looked like twenty.

"I'll give you a boost. You need to get over and behind the bush in fifteen seconds," Tony repeated, his eyes on his comtab. "Get ready. Twenty seconds. Nineteen." He stuck the comtab in his pocket and made a basket out of his hands. "Up you go. Sixteen seconds."

Taking a deep breath, Quinn put one foot into Tony's hands.

"Three, two, one, now!" On the last word, she pushed against his hands, forcing herself upward. Tony grunted.

"Sorry." She knew she was no lightweight. She pulled on the rope, her fingers burning. With another grunt, Tony launched her upward. She scrabbled at the top of the wall and got an elbow over. Tony pushed again, and she managed to roll onto the wide top.

"Go," Tony hissed. "You've got eight seconds to get down and behind that bush."

With a heave and a twist, she flipped around and dangled her legs over the side. Not taking time to think, she dropped, rolling as she hit the ground in what she hoped was the right direction. She scrambled to her hands and knees and scuttled behind the bush.

After ninety-five seconds that felt like hours, she heard a ripping sound.

"Crap," Tony whispered with a thread of a laugh. "Caught my pocket on the damn grappling hook." A soft thud and he dropped beside her.

The back of the house was visible through the trees, glowing brightly. "They don't usually have all the lights on, so I'd guess they're expecting us. But I know where the cam-free areas are." Tony pulled a pair of goggles out of his backpack and dragged them onto his face.

"How did you figure that out so quickly?" Quinn asked. "I just installed the snooper plug this afternoon."

"The family does a lot of business here, so our dirtside connections have created a comprehensive map of all surveillance cameras. I asked them to add the LaRaine system to the program when you were arrested."

"I thought Mrs. Ricardi was your contact," Quinn said. "We can't trust anything she's touched."

Tony chuckled. "This ain't my first rodeo." Ignoring her questioning look, he continued. "We have multiple contacts on any planet—contacts who don't know about each other. It's the safest way to do business." He stood, staying hunched over, his head swiveling. "Stay right behind me and keep an eye out for actual people watching us."

After a long pause, he ran across an open stretch of grass. Quinn scrambled to catch up without stepping on his heels. They paused in the shadows of a stand of decorative trees. The scent of dying flowers smothered them, and Quinn choked back a cough. She'd always hated these things. Lovely orange flowers, but they smelled like death.

From here, they could see the entire back of the house. Every window was lit, but curtains were drawn across most of them, showing only cracks of light along the edges.

"Go." Tony lunged forward to dart across the next open stretch.

"Wait!" She grabbed his arm. Her heart rate increased from quick march to drum roll. "Upper window."

Tony froze, his head slowly turning to look where she indicated. A curtain fluttered. "Good catch. Definitely someone watching. This way."

They drifted behind the death bushes and across a narrow, gravel walkway. They crouched in the shadows under a thick hedge for a few minutes before creeping along the base toward the house.

"Don't they have heat sensors?" Quinn asked.

"They do," Tony said. "But for some reason, they aren't working properly. They kept getting false positives last week, so they're shut down and waiting for a maintenance tech. He's scheduled to come tomorrow."

"They won't think that's a bit suspicious?"

"You were in prison last week. How could that have anything to do with you?"

Quinn shook her head slowly, marveling at the extensive prep work Tony had done. How did she deserve a friend like him? And what would she owe his family after?

With a few more false starts, they reached the vegetable garden behind the kitchen. "From here on out, we're under surveillance," Tony said. "Aside from cutting the power, there's no way to evade the cameras. We're going to try to draw Reggie off, then get inside."

"Don't you have someone else inside the building? Seems like you have connections everywhere."

He shook his head. "Mrs. Ricardi was it. I never dreamed she'd switch sides. I mean, it's always a possibility, but I thought she was the last one..." He rummaged through his bag, then handed her something. "Put this on."

"What is it?"

"Uniform." He tugged a cap low over his eyes. Pulling a knife from his pocket, he cut a swath of vegetation from the garden and piled it up. "I'm the chauffeur. You're one of Ricardi's minions."

"Don't they have ID cards and stuff?" Although she'd spent many family vacations at this estate, she had never paid much attention to the security measures. She pulled the thin jacket over her clothing. The word "LaRaine" was emblazoned above the left chest pocket in bright pink.

"Of course. They check that stuff at the gate." Tony cut a few more stalks, then handed the bundle to her. "But we're already inside. The key is to look like you know where you're going. Nobody will bother you if you walk with purpose. Stay behind your lovingly prepared bouquet and hope we don't run into anyone who knows you. Come on."

He straightened up and strode out into the light shining down from the back of the house. Quinn ducked her head over the armful of plants and scurried along behind him. At the back of the house, he fiddled with the doorknob and opened the door. They stepped into the garage, and Tony locked the door behind them.

"Did you pick that lock?" Quinn asked. "That was really fast."

"No, I grabbed a house key when I got the car keys." He grinned, and the dim light from his comtab screen glinted on his teeth. "They really shouldn't leave those things lying around."

"What am I supposed to do with these plants?"

"Dump them in the trash," Tony said. "That was camouflage for the walk across the back yard."

"You know there's nothing edible in season right now, right? This is a shrub."

"Oops. Of course, no one watching is likely to know that either, right?"

"We can hope not." She dumped the dry stalks into a can and followed him out of the garage. They turned down the side hall and returned to the mechanical room.

"We won't go in there." Tony pointed at the spy post they'd used earlier. "I don't want to be cornered."

"Do you think they found the exit?" Quinn gestured to the slot between the heater and the wall.

Tony shrugged. "I left some sensors when we went through, and they haven't been tripped. Maybe they found them. Or maybe they know it's there, and they're watching the exit."

She glanced around the cluttered room. "Was this too easy? Is their security that lax?"

"Maybe," Tony said. "Think about it. Reggie doesn't think you're smart or strong enough to pull this off. If he did, they'd have beefed up the staff. Or called in the Feds. Or moved off-planet. I mean, the safest place for them right now would be a military base."

"But you said he was forced to retire."

"Yeah, but I'm sure he could have gotten a place in the temp officer quarters. Especially if he convinced them you might come looking. They want to catch you as badly as Reggie wants you gone. But they don't want to expend the manpower for a full-on search."

Even knowing her husband was a cheating scumbag, the pain struck like an arrow to the heart—to know he thought so little of her. Intellectually, she knew he'd moved on long ago—maybe years ago—but the off-hand comment didn't hurt any less. She took a deep breath, pushing the pain deep inside. "Let's do this."

In the glow of his comtab, Tony's eyes crinkled in sympathy. He patted her shoulder awkwardly, then tapped his device. "I've got video—and audio—from the house patched into my comtab." He handed her an earbud. "You can listen in. Sending the text, now." He angled the comtab so Quinn could see the screen.

The video feed showed a comfortable living room. "Reggie's suite," Quinn whispered.

Tony nodded.

Reggie and Ellianne sat on a couch. Ellianne was curled up next to her father, her head against his arm, while she watched something on the large screen above the fireplace. A small fire burned below. Reggie ignored his daughter, swiping at something on his comtab.

Quinn's heart squeezing with longing. "Wait—where's Lucas?"

On-screen, Reggie tensed. Ellianne glanced up at him. "Son of a bitch!" He leapt off the couch. "Stay here." He stormed out of the room.

Ellianne stared at the door that slammed behind him. "Daddy?"

Before Quinn could grab the comtab out of his hand, Tony swiped to another camera. Reggie stomped down the hall, yelling, "Francine!" He ran down the steps, poking at his comtab. "Francine! Get down to my suite and watch Ellianne. I need to go." He stumbled on the landing, then whirled and continued down the next flight. "I don't care if it's your day off. Get down there and watch the kid!"

"Here he comes," Tony whispered.

They heard the slamming of doors. "What do you mean the Citralus is out of commission?! It was working perfectly yesterday!" There was a pause. "No, she hasn't been into the house. I checked the video myself. Besides, she's too cowardly to come here. My mother scares the crap out of her."

Tony raised an eyebrow at Quinn.

"Not anymore," Quinn hissed, her eyes narrowed. "I've got nothing left to lose."

"Just send the damn Seridia around," Reggie's voice snarled. "Why the hell do you keep that thing way in the back?"

Quinn rolled her eyes. "Because you wanted room in the garage for your precious Citralus."

"And get someone watching the front door!" Reggie yelled.

Tony pointed at his comtab. "There are three people watching the front door, idiot." He zoomed in on a man standing in the shadows. "Him, the guy in the woods—" He swiped and zoomed again. "—and whoever is in the control room." He swiped back to the front steps as Reggie stormed down them. Within seconds, the huge, boxy Seridia pulled up in front of the house. Reggie climbed into the back seat, and it whooshed away.

"Let's go." Tony tapped a few commands into his comtab to engage the interface Quinn had installed on the security computer. "As we approach each camera, a five-second loop of empty room will transmit in place of the live footage. If we don't get out in time, we'll be on screen for whoever is watching."

"Do we know if there's someone in the control room?" Quinn led the way through the kitchen.

"No, but safer to assume there is. I only know my device hasn't been tampered with."

"We still don't know where Lucas is," Quinn whispered as they slipped through the butler's pantry. She paused at the door to the servants' lounge. "Is anyone in there?" Normally, the staff didn't hang around after their shifts—they all had homes and families of their own—but these were not normal times. She didn't know who—or how many—Reggie might have conscripted.

"Empty." Tony angled his device so she could see the screen. "Go."

They pushed through the doors into the empty room. This one was more cheerful than the rest of the house, with pale yellow walls, overstuffed couches, and plants on the windowsill. It must have been planned and decorated by a human. Quinn had always suspected the rest of the house had been decorated by an artificial intelligence with a penchant for ancient stone temples.

Another door led to a narrow, dark stairway. They climbed to the third floor, then paused. Quinn pointed. "Reggie's suite is the first door on the right."

Tony nodded. "Go."

They ghosted down the hall, and Quinn paused to enter a code into the access-panel. "He always keeps this locked when he's here. I don't think he trusts the staff."

"Why would he?" a female voice asked.

CHAPTER 17

LOU GRABBED End's shoulder and shook. Hard. "Get up! Standing watch means staying awake. From now on, you will *stand* watch, not sit."

"*Futz*, Gramma!" End leapt out of the chair. "You scared the crap outta me!"

"You're lucky that's all I did!" Lou slapped the back of his head, but just hard enough to get his attention. "Straighten up, kid, or it's back to scrubber duty for you."

"Not the scrubbers," End whined, rubbing his head. "I hate those things. All those finicky little pieces. You know they make bots to do that kind of work, right?"

"If I had bots to do it, I would lose an effective threat, wouldn't I? Where's your sister?"

"I dunno," End said. "She left. Said she had to make a delivery for you."

Lou's eyes narrowed. "A delivery for me? Have you been drinking as well as sleeping?"

"N-n-no, ma'am." End covered his mouth with his hand.

Her nostrils flared. "Out!" she said, her voice cold and low. She pointed to the door. "Back to the scrubbers. Send Maerk up here."

End scrambled around Lou and ran for the door.

"Wait!" Lou said.

End stopped, but he didn't turn around.

"When did Dareen leave?" Lou's eyes bored into End's back.

He squirmed as if he could feel her gaze. "I told you, she said she had a delivery run." He glanced at the clock. "About three hours ago. She got the box and took the shuttle."

Color drained from Lou's face. "The box? The box she brought up earlier today? She took it and left?"

"Yes, ma'am. I wasn't drunk. You can check the logs."

"Get out," Lou dropped into the chair. The door whooshed open and closed again. She pulled up the logs. Video recordings sped by as she scrolled through the feed, looking for the appropriate time. End's memory was off—it was only two hours ago. She stopped on a thumbnail showing Dareen, then scrolled back to when she walked onto the bridge.

She watched the video in silence. What the hell was that girl up to? Lou was so tired of teens. Tony had been terrible. Sending him off to the academy had been a relief. She'd missed the scamp, of course, but all those hormones and poor decisions! Hard to believe that had been twenty years ago. Now she had Dareen and End, and it was the same thing all over again. She slapped the comm, bringing up Maerk's lab..

"Maerk, what's that girl doing?" Lou barked.

"Dareen? Or Liz?" Maerk didn't look up from his workbench.

"Dareen, of course. Why, is Liz up to something, too?"

"Not that I know of." Maerk set down his tool and looked up at the camera. "I think Dareen is in her room. She was upset—you know, the usual. Not being treated like an adult, nobody trusts her, yada, yada."

"Well, apparently there's a reason nobody trusts her," Lou growled. "She took a shuttle and headed dirtside. Who knows where she is."

"Have you tried calling her?" Maerk asked.

Lou fumed. She didn't need her ex-son-in-law being all reasonable—she wanted to be mad. "Not yet. I wanted to have my facts straight. Out." Before he could reply, she slapped the off button and flipped to the shuttle comms.

"Dareen, what are you doing?" Lou ignored the usual communications protocol, letting her frustration color the words. "Answer, girl. What are you up to?"

"I'm saving the day," Dareen said. "You don't have a need to know."

And the connection went dead.

CHAPTER 18

QUINN WHIRLED. "WHO ARE YOU?"

A gun appeared in Tony's hand, pointed at the woman.

She lifted her hands. Long, blonde hair spilled over her shoulders and piercing blue eyes bore into Quinn's muddy brown ones. "You must be Quinn." She looked at Tony. "And is this the Krimson spy?"

"Who are you?" Tony repeated Quinn's question. Without waiting for an answer, he jerked his head at Quinn. "We need to get out of video range now."

Quinn slid into the room, holding the door open. The woman strolled in, ignoring Tony's gun. Tony followed, keeping well out of reach but making sure nothing got between him and his target.

In the formal parlor, a leather couch sat in front of a low marble table, a deep blue armchair on each end. A vast marble fireplace took up one wall, while wide windows, currently covered by thick velvet drapes, faced them. The third wall held tall bookshelves and a door.

"That's the family room from your video feed." Quinn pointed at the door. Then she turned slowly and looked at Tony's device. "Wait a minute—that room doesn't have a camera. I looked this afternoon. Where are you getting that feed?"

Tony grinned. "A bug. Leave it be." His eyes locked on the other woman. "Before we go any farther, I need some answers from *you*." He jerked the gun toward her. "Who are you?"

"I'm Ellianne's tutor." She strolled to the blue wingchair, turned it to face Tony and sat gracefully, crossing her legs.

"You're pretty dressed up for a tutor." Quinn eyed the pencil skirt and high heels.

"I was supposed to have a date tonight. Thanks to you, I'm babysitting instead."

"Don't blame me," Quinn said. "Blame Reggie. As far as I'm concerned, you're welcome to party all night."

The woman laughed. Even her laughter was exquisite.

"Name?" Tony barked.

"Francine Zielinsky."

Tony's face paled. "Zielinsky?"

She shrugged. "Here I go by Terrence."

"Who is Zielinsky?" Quinn asked.

Tony's lips twisted. "The Zielinsky family is connected to the Russo Mafia. They, uh, don't usually get along with other families. Lou would have a fit…"

"Lou?" Francine's eyes snapped to Tony's. A look of recognition crossed her face. "You're a Marconi. Of course! I wondered how Quinn got here so fast."

Quinn glared at the woman. "Don't talk about me like I'm not here. Why are you here?"

"Believe it or not, I really am Ellianne's tutor," Francine said. "I'm on walkabout."

Quinn glanced at Tony. He shrugged.

"I'm on sabbatical from the family," Francine clarified. "Didn't want to live the family life, so I ran away and joined the circus."

"I guess the family thing explains why you're so calm about having a gun pointed at you," Quinn said. "Nearly made me hyperventilate the first time."

"You get used to it," Francine replied.

"You aren't here on Russosken business?" Tony's eyes narrowed to slits.

"Nope. Took a break." She smoothed her skirt. "Moved to the boonies. But the boonies suck. I'm used to the finer things in life." She gestured around the room. "When LaRaine advertised for a tutor, I grabbed at the chance for a better living situation."

Tony stared hard at her. "You expect us to believe that?"

She shrugged. "I don't *expect* you to believe anything. I'm just sharing my story."

Quinn glared at the woman, a cold finger of dread sliding down her spine. "And distracting us until Reggie gets back?" She turned to Tony. "We need to go. Now."

He nodded. "Go get Ellianne. I'll watch the *tutor*."

Quinn raced across the room and yanked the door open. It was dark, with only the low fire and the video providing illumination. Her daughter lay on the couch, eyes closed, head pillowed on the armrest, a furry thing clutched in her arms. Her curly, dark hair shone in the flickering light, and Quinn's breath caught in her throat. Her baby.

"Ellianne?" she whispered.

"Mommy?" she muttered, her voice fuzzy and warm.

Quinn slipped across the room. She put a hand on her daughter's shoulder. "Ellianne. Sweetie."

Ellianne's eyes drifted open, and she looked up. The pupils went wide, and her head snapped up. "Mommy!" Dropping the furry thing, she flung herself into Quinn's arms.

Quinn pressed her daughter tight against her chest, breathing in her warm, flowery scent, reveling in the thin arms gripped tight around her neck. Until they cut off her airflow.

"Baby, let me breathe!" Reaching behind her head, she pulled one of Ellianne's arms down and wrapped it around her waist instead.

"Are you staying, Mommy?" Ellianne asked. "Please stay."

"I can't stay," Quinn said. "But you can come with me."

The little girl's arms loosened, and she leaned back. "Daddy said you didn't want us anymore. I knew he was wrong."

"He said what?" Quinn's blood ran cold then hot with anger. "I will *always* want you. You and Lucas are my reason."

"Reason for what, Mommy?"

"Everything."

Ellianne's arms tightened around her again.

"Quinn, we gotta run," Tony called from the door.

"Where's your brother?" she asked the girl.

"He went to Tyrel's house. He and Daddy had a fight, and he ran off." Ellianne tugged on a strand of Quinn's bleached hair. "I like your new hair."

"Thanks. Where does Tyrel live?"

"I dunno, but Daddy said that's where he went."

"Okay, come on." Quinn picked up the furry toy.

It hissed.

Quinn dropped it. "Crap, what is that?"

Ellianne gathered up the furball. "This a Sashelle, Eliminator of Vermin. She's a caat."

"That is not a caat." Quinn pushed her daughter gently toward the door. The animal draped itself over the girl's arm, like an enormous, breathing blanket. "Caats are small. That is a mountain lion. Or a rug."

Ellianne giggled. "She's not a mountain lion, are you, Sashelle?" She rubbed her face against the caat's head, then looked up, her eyes big. "We can take her with us, can't we?"

"You'll have to ask Tony." Quinn urged the girl through the door.

"Tony!" Ellianne launched herself at the short man.

"Elli-belly!" Tony scooped her up, caat and all.

"Can we take Sashelle, Eliminator of Vermin, with us? She's really good at catching meece."

He looked at the caat, then scratched behind its ears. It made a rumbling noise. "Spaceships always have meece. Gotta have a caat."

"A spaceship? Cooool."

"Tony, where's Francine?" Quinn asked sharply.

He set the girl down. "I convinced her she should go on her date."

"You let her go?" Quinn demanded. "What if she sells us out to Gretmar?"

"She won't. Let's go."

"How do you know she won't?" Quinn grabbed his sleeve.

"I know." He squeezed her hand. "Trust me. Where's Lucas?"

"He's at a friend's house," Quinn said. "And I don't know where the friend lives. I didn't know he had any friends here."

"Tyrel is a new friend," Ellianne said. "We met him at *the club*." She said the last two words in a very posh accent.

Quinn shivered. The girl sounded exactly like her grandmother.

"You can look at Daddy's tracker," Ellianne said.

"What tracker?" Quinn asked.

Ellianne grabbed her hand, pulling her back toward the living room. "It's in his bedroom. I'll show you."

Quinn looked at Tony.

He made a shooing motion. "Is there a back way out of this suite?"

"Yeah, come on." She followed the girl through the living room and into a short hallway. Four doors opened off the hall—three bedrooms and a bath. "Do you have a bag packed?" Quinn asked her daughter.

"Yup, in my room." The girl skipped to the second door. When she flicked on the lights, an explosion of pink blasted their eyes. "Mrs. Ricardi said we needed to be ready, 'case Daddy got deployed." She ran across the thick, pink carpet and opened the closet where she pulled out a small, pink wheeled case. "Here's my go bag!"

Tony bit his lip, the corners twitching. "I'll see if Lucas has one." He retraced his steps and went into the first door.

"Where's Daddy's tracker?" Quinn asked.

"I'll show you." Ellianne headed into the hall. Grunting, she dragged the case with one hand, the caat still draped over her other arm. She opened the third door and struggled across the huge room toward an equally enormous bed.

"How about I take the suitcase?" Quinn suggested.

"Okay." Ellianne pulled open the bedside table. "Here's the tracker."

Quinn gazed around the room. It hadn't changed since the first time she'd visited Hadriana—one hundred percent Reggie's room. Heavy wood furniture, leather upholstery on the chairs, thick, dark curtains. There were two pictures on the dresser—formal portraits of each of the children. Gretmar insisted on having them taken each time they visited. These were new.

A chill ran through Quinn's shoulders. This room was one hundred percent Reggie's. He'd grown up here, and after they'd married, they'd stayed here any time they visited Hadriana. After fifteen years of marriage, the room should hold something of hers, but it didn't. It never had.

She pulled her attention back to the drawer Ellianne proudly indicated. It held a jumble of papers and a large rectangular device. It looked like a comtab but bigger, and when she touched the screen, it didn't light up.

"You have to turn it on." Ellianne grabbed the object. She pressed something and handed it back to Quinn. "See. That blue dot is Lucas, and the pink one is me."

A thick sheaf of papers lay folded in the open drawer, but her name peeked out. She withdrew the bundle and spread it out.

Tony poked his head through the door and saw her face. "What?"

"That bastard was divorcing me!" With a growl, she shuffled through the pages, signed the last one with a flourish, and tossed the wad on the bed.

"I'm done here. Let's go."

CHAPTER 19

"LET'S figure out this tracking business," Quinn said.

Tony took the device. "Tracking how?" He flipped it over and squinted at the tiny print on the back. He looked at the girl. "Do you know how he's tracking you?"

Ellianne nodded. "We went to the Bod Mod Pod and they put in the tracker." She rubbed her upper arm.

Quinn lifted her daughter's sleeve. There was a small, hard bump on the back of her bicep. It moved under the skin.

"I wanted to get a tattoo, too, but Daddy said no," Ellianne continued as Quinn examined her arm. "I was going to get one of Sashelle chasing a meece."

"If we take her out of the house, he'll know." Quinn looked up at Tony.

"He left this here." Tony took the device from Quinn. "Is that because he's got an app on his comtab, or because he assumed the kids would stay put?"

"That would be stupid," Quinn said. "Why bother if you're just going to ignore it?"

Tony nodded. "We'll have to assume he has an app."

"It's on his comtab," Ellianne said. "He didn't want to carry that thing."

"How are we going to sneak away with that tracker in her arm?" Quinn asked.

"Duct tape," Tony said.

"What?"

"We'll wrap foil around her arm, then duct tape it in place," he said. "It works perfectly."

"Won't he notice if she suddenly disappears?" Quinn asked.

"Yes, but he won't be able to trace us." He slid the tracking module into his pocket and nodded. "I can see why he wouldn't want to carry this—it's huge."

That surprised a snort of laughter out of Quinn. She shook her head and headed back to the living room. The others followed. "There's probably some foil in here." She rummaged through the drawers under the wet bar. "Nothing."

"My baked 'tato has foil," Ellianne said. "In the fridge."

"That's my girl—way to think outside the box." Quinn fought the urge to leap across the room and hug the little girl again. She never wanted to let her go. Instead, she opened the fridge. Piles of takeout boxes filled two shelves. "There's a goldmine of foil in here. Did you eat out every night?"

Ellianne shook her head. "Only the days Grandmother wasn't home."

"So, most of them." Quinn pulled a couple packages out of the fridge and started unwrapping food. "Here we go—enough to cover your arm."

"I have some duct tape." Tony patted his backpack. "We'll wait until the last minute to wrap it. Where's the back door?"

Quinn took Ellianne's hand and crossed to the curtained wall. "Hit the lights, Tony."

Darkness fell, leaving only the glow of the big screen to light the room. Quinn pulled back the left side of the curtain, revealing a glass door that led to a balcony. "There's probably someone on guard down there—at least there should be. We might be better off to go through the house."

"Let's check it out. Is there an alarm system?" Tony asked.

"Sh— Sugar." Quinn glanced at her daughter. She dropped the girl's hand and ran across the room. Yanking a cupboard open revealed a computer system. Quinn hit the start button and typed in something. "Idiot hasn't changed his password in years," she muttered. "Looks like there's an alarm. Can you check for cameras?"

Tony nodded, pulling out his comtab. "Got 'em. Cameras on the door and the stairs. Gimme a second and I'll take them out of the rotation. They'll notice eventually, if they're watching, but that's a hazard of so many cameras—people don't notice when one is missing."

"Alarm is off. I set it to restart in five minutes, so we need to go now." Quinn logged off and jogged across the room.

"There isn't anyone at the bottom of the stairs." Tony pointed at his comtab, his tone disbelieving. "There should be a guard. At least, I'd put someone there."

"Let's just get out of here," Quinn said. "We can deal with problems when we get there."

"Me first." Tony put a hand in his pocket.

Quinn glanced at the weapon-shaped bulge and nodded, grateful he'd kept the gun out of Ellianne's sight.

The door opened quietly, and the three of them slipped out onto the balcony. Quinn leaned down to whisper in Ellianne's ear. "We have to be really quiet. We don't want to wake Grandmother."

Ellianne gave her mother a scathing look. "Grandmother isn't here. I'm not five."

Biting her lip, Quinn nodded gravely. She pointed at Tony, who had started down the spiral steps. Ellianne followed, lugging her huge pet. Quinn brought up the rear, carrying the pink suitcase.

"What are you doing here?" Tony hissed.

"Helping," a female voice answered.

Quinn grabbed Ellianne's shoulder, stopping her halfway down the stairs. She peered over the railing but couldn't see who had answered Tony.

"Quinn, get down here," Tony called softly.

Ellianne looked up at her mother, and Quinn nodded. They hurried down the stairs as quietly as possible, but they still made way too much noise to Quinn's ears.

At the bottom, Tony shone his comtab screen on Francine.

"I thought you had a date," Quinn muttered at the blonde.

The other woman shrugged. "I thought this would be more fun. Besides, when they discover Elli is missing, my job will be toast. They'd probably throw me in prison for abetting a kidnapper. And prison around here doesn't come with a 'get out of jail' card. We need to work together."

Tony's eyes narrowed. "Why would we trust you?"

The woman shrugged again. "Because I didn't set off the alarm? Because I took out the guard standing at the bottom of these steps?" She jerked her head toward the bulk of the house.

In the shadows near the foundation, Quinn saw a body. She went cold. "Is he...dead?"

Francine snorted. "Squeamish? No, he'll be fine. I stunned him and shorted out his cybernetics. When he wakes up, he'll need some chips replaced, that's all. Where's your transport?"

Quinn dumped the suitcase on the ground and pulled the foil out of her pocket. "I have to get Ellianne's arm wrapped first."

"Don't bother." Francine held out a hand. "Give me the tracker. I can hack it."

Tony narrowed his eyes, but he slowly extended the device. "We're in this together."

Francine smiled. "Of course." She tapped the screen and plugged something into a port on the bottom. Then she pulled out her comtab. She glanced at Quinn. "You're a comm-geek, right? Let me show you." She angled the screen so Quinn could see. "The signal comes from the tracker to this device, then gets broadcast to the app on

Reggie's comtab. I'm hijacking the signal and replacing the variable with a constant."

Quinn's eyes widened in comprehension. "The current location gets hard-coded to this spot."

"Exactly. Easy, peasy, once you get into the device." Francine handed it back to Tony. "This says Lucas is at Tyler's house. I've hardcoded him there, too."

Tony's eyes flicked from Francine to the device in his hand and back. With a jerky nod, he turned. "Let's get out of here."

They crept around the house. "There's a guy at the front door," Francine whispered, "and another at the side door to the garage."

"Got him." Tony crouched, running under the heavily curtained windows along the back of the house. At the corner, he paused, then gestured for the others to stay in place. He disappeared around the house, returning a few minutes later. He crooked his fingers to call them over.

They eased around the corner, and Tony pointed to the side door. The stunned guard lay inside, staring up at the ceiling.

"Get in the Citralus," Tony whispered. While they climbed in, he popped the engine cover in the back. "I need to reattach the cables I disconnected earlier."

"Not much room back there," Quinn muttered as Ellianne scrambled into the narrow space behind the front seat, the caat cradled in her arms. "I've never ridden in the back. This suitcase takes up a lot of space."

Tony grunted. He lowered the hood carefully, snapping it into place. Quinn climbed over the front seat and folded her long legs into the tiny back seat. Ellianne grinned at her, and Quinn felt a surge of love. Her little trooper was always game for an adventure.

Tony climbed into the driver's seat beside Francine. "Try to duck down, Quinn."

Quinn twisted sideways and leaned forward, curving her body over her daughter.

"Good. Here we go." He pressed a button and the garage door

rolled open. The car rumbled to life and rolled out onto the gravel drive. "This thing is damn noisy," Tony muttered. The car surged forward, knocking Quinn's shoulder against the seat back. Ellianne giggled.

"Do you think the guards know there's no one home who should be driving this thing?" Francine asked conversationally.

"They haven't exactly impressed me with their skill and intelligence," Tony said. "But if something's going to go wrong—"

Bright lights stabbed through the rear window. A magnified voice shouted, "HALT!"

"Speak of the devil," Tony muttered. "Hold on, folks. Time to try out the booster."

With a roar, the vehicle slammed forward, shoving them all back into the seats. Quinn wrapped her arms around her daughter and squeezed her eyes shut.

"The gate isn't opening!" Francine's voice was shrill over the roar of the engine.

"It will," Tony yelled. "Or we'll open it. That flimsy metal isn't stopping this rocket."

The engine spooled up, shaking the car and pounding their ears. Quinn clutched Ellianne, wishing the back seat had safety restraints. Metal shrieked on metal, and they jolted as something seemed to grab the car.

Quinn's eyes popped open. The partially open metal gate gripped the car in its open maw. The sharp stench of burning tires bit her nose. The engine whined then the car tore free, pieces of gate flying into the air.

"Yes!" Tony whipped the Citralus around the tight corner into the street. The power surged again, shoving them against the thick upholstery.

"Now what?" Quinn yelled over the engine noise. "This car is impossible to miss. Even without significant body damage. Now that they know we have it, they'll corner us in minutes."

"Maybe," Tony hollered. "The guards might try to chase us for a while before they call in reinforcements—in hopes they won't get fired—but we shouldn't count on that. I have a plan."

The car rocketed down the road, turning at seemingly random points. They stormed through a suburban neighborhood, then across a parking lot and through a busy fast-food drive-through. Quinn wasn't sure how Tony had missed the cars in the driveway.

"Francine," Tony said. "Can you set up an auto route for this car? So we can ditch it, and it will keep going? Lead them on a crazy chase."

"My pleasure." Francine grinned, her white teeth flashing in the lights from oncoming traffic.

Quinn peered through the back window, but she couldn't tell if they were being followed or not. No police lights, so that was a good thing.

"This is fun!" Ellianne's eyes shone. "I like going fast." The cast purred in her lap.

"This is crazy dangerous," Quinn said. "We'll be lucky to escape alive."

"Got it?" Tony asked Francine.

"Give me a couple minutes. This thing is slower than dirt."

"Is dirt slow?" Ellianne asked.

Quinn bit back a smile.

"Soon?" Tony asked.

"Almost there," Francine said.

"I'm heading to our jump-off now. You need to be done in thirty seconds."

"I told you, this thing is slow! Next time, you need to upgrade."

"Not my car, not my fault," Tony replied. "Twenty seconds." Ignoring Francine's growl, he called over his shoulder to Quinn, "I think I've lost them for now. We're going to stop in about fifteen seconds. Get out as fast as you can. We need to hide as soon as we get out."

Francine muttered under her breath, but Quinn ignored her. She turned to her daughter. "You heard Tony. As soon as we stop, get out. Go that way." She pointed to Francine's door. "I'll go this way and meet you outside."

Ellianne nodded, squeezing the caat.

"Ready?" Tony asked.

"Almost," Francine said. "Just one more..."

"Five...four...three..." Tony counted down as the car veered around a corner. "Two...one..." They slammed to a halt.

"Got it!" Francine yelled.

"Out! Out! Out!" Tony slammed his door open and lunged out.

Francine shoved her door wide and dove out. Quinn boosted Ellianne over the seat. The caat hissed and squirmed free, scrambling away. Tony paused long enough to fold his seat forward. From the corner of her eye, Quinn saw Francine grab Ellianne's hand and drag her away from the street. Tony yanked her arm.

"My foot is stuck!" Quinn yelled.

"The car is going to leave in five seconds!" Francine called. She and Ellianne were already pushing into a thick hedge on the side of the road. "Hurry!"

"Take Elli's bag." Quinn shoved the pink suitcase at Tony. "I'm fine!" She twisted her foot, trying to pull it out from under the front seat. Pins and needles lanced up her right leg. She flung herself forward, over the folded seat, dragging her sleeping leg behind her.

The car shifted into drive and started rolling forward. Tony threw the suitcase onto the grass beside the road and ran to the still-open door. Quinn grabbed his outstretched hand and pushed with her other arm and her left leg.

A loud ripping noise echoed in her ears as Tony yanked her from the car. The Citralus sped off into the dark, doors slamming shut. She collapsed against Tony, breathing heavily.

"Come on," Tony said. "We need to get out of sight." They limped to the thick hedge and pushed through a low, dark opening. Sticks caught in Quinn's hair and scratched her face.

"Come on, Mommy," Ellianne called. "You're almost through."

She pushed harder, anxious to reach her girl. Branches snapped and her sleeping leg gave way. She fell face-first into the dirt.

"You made it!" Ellianne said. "Where's your shoe?"

CHAPTER 20

DAREEN LANDED the shuttle and ran through the shutdown procedures. She'd argued with herself all the way, but new, rebellious Dareen had won each time. Tony needed help. She could *feel* it. And she had the means to help him. She clutched the box in her hand. This thing was magic, and she was going to use it to save the day.

Logical Dareen tried one last time to talk reason, but emotional Dareen had spun up to high speed. No one understood her! No one knew what she could do! She'd show them all!

The screen pinged, and she paid the automated parking fees. Then she pulled a mini-blaster from the weapons locker and a comtab out of the charger. After logging in to her account, she sent a message to Tony's drop box.

"This is Dareen. I have something you need. Where can we meet?" She slapped the disconnect and left the bridge. In the hallway outside, she opened a closet. Various pieces of clothing hung inside, crammed tightly together. She yanked out a coverall and tossed it over her shoulder. Crouching, she pulled open a drawer and grabbed a utility belt.

She stepped into the dark coverall and slid her arms into the sleeves. Then she strapped on the belt and tucked the invisibility box into an empty pouch. Mini-blaster went into the holster. She checked the other pouches—hard currency issued by several different governments, survival gear, protein bars. She wrinkled her nose. She didn't expect to need those on a civilized planet, but you never knew when you might be in a place where you couldn't get to a vending machine.

She shut the closet and headed to cargo to unload the bike. It was fully charged, but she put an extra battery in the cargo pod and made sure the solar charger was still inside.

What else might she need? Kidnapping was not something she'd done before, so she wasn't sure what might be required. Duct tape? She always had that. Food? Kids liked food, right? She jogged back to the tiny galley and grabbed a bag of chocolate bars and a couple water packs. Those went into the cargo pod, too. Maybe a blanket? She tossed one into the basket.

Now what? She pulled up the files Tony had accumulated while planning this mission. They'd been stored in the shuttle's memory. There must be something in there to give her a clue.

"MY SHOE IS STILL in the car," Quinn told her daughter. "It got stuck. That stupid back seat was not built for real humans." She'd told Reggie that when he bought it, but he'd insisted. Mid-life crisis.

Sirens screamed in the distance, getting louder by the second.

"Come on," Francine whispered. "We need to get away from the street."

Tony grabbed her shoulder. "Wait."

Before they could move, a half dozen cars sped by, brilliant lights flashing. Quinn blinked rapidly, trying to clear the afterimages from her eyes.

"Let's go." Tony crept deeper into the foliage. "Our ride is this way."

They slipped between the trees and found a paved path. Tony led them forward, his hand in his pocket. Francine brought up the rear. Quinn glanced back at her, grateful for the help but still distrusting the woman. Why was she helping them?

"Where are we?" Quinn asked. "This looks like someone's backyard."

"It is." Tony pointed to his left. Light filtered through the trees, providing dim illumination. "The house is over there. It's a huge lot, so we're going to sneak through their side yard."

"What if they have a dog?" Quinn asked.

The caat in Ellianne's arms hissed. Quinn had forgotten the beast was with them. "Is that thing too heavy?"

"Sashelle isn't a thing," Ellianne said, outraged. "She's my friend."

"Of course. Sorry." She glanced down at the furry head. "Sorry, Sashelle." Why was she apologizing to a caat?

Ellianne beamed. "She's not too heavy." She shifted the animal to her other arm.

"Are you sure?" Quinn asked. "I can carry her, if you want."

The caat and the girl looked up at her. Ellianne shook her head. "I'm okay."

"Quiet," Francine whispered. "We're getting close to the house."

They eased up the path, keeping an eye on the house as they approached. At the fence, Tony reached up to unlatch the gate. It swung open, screeching loudly.

"Down!" Tony hissed.

They ducked behind the low bushes as a spotlight speared the gate. The back door of the house opened, and someone stepped out. "Who's there?"

Tony, barely visible in the shadow of the bushes, put a finger to his lips. Quinn put a hand on Ellianne's head.

"Who's out there?" the voice demanded again. "The gate is open! I know you're there! I have a blaster."

Quinn peeked through the foliage. An ancient-looking man holding a cane—and no weapon—stood in the doorway. She grinned. *Points for courage, old man.*

"Come out!" The man shook his cane.

Sashelle squirmed out of Ellianne's arms and shot across the yard, heading directly for the back door. Ellianne gasped, but the caat meowed loudly at the same instant.

The caat shot between the man's legs, dashing into the house. The man stumbled, grabbing the doorframe. He recovered, swinging his cane after the caat's retreating tail. "Get out of my house, you damn caat!"

"Come on," Tony muttered. "While Sashelle has him distracted."

"We can't leave her!" Ellianne cried.

Quinn pressed her fingers against child's lips. "She'll catch up."

Ellianne's eyes lit up. She scrambled to her feet and followed Tony through the gate. Quinn and Francine followed.

The front yard provided little cover. Tony darted into the shade of a scrubby tree. A light from the front of the house cast lacy shadows across his face and body. Ellianne slid next to him, disappearing behind the slim trunk.

Quinn took a step toward them, but Francine grabbed her arm. The younger woman jerked her head at another of the slender trees, then eased down behind a birdbath. Quinn ducked under the tree branches and sucked in her stomach, hoping she wasn't as painfully obvious as she felt.

The furious cries of the caat echoed from inside the house. Loud thumps and curses followed. "Get out of my house!" the old man cried repeatedly.

Tony caught Quinn's eye and jerked his head toward the street. They raced across the damp grass. Quinn stumbled, pain lancing through her bare foot and up her leg. She flailed her arms, scrambling to maintain her balance. Ignoring the pain, she hurtled across the yard and behind a car parked in the road.

"Did you trip on one of the gnomes?" Tony grinned from behind a low fence in front of the neighbor's yard.

She scowled at him, then turned to look at the house. Francine leapt gracefully over a short, pointed statue and slid in next to them. "Stupid garden gnomes. Why do people have those things?"

"And stay out!" The old man's yell was punctuated by the slamming of a door.

"Where's Sashelle?" Ellianne whispered, her high-pitched voice sounding loud in the sudden silence. Quinn shushed her.

"There she is." Francine pointed.

They peered around the car they hid behind. The caat strolled across the grass, her thick tail waving over her back as she went, hips swaying. She sat down beside a gnome dressed in the blue and gray of the Federation and licked a paw. Then, lightning-fast, the paw whipped out and smashed the garden ornament to the ground with a crash. The caat stretched, arching her back and kneading the grass.

"Sashelle," Ellianne whispered.

With one last flick of her tail, Sashelle streaked across the grass into the little girl's arms.

Quinn stared. Beside her, Francine chuckled. "Don't mess with the Eliminator."

CHAPTER 21

DAREEN STOPPED the bike in the shadows at the base of the high wall surrounding the LaRaine Estate. Sirens screamed, growing softer as the patrol cars sped away. She looked at the gate, swinging closed. She could probably get through the opening before the gate snapped shut, but then what? Obviously, Tony and Quinn had left, or the rent-a-cops would still be inside.

Dareen chewed a fingernail. She could follow the sirens and hope to catch up to her cousin without getting caught, or she could try another location. With a nod, she tapped the comtab clipped to the handlebars and clicked the secondary target she'd loaded into the system.

The bike hummed under her butt. She put it into gear and pulled a U-turn in the middle of the street. She'd probably been caught on a traffic camera, but she wasn't worried about that. By the time the system figured out who to bill for the ticket, she'd be long off-planet. Besides, according to the data from the shuttle, the bike's plates were registered to the LaRaine Estate. She chuckled.

Following the glowing map on her comtab, she sped away. The map led her down the road and to a narrow highway. A few klicks along, she turned into a more urban area, with taller buildings. She stopped in a lot and parked the bike. Then she dropped a couple coins into the meter. No point in tempting fate. She hitched up her belt and strolled across the street.

It was late, at least for a place like Hadriana. The streets were deserted except for the occasional car. No one loitered in the recessed doorways. A few lights glowed in the apartments above, but the street was quiet.

Dareen stepped into a recessed doorway, leaning back so the streetlights couldn't reach her. She stared up at the lighted window on the fourth floor. According to Tony's research, that apartment belonged to Malinia Sinclair, Reggie's girlfriend.

"What are you doing?"

Dareen's heart slammed into high speed, and she jerked upright. A shadow stood next to her in the doorway. "Who— What— Who are you?"

A snort, quickly stifled, was the only reply.

Dareen flicked her comtab and shined the glow at the figure. It resolved into an adolescent boy, with messy brown hair, green eyes, and a smattering of freckles across his nose.

"I'm Lucas," he said. "Who are you?"

"Lucas? Lucas LaRaine?"

The boy's eyes narrowed. "Who wants to know?"

"I'm Dareen Whiting. Are you Quinn's kid?"

"You know my mom?" His eyes widened.

"Yeah, we brought her to Hadriana," Dareen said. "What are you doing out here?"

"Watching him." The boy jutted his chin at the lighted window. "He thinks I'm at my friend's house, but I've been following him. Jerk."

"Your dad?"

Lucas snorted. "Who else? I can't believe he's cheating on Mom."

"I'm sorry. That must suck."

"You think having your mom on death row and your dad cheating on her sucks?" The boy's voice cracked painfully. "That's the understatement of the year."

"What do you want to do about it?"

"What can I do about it?" He turned away, looking down the dark street. "He can do whatever he wants. Grandmother owns this planet."

"How about running away?" she asked. "You can go with your mom."

He shook his head. "Go where? They're going to catch her. The Federation doesn't let convicted traitors escape."

Dareen shrugged. "Not usually. But most of them don't have the Marconis to help."

"The Marconis?" The boy jerked around. Then he laughed. "A fictional crime family is going to help my mom?"

She planted her fists on her hips. "We aren't fictional! Why does everyone keep saying that?"

"You're a Marconi?" Lucas raised his eyebrows at her. "Really? Why didn't you introduce yourself that way?"

"My last name isn't Marconi," Dareen said. "It's Whiting. And we usually like to keep a low profile. But my mom is a Marconi. And my gramma is the head of the family."

"Who *are* you?" Lucas asked.

"I just told you!"

"Whatever." Lucas crossed his arms over his chest. "Do you know where my mom is?"

"Not right now—"

He cut her off. "Then forget it."

"I can find her!" Dareen stomped her foot. Even this little twerp didn't take her seriously. "My cousin Tony is with her right now. And I'm meeting him."

"When? Where?" Lucas grabbed her arm.

She yanked free and narrowed her eyes at the boy. "Now you believe me?"

"Are you meeting my mom?" Lucas asked, his voice raw with longing.

Dareen looked away. "Yes, I'm here to extract them. And I have this." She pulled the device from her belt pouch.

"What is it?" Lucas asked.

"It's an invisibility cloak." She flipped the lid open.

Lucas rolled his eyes. "Right."

"Seriously, watch." She pressed the activation button. The humming started in her jaw.

The boy rubbed his ear. "What is that noise?"

"It's the cloak."

"I can still see you."

She nodded. "That's because you're inside it. But watch this." She walked out of the doorway and across the sidewalk. His gasp told her the device was working.

"Where'd you go?" Lucas whispered.

She turned and stepped closer, bringing him inside the cloak. "I told you." She smiled.

"How does that thing work?" Lucas stretched out a hand.

She batted it aside. "Don't touch. I don't know how it works, just that it does."

"Awesome! Now what?"

Dareen glanced at the box, then back at the boy. "I— I don't know."

THE CAR SLID to a stop outside a large house. It looked like every other house in this neighborhood, with a two-car garage, a small square lawn, and a narrow front porch.

"Tyrel's house is gray." Ellianne pointed to the houses on either side. "That one is green, and that one is blue. But you can't tell in the dark. Plus, they're kind of muddy green and blue, so they look the same."

In the front seat, Francine snorted. "This whole planet looks the same."

"Not really." Quinn felt a strange compulsion to defend her in-laws' home. "There's desert on the other continent."

"That's not what I meant," Francine said. "You know the government works hard to make everything the same, so no one feels, uh, dissatisfied. I was going to say unhappy, but they really don't care about that. They want to keep the masses pacified."

Tony shook his head. "Let's not talk politics. We have a mission."

"Right." Francine opened the door. "I'll be right back." She climbed out of the car and strolled up to the front door.

"I'm not sure this is a good idea," Quinn said. "Surely Reggie told them I'd be looking for him."

"Do you think so?" Tony twisted around to look at her. "His mother doesn't want people to know you're here. Having a daughter-in-law tried for treason was a serious blow to her social standing."

Quinn laughed, a single hard bark. "I'm so sorry my little *difficulties* reflect badly on her. Besides, she practically owns this planet. I don't think anything could hurt her social standing."

"Maybe not," Tony said. "But she's not going to take a chance."

"Okay, I'll give you that one. But now that they know I'm on Hadriana, they must have taken precautions. They'll know I'm looking for Lucas."

Tony shrugged. "Maybe Reggie thought sending Lucas to a friend's house was safe. He seems to think you're operating on your own—how would you know where the friend lives?"

She shook her head. "He's delusional. He must know I'll do anything to get the kids back. And he knew you were involved in my escape."

Tony shook his head. "He knew I was involved in the Fort Sumpter thing. Hell, everyone knew that—it wasn't a secret that I was there—but Reggie hasn't seen me here, and the person who helped you escape Romara was reported to be two meters tall and half-android." He grinned.

"Your actions were larger than life," Quinn said. "What about Mrs. Ricardi? She knew you were here."

"She doesn't know me as Tony Bergen. It's quite possible she has no idea."

"She said Tony Macaroni was at Grandmother's house," Ellianne piped in. "And 'that dreadful woman.' I heard her."

Tony winked. "See? Not me, some guy with an unfortunate rhyming name."

"I think she meant you," Ellianne said. "She said it wrong. But I didn't see any dreadful women. Just Mommy." She leaned her head against Quinn's arm.

The car door opened and Francine leaned in. "Not here. The guy said his kid hasn't seen Lucas in a couple days. Toby?"

"Tyrel." Ellianne yawned again.

"Tyrel is at home. No friend visiting." Francine climbed into the car and shut the door.

Tony hit the start switch, sending the car silently down the street. "So, he already figured out how to trick the tracker. Before you hacked it."

A wash of pride swept over Quinn. She'd be furious if one of the kids tried that on her, but now it was funny. And helpful. Except— "How will we find him?"

"Where would he go?" Tony asked. "Somewhere he doesn't want his dad to know about. Party? Girl's house?"

Francine and Quinn both shook their heads.

"He's never been the rebellious type. At least, he never was before." Quinn looked at Francine.

The other woman shook her head. "If he's snuck away, it's because he wants to do something Reggie wouldn't like. Not like a party or to get into trouble, but to find out something. Or maybe he's trying to get to you?"

Quinn considered that. Would Lucas try to find her? He'd run away from her earlier in the day, but he was a moody kid. He reacted emotionally, then had to backpedal when he realized his first reaction had been too extreme. Quinn figured he'd grow out of it. But for now, yes, it was likely he'd decided to find her.

"Did he say anything when you talked to him this afternoon?" Francine persisted.

Was it only this afternoon? Quinn's eyelids suddenly drooped. She was exhausted. She hadn't gotten a decent night's sleep since the evacuation—death row was not conducive to pleasant dreams. Since then, she and Tony had been on the move, every night.

Every night. She glanced down at Ellianne, but the child's eyes were closed, and her face peaceful. "Does he know about Reggie's girlfriend?" Quinn asked softly.

"If he didn't before, he does now," Tony said. "You told him."

Quinn stared at Tony. "I did?"

He nodded. "At the cave? You mentioned Reggie's old girlfriend."

Quinn dropped her head into her hands. "I used to be so good at momming."

Francine coughed quietly. "He knew. Before Quinn said anything. I don't think he believed it—or at least he tried not to. But when he got back from his ride this afternoon, he asked me where Reggie went every night." Her face tightened. "I told him he went to his club. That was his cover story."

"*The club,*" Quinn mimicked Ellianne's upper crust tone from earlier. "You think he is trying to find out where Reggie's been going? How would he know where she lived?"

"Maybe he was tracking Reggie," Francine suggested with a laugh.

"That would not surprise me at all," Tony said. "That kid is smart. We may as well check it out—it's the best lead we have at this point."

CHAPTER 22

LOU PACED across the bridge—three stomping strides in each direction. She turned and pinned her son-in-law with a glare. "What the hell was that girl thinking? What kind of ungrateful child did you raise?"

Maerk stood by the door, arms crossed over his chest. He stared right back at Lou, his eyes hard. Usually, he did what he was told—Lou was a good captain and ran a profitable business—but this concerned his daughter. "You sent my teenage daughter on a dangerous mission without my knowledge, and now you expect *me* to take the blame for her going AWOL? How about you explain exactly what you got her into?"

Lou eyed Maerk. "She's an adult," she said sulkily.

"If she's an adult, you should have trusted her with all the information," Maerk said. "She told me you left her in the dark. If you expect her to run missions, she needs all the details."

"You think she's sulking because I didn't give her enough information?" Lou shook her head. "I'm not going to trust her at all if she's behaving like a child."

"Seems to me, you're the one who's sulking. What are you not telling me?"

"I don't know what you're talking about." Lou swung away to look at the ship's console.

Maerk took a couple steps forward and grabbed Lou's arm. "I know that tone of voice. Spill it, Lou."

The old woman looked up, then sighed. "Fine. You're right. I didn't give her all the details. I should have told her what the device did, and that she'd need to verify its use." She rubbed her hand through her gray hair, making it stand on end. "I also should have told her about the side effects when I found out she'd turned it on again."

Maerk went still. "What side effects? What does this thing do?"

"It uses elastic-optic technology to mimic the environment."

"Elastic-optic technology? It's a stealth tech? Those things aren't very good yet." Maerk's eyes narrowed. "At least, last I heard, they were still in the experimental phase."

"This one works," Lou said. "It's effective enough to be used in the field. The problem is, the electromagnetic shielding isn't perfect—it can't be. It amplifies the visual dampening. But it has some weird effects on the brain."

"What kind of effects?"

"Nothing inherently dangerous." She held up her hands to ward off his explosion. "From what I know, it kind of introduces static to the connections in the brain. The effects are minor, but cumulative."

"Static in the brain?" Maerk's hands clenched. "The part of the body that isn't fully developed until you're well into your twenties? And the effect is cumulative? What the hell does that mean? Is it permanent?" His voice got louder and more agitated with each question.

"No—no!" Lou cried. "It just means the longer you use the device, the more static it introduces. If you turn it off, the static goes away, but if you turn it back on, it starts at a higher level. At least, I think that's what it means. I'm not a neuroscientist."

"You need to fix this." Maerk stepped closer to Lou, leaning over her, his voice dangerously low. "Call her. Call Tony. Get them back up here!"

"I can't call them," Lou said. "Tony is running silent. And calling Dareen would bring attention to her. She won't listen to me anyway—not if she's under the influence of that thing."

"Then go get her. You need to find my daughter and bring her back to the ship before she unintentionally does something stupid. And when she gets here, we are going to pack our things and leave. I won't stay on a ship where the captain puts her own pride ahead of her crew's welfare."

"Don't leave," Lou said. "I know I was stupid. I was trying to protect her. I'll get her back. *We'll* get her back."

Maerk slapped the comm button on the console. "All hands to the bridge. NOW!"

DAREEN STOPPED at the top of the steps and glanced back at Lucas. "This doesn't seem like a great idea." Logical Dareen was whispering in her brain again.

"If you're chicken, I'll take the box and you can wait here." Lucas extended his hand.

"I'm not giving you this thing," she replied. "It's Marconi property."

"Do you have a better idea?"

Dareen wracked her brains. "Nope."

"Then let's go." He pushed open the door. "Is it on?"

"Yeah. Can't you feel it?" She rubbed her jaw.

They stepped into the fourth-floor hall. Rough, brown carpet covered the floor. Flat, brown doors stood at intervals with cheap watercolor prints hung between. Dareen counted the doors as they walked along the hallway. "This one." She pointed to the light shining under the door.

They leaned in close, listening. Lucas shook his head. "Nothing."

"What's the plan?" Dareen asked. "Are we going to just open the door and walk in?"

"Why not?" Lucas replied. "They won't see us, so they won't know we came in. Maybe they'll think it was the wind."

Dareen stared at him. "There's no wind in this hallway."

"Wait here." Lucas ran to the far end of the corridor, where a window looked down into the narrow space between this building and the next. The window slid open easily. Then he sprinted back, almost slamming into Dareen. "Whoa! Didn't see you there!"

Dareen snickered. "That's pretty funny. You didn't see me!"

Lucas laughed too, making weird faces at her.

That got her laughing harder. She wasn't sure what was so funny about it, but she couldn't stop. "You couldn't see me!"

"Keep it down out there!" a voice called through the door on their left.

Their giggles cut off and their eyes met. Then they laughed even louder.

"Hey! I said shut up!" The door rattled with the sound of locks turning.

"These walls must be paper thin," Dareen whispered, putting her hand over her mouth to stifle the giggles. "Be quiet."

"You be quiet." Lucas bit his lips, but his eyes crinkled, and a snort escaped.

The door behind them opened. A man stuck his head out, looking up and down the hall. "What are you kids doing?"

Dareen grabbed Lucas's hand and dragged him farther away. She was pretty sure the guy hadn't seen them, but what if he'd been inside the invisibility bubble?

Other doors opened. People looked out and then went back inside, slamming doors behind them. Reggie stepped out of the apartment closest to them. Lucas lunged forward, but Dareen grabbed his arm, pulling him back.

"Why's that window open?" Reggie demanded. No one answered. He stomped to the end of the hall.

"Now." Lucas dragged Dareen into the apartment.

The industrial blah aesthetic of the building ended at the door.

Slick black and white marble tile covered the floor. An angular metal table stood in the middle of the room on a thick red carpet. Black metal shelves held sleek silver ornaments. A shiny black couch sat by the table, and a woman lounged on the couch, drinking a glass of wine.

"Is that her?" Dareen whispered.

The woman looked up, her face puzzled. She wore an expensive-looking robe and her blonde hair was teased into a huge bubble around her face. Heavy makeup lined her eyes and covered her cheeks. She looked like a middle-aged woman who couldn't admit time was catching up with her.

Lucas shrugged and made a face. "I guess. Now what?" he mouthed.

Dareen grimaced. "This was your idea," she mouthed back, pointing at him.

He looked around the room, then pointed at the still-open door. "Let's get out—"

Reggie came back in and shut the door.

"Who was causing all the trouble?" the woman asked.

Reggie shrugged. "Probably neighbors. Look, Malinia." He caressed the woman's shoulder. "I gotta go. I shouldn't have stayed this long. Obviously, that call was designed to get me out of the estate. Who knows what Quinn is trying? If we didn't have such good security—"

"I'll be so glad when that woman is caught. I can't believe the nerve of her, coming here!"

"I know," Reggie said. "But she wants the kids. I gotta make sure that doesn't happen. Or at least make it look like I don't want that to happen."

The woman smirked. "It *would* be convenient if they disappeared. Why don't you stay here and let her take them? It wouldn't be your fault."

"My mother would have a fit." Reggie went pale. "She keeps squawking about family legacy and descendants."

"Maybe if we're lucky, Quinn will take her, too." Malinia cackled.

Something brushed against Dareen's arm. Her head snapped around but before she could stop him, Lucas lunged forward and slammed his head into Reggie's gut, knocking him to the floor. "You want to get rid of us?"

Malinia shrieked.

"What the hell?" Reggie hollered, glaring up at his son. "How'd you get here?"

Through the door, someone shouted, "Shut up!" No one but Dareen seemed to notice.

Reggie leapt up and grabbed Lucas's arm. "Where were you hiding? Who brought you here?"

"Don't change the subject," Lucas spat. "You just told your girlfriend you don't want me and Elli!"

"You misunderstood," Reggie said. "I—"

"Tell him the truth, Reg," Malinia drawled with a negligent shrug. She looked at Lucas. "He *doesn't* want you. Why would he? You're a constant reminder of that *crepiva*." She turned to Reggie. "Get rid of him. I don't want this ungrateful *zerek* in my house." She crossed her arms over her ample chest.

Reggie glared at Malinia then turned back to his son. "That's not true! You're my son. Of course I want you."

"You don't give a *zerek* about us," Lucas said. "I think you just don't want Mom to have us, either."

Dareen stepped back slowly, easing toward the kitchen. She didn't need Reggie or Malinia stumbling into the cloaking bubble. She wasn't sure what to do about Lucas, but she sure as hell wasn't going to get caught, too.

CHAPTER 23

MAERK STOOD before of the viewscreen on the bridge facing the family. Behind him, the curve of the planet glowed brightly as they approached the sunward side. Lights picked out the edges of the large equatorial continent.

The family crammed into the bridge. It usually felt spacious, but not today. Since he was essentially staging a mutiny, Maerk wanted the entire family to know *he* was calling the shots.

Lou sat in the navigator's chair, head down. She'd screwed up, and she was letting him take charge. This was a temporary situation—he'd known Lou long enough to make that one hundred percent clear. For now, she was going to let him run the show. But this was her ship, and she would take it back. Fine with him. He was going to rescue his daughter and take his family somewhere safer. Somewhere saner. Normal, even.

Liz stood near the captain's chair. Her older brother, Kert, leaned against the back wall, next to End. Stene, Lou's middle child and Tony's dad, sat at the communication station. Ironic, since he rarely spoke.

"We know Dareen has this cloaking device," Maerk said. "It hides the user visually but doesn't affect the other senses. If she makes noise, for example, it's still heard. Anyone using a heat sensor or sound detection would notice her. There are also minor visual anomalies that might be noticed—if the target is looking for them. However, on an unsuspecting audience, it's quite effective."

"I want to know more about these side effects." Liz turned her piercing green eyes on her mother. "What's the actual effect? Poor judgment? Clearly. But how will that manifest? And what's the long-term effect?"

Lou shook her head, not meeting anyone's eyes. "We don't know. Presumably, in a person with incomplete frontal lobe connections—that is, a teen—the device would make those connections even less robust. So, yes, poor judgment. A feeling of invincibility, perhaps? This is black-market tech, though, so I doubt those things have been studied."

"And you let my teenaged daughter mess with this device without supervision?" Liz accused. "What were you thinking?! Oh, yeah, you weren't!"

Maerk felt a grim sense of satisfaction in hearing Liz spout the phrase he'd often heard Lou say to the younger members of the family. Apparently, it applied to all generations.

"If we could warn her," Kert said, slowly, "would it help? I mean, if we made her aware of the problem, could she monitor herself?"

"Maybe?" Maerk rubbed his hands over his head. "If she's using it, we need to get her to turn it off."

"If she's using it, we can find her!" Lou jumped up from her seat. "We should be able to scan for the frequencies it's emitting."

"You know what those are?" Maerk leveled a look at her.

"No, but I know when she activated it yesterday," Lou said. "We always monitor missions, so we have a recording of the location dirtside when she did the pickup. That should allow us to determine a unique signature and look for it again. End, get over here."

End slunk between the adults and slouched into the chair Lou had vacated.

"The device was activated briefly around the time she transmitted the payment release," Lou said. "And it was turned on again shortly after that and continued operating until she returned to the *Peregrine*."

"She had it on that long?" Liz sounded shocked.

"It got switched on accidentally, and she couldn't figure out how to switch it off," Lou said over her shoulder. "She left it in the cargo bay, so she was outside the effect most of that time. Plus, the shielding in the shuttle should have protected her." Lou's voice was authoritative, but Maerk detected a faint whiff of bluster. She really didn't know squat about this thing.

"You don't know squat about that thing." Liz repeated his thoughts word-for-word. "Don't try to talk around me with your technobabble, Mother."

Lou spun around, her hand clutched to her chest. "Ouch. You wound me." She rolled her eyes. "I've put up with worse from the lot of you over the years."

"Yes, but you're the captain." Liz thrust a finger at her mother. "You are supposed to be responsible. The logical decision-maker. The parent."

Lou drew herself up, ready to launch a counter attack.

"Got it." End interrupted the standoff. "There *is* a unique signal. Scanning for it now."

"I hate to mention this." Stene raised his hand slowly. "If there's a unique signal, we might not be the only ones looking for it."

THE CAR SLID up to the curb and stopped. Tony looked up at the building, then at Francine and back at Quinn. "We need to find out if he's here. If he is, we need to extract him. Suggestions?"

They stared blankly at each other.

"You could go knock on the door," Quinn told Tony. "*She* doesn't know you."

"Does she know you?"

Quinn shrugged. "She's probably seen a pic of me. My face was plastered all over the planet when I married Reggie."

"What good will knocking on the door do?" Francine demanded. "The kid isn't going to be in her apartment—unless they caught him. And they aren't going to just hand him back to us if they have."

"She's right," Tony said. "If he's here, he's spying on his dad. He isn't going to visit the girlfriend."

"Stop saying girlfriend," Quinn muttered. "It sounds friendly."

Francine chuckled. "Now that Ellianne is asleep, we could use whore, I suppose. Bitch? Slut?"

Quinn glared at Francine. "Fine. Stick with girlfriend, just until we don't have to mention her ever again." She glanced at her daughter, whose head lay in her lap. "But I think you're right. If he came to spy on his dad, he'll be out here. Or maybe in the lobby. We should check. But someone needs to stay with Ellianne."

"I'll look for him." Francine open the car door. "He seemed pretty upset earlier. I'm not sure he'd go with either of you." She hopped out and shut the door before they could respond.

"Why do you trust her?" Quinn watched the other woman cross the street. "You said she's from a rival family. How do we know she isn't going to…" She waved her hands in a vague motion.

"Kidnap him?" Tony asked with a chuckle. "She's been working for the LaRaines for weeks. If she wanted to take your kids away, she could have done it any time before we got here. I think she's exactly what she says—taking a break from her family and working an honest job for the first time in her life."

"That's exactly what scares me!" Quinn said. "If we're successful, she'll have lost that job, so why is she helping us?"

"I trust her. I can't share the details with you, but I have very valid reasons." He lifted his comtab to read a message. "She's checked the perimeter. Now she's going in."

A light flared as the front door opened. Then it closed, leaving darkness.

Moments later, the door opened again. "That's Reggie!" Quinn pointed through the gloom. "And he has Lucas with him! I'm going—"

"To what?" Tony slapped an arm against the passenger seat so she couldn't push it forward and get out. "Stop them in the middle of the street under full view of urban surveillance? We'll be better off to follow them back to the estate at this point."

Reggie pushed Lucas ahead of him toward the boxy Seridia she hadn't noticed sitting under the trees by the street. Lucas climbed into the open back door, then out the other side. Reggie hollered and raced around the back of the car to grab his son's arm. He dragged the boy into the car, and it pulled away from the curb.

"Follow him!" Quinn said.

"What about Francine?" Tony said.

"She's on her own. Follow him."

"We know where he's going." Tony started the car and tapped on the control screen. "We're locked on to that car."

"You can do that?"

Tony grinned over his shoulder. "It's not a standard upgrade."

DAREEN TRIED to follow Reggie and Lucas out of the apartment, but Malinia got in the way. Desperate to stay hidden, she backed into the kitchen as the woman closed the door.

The kitchen was a tiny, galley-style space, separated from the living room by a half-wall and overhead cupboards. Dareen was tall, but if she ducked, she could see into the living room.

Malinia closed the door and strode to the kitchen. Dareen swallowed a curse and backed up against the narrow closet door at the end of the room. She pulled the device out of the belt pouch and popped the lid open. Maybe there was a way to dial down the radius of the bubble. If Malinia came more than two steps into the room, she was toast.

The older woman opened the refrigerator and pulled out a bottle.

She crossed to the counter, moving closer. As Malinia pulled a clean glass from the cupboard, Dareen twisted the device, wildly searching for controls she knew weren't there. Panic sat on her chest, her breath getting louder.

Malinia set the glass down and looked around the kitchen. Dareen clamped a hand over her mouth, holding her breath. With a shrug, the older woman picked up the bottle and glass and moved out of the kitchen.

Dareen sucked in air, her heart pounding in her head. That was too close! She bolted out of the kitchen, knocking into Malinia in the tiny foyer. The older woman tumbled to the floor, her eyes wide. The glass flew out of her hand and shattered against the marble floor.

"What the—" Malinia said, staring up at Dareen.

Too close—she was inside the stealth bubble! For a second, Dareen froze, her eyes locked onto Malinia's. Then she leapt over the prone woman, yanked the door open, and fled.

CHAPTER 24

A MAP of Hadriana glowed on the big screen, a pinpoint of bright green expanding into a circle, growing larger before disappearing and starting again. Maerk pointed. "What is that?"

"It has to be Dareen." End cocked his head, reconsidering. "Or whoever is using the device."

"That's a suburb of Hadriana City—not too far from the LaRaine Estate," Kert put in. "Is she working Tony's gig?"

"I told her the device was to help Tony." Lou hung her head. "She probably figured she should take it to him."

"That doesn't make sense to me," End said. "The device was off when she decided to take it from the weapons locker. It wasn't influencing her decisions at that point."

Maerk looked up, sharply. "You're saying the effect is persistent, even when the device is off?"

"I'm not saying that," End said. "I'm a stupid teen with a disconnected frontal brain case or whatever. But I *am* saying that taking the thing to Tony in the middle of a mission is a stupid idea—she knows he runs deep. Even I wouldn't try that. So why did she do it?"

Maerk ground his teeth. End was right. There was more going on than Lou was owning up to. "Let's just find her and bring her back."

Lou stood. "We'll do a covert extraction."

"No," Liz said. "I'll fly the second shuttle down. Maerk and I will go in through normal, official channels. Two parents looking for their kid who's run off. Happens all the time. No one will think twice about it."

"Doesn't usually involve a shuttle and a magic cloaking device," End muttered.

Maerk glared at the boy. "You're staying here."

"I hate to be the bearer of bad news," Kert said, "but the secondary shuttle is inop. Got a short in the auto-drive."

"I don't need the auto-drive," Liz said. "I've been piloting shuttles my whole life."

"Yeah, I know," Kert said. "Who taught you? The problem is, I've got the thing torn apart."

"Why would you tear apart the shuttle when we're on a mission?" Liz demanded.

"Number one," Kert said, "this is not a normal mission. We were providing minimum support to Tony, and one shuttle should have been sufficient for that. Number two, *you* approved the work order when I made the request. Number three, I started pulling—"

"Shut up, Kert," Liz said. "I get it. Not your fault. We'll have to use the drone."

"Saint Joseph protect us," Maerk muttered. "I hate riding the drone."

DAREEN STUMBLED out of Malinia's apartment and raced down the hall. She slammed her finger on the elevator button but thought better of it and lunged for the stairwell. Hands slippery with sweat, she juggled the device, trying to put it away so she could open the door.

She'd just stowed it when the door opened. A woman she didn't recognize looked right at her and smiled. "I'll take that," she said. Her hand darted into Dareen's open pouch.

"Hey! Give that back to me!" Dareen grabbed the woman's arm. The woman swung around, slamming Dareen into the open door. Dareen yelped as pain zinged through her shoulder.

She barely noticed a sting in her arm. Her head swam. The woman went all wavy, like an ocean. A warm feeling of contentment spread through Dareen's body, like a thick blanket and hot chocolate.

"Come with me," the woman said.

Dareen smiled. "Okay."

THE BOXY SERIDIA carrying Reggie and Lucas slid along the street at a stately pace. Quinn itched to jump out at each stop and yank Lucas to safety. Then smash Reggie's smug face again. But Tony kept the little blue coupe at a distance, following with the lights off. The auto-drive was locked onto the Seridia, and traffic was almost nonexistent this late in the evening. Once they left the residential areas, Tony increased the distance even more so Reggie wouldn't notice them.

"If they get back to the estate, we're screwed," Quinn said. "They've got to be on high alert. They'll know we have Ellianne, and they'll be watching for us."

"Then we'll stop them before it gets there," Tony said. "I'm just waiting until we reach an area without cams."

"How are we going to do that?"

"Drone," Tony said.

"What? You're going to use a drone?" Quinn asked when he didn't elaborate.

"No, look," He pointed through the windshield. "That's the family drone. What the heck?"

Quinn squinted upward. "I don't see anything. Too dark."

"Oh, yeah," Tony replied. "I've got, um, let's call it an 'augmentation' that allows me to see family assets."

"Augmentation? In your eyes?" Quinn stared at Tony.

"Contact lenses."

Quinn filed that away for later. "Can you contact the drone and find out who's coming down and why? Could they be coming to get us?"

Tony shook his head. "I haven't called for extraction yet." He punched a few buttons on the dash. "But if it's here, we should hurry up and catch a ride. I'm going to force them off the road."

"What?" Quinn squawked. The car surged forward, the seatbelt cutting off her air supply and her question.

With smooth, competent movements, Tony guided the speeding car along the highway. In the back seat, Quinn clutched her sleeping daughter. In moments, they overtook the Seridia and swung out to the left as if to pass. The deserted road stretched ahead of them, the gates of the estate not yet in view.

Tony jerked the joystick and stomped the brakes, skidding the car across the path of the Seridia. They rocked to a halt, blocking the right lane. The bigger car swerved to the left, but Tony was ready. He jammed the coupe into reverse and blocked the left lane. "Go!"

Quinn dove over the passenger seat and slammed into the car door. It swung open and she rolled into the street.

"Ow!"

"Go!" Tony yelled again.

Quinn jumped up, raced to the Seridia's door, and yanked it open.

"Quinn!" Reggie cried.

"Give me my son."

"No. Go away." He leaned forward to tap the auto-drive screen.

Quinn grabbed his shoulder and pulled him back. "That's not going to happen." She leaned down to peer into the car. "Lucas, come with—" She shook Reggie's shoulder. "Where is he?"

Reggie twisted out of her grip. "What the—"

"Come on, Mom!" Lucas called from near Tony's car. When she looked up, he waved and climbed inside.

Quinn laughed. "That's my boy!" Leaving Reggie alone in the luxury sedan, she ran to Tony's car and jumped into the front seat. "Let's go!"

"Leave it open." Tony leaned across Quinn's lap, his mini-blaster in his hand. He fired a sustained blast into the Seridia's grill. The hood glowed red, heat rolling off it. With a muffled "boom," a wave of hot air pulsed against them. Tony sat up and motioned for Quinn to shut the door. He backed the car, turning it away from the LaRaine Estate, and hit the accelerator.

"What *was* that?" Lucas between the seats, his eyes wide.

Tony grinned over his shoulder. "Most folks don't know that'll take down an engine. Handy technique." He tapped on the navigation screen and entered some data.

"That was wicked!" Ellianne said.

"Great, your sister is awake. Put your seatbelt on, Lucas." Quinn glared at her son until he slid back. "We may be fugitives, but we need to be safe."

With a grin, Lucas buckled in and checked his sister's restraints.

"So, are we going to find the drone?" Quinn asked Tony.

"Drone?" Lucas leaned forward as far as the seatbelt would allow.

"Drone," Tony confirmed, his lips twitching. "I lost track of it while we were waylaying Reggie. The car nav hasn't locked on yet, so they may be running dark. I might need to break radio silence."

"What about your— What did you call them? Augmentations?" Quinn asked.

"I don't have any direct body augmentations—couldn't risk anything the Federation might find if I got hauled in."

"That's a real thing—direct augmentation to the eyes?" Quinn asked.

Tony shrugged. "I'm not saying they *don't* make them. But that's not what I have. My contacts identify and filter signals. Then my comtab IDs any assets bearing the family tags."

"Isn't tagging your assets kind of dangerous?" Quinn asked. "I mean, if Francine's family got ahold a pair of these contact lenses, they'd be able to find your stuff."

"We have safety procedures. For example, I have to run an activation code before they'll work, so Francine would have to have that as well. And there are decoy tags."

"Francine?" Lucas asked. "Our tutor?"

"She's a secret agent." Ellianne's eyes sparkled with excitement. "So's Tony!"

"Francine?" Lucas said again, with disgust. "She reads fashion magazines and wears high heels!"

"Excellent cover," Tony muttered.

Lucas stared at Tony, his jaw dropping. "Genius."

"She's not an active agent," Quinn said. "She quit. She's just a math tutor." And not a very good one, from what she'd seen in the library.

"Don't underestimate her," Tony said in a low voice. "She might not be 'active,' but she's got skills. And family she can call on." A soft ding drew his attention. "We've got the drone signal. Looks like they're headed for the floozy's neighborhood."

Quinn glared at Tony, jerking her head at the back seat.

"Did I miss the floozy?" Ellianne said with a huge yawn.

"You didn't miss anything," Quinn growled.

"Yeah, she did," Lucas said. "She missed Dareen and her magic box!"

Tony's head snapped around. "What did you say?"

Lucas blinked at Tony's tone. "I said she missed Dareen's magic box."

"How do you know Dareen?"

"I met her when I was casing *the club*." The boy's voice cracked on the sarcastic label. "She was watching it, too."

"Why?" Quinn asked.

"She said she was meeting you two." He looked at the adults. "She wasn't, was she?"

"We weren't expecting to meet her there," Quinn said. "She was supposed to pick us up when we called for extraction."

"Extraction," Ellianne said gleefully. "That means going to the spaceship."

"I figured." Lucas shot his sister a condescending look.

"Tell me about this magic box," Tony said.

"It was so cool!" Lucas's eyes lit up. "It made us invisible!"

"Cool!" Ellianne echoed.

The adults made disbelieving faces. "Go on," Tony said.

"Uh, isn't that enough?" Lucas demanded. "She has an invisibility cloak. What else do you need to know?"

"She said she was meeting us at—" Tony glanced at Quinn. "—that woman's building, and she had an invisibility cloak?"

"Yup."

"How did you get caught?" Quinn asked in her best mom-voice. "If you had an invisibility cloak? And you were outside, casing the joint?"

Lucas looked away, his shoulders twitching up around his ears. "We went inside. It was stupid, but it seemed like a great idea at the time. We snuck into that woman's apartment and Dad was there. Then he said—" The boy broke off.

"He said what?" Tony asked.

"I don't want to—" Lucas jerked his head toward his sister. "He said something that made me mad, and I..."

"What?" Quinn asked when he didn't continue.

"I did something stupid, and he caught me," Lucas finished with a rush. "That's all. Dareen was still in the apartment when we left. I think. She was invisible, so it's hard to say."

CHAPTER 25

THE DRONE TOUCHED down on a roof in a residential neighborhood. Liz released the breath she alway held when landing this way and scooted around to unlock the hatch.

Maerk put a hand on her arm. "Now what?"

"Now we find our daughter." She shook off his grip and hit the release.

"How?" Maerk gestured to his comtab. "Our readings aren't precise. She could be anywhere in a five-block radius. We really should have discussed this on the way down."

Liz glared. "I tried to. You were too busy praying for a safe landing."

Maerk grinned. "Saint Joseph of Cupertino, patron saint of flyers."

Liz rolled her eyes. "Yeah, I heard. But we don't have a plan. Unless you were inspired by the spirit."

"Don't mock my faith, woman," Maerk said. "We made it here alive."

After all these years, Liz still couldn't tell whether he was yanking her chain or deadly serious. "All right, then, what are we going to do?"

Maerk's comtab buzzed. "It's End. He's sending a refined estimate." He swiped and clicked in silence for a few moments. "That's my boy! He reduced the radius to a hundred meters. She should be in the next block." He pointed. "Or at least that's where the device was ten minutes ago. End says it's off now."

Liz opened the pod. "Let's go!" She vaulted out, mini-blaster in her hand. Maerk followed more sedately. "There's a door over here." She trotted across the roof.

Maerk's long legs got him there first. He rattled the knob. "Locked. Hold one." He fished some tools from his belt and plugged his comtab into a port at the base of the access-panel. Swipe. Flick. Click. "Ta dah." He shook his head as he put his gear away. "Why do people think zero zero zero zero is a secure password?"

Liz grinned at her ex-husband. "No alarm?"

Still shaking his head, Maerk gestured for her to open the door.

They tiptoed down to the top floor, then broke into a jog. Liz hadn't gone on a mission in many years, but some of the craft came back to her easily. Like acting as though you belong somewhere. Descending the first flight from the roof quietly made sense but sneaking down the rest of the stairs was a sure sign they were up to something.

Luckily, these buildings were big. Most occupants probably recognized only a handful of neighbors. If someone stopped them, they could claim to be visiting a friend on a different floor.

They reached the ground level without incident. Maerk put a hand on the external exit, but Liz pointed at a sign. "That's alarmed. Let's go out through the lobby."

Dim light illuminated a utilitarian lobby. These buildings were worker accommodations—stark, rent-controlled apartments for the working class. Liz shivered as they exited the building and crossed the poorly lit street. "Where is she?"

Maerk said. "Maybe we should text her?"

"If she doesn't have her sound off, we might give away her position."

KRIMSON RUN

"So?" Maerk paused on the sidewalk. "She's not a fugitive. She flew a shuttle down here and paid for parking on a public runway." End had found the receipt before they'd left the ship. "Even if she's in an apartment, so what? Some hotel housekeeper or potato farmer might see or hear it. Big deal. Sure, it would be better if we can extract her without creating a fuss. But as far as I'm concerned, this is a runaway teen issue. The stupid cloaking device is irrelevant."

"And Dareen is smart enough to keep her volume off when she's on a mission," Liz said. "Or at least she was before she tried out that irrelevant device."

Maerk held up a finger, then swiped his comtab. "End, did you complete an evaluation of activity in this neighborhood?"

End's voice came through the tiny speaker. "We have no contacts in that area. Nothing pops up on the local searches. That place is about as boring as it gets. You're in a normal, average neighborhood."

Liz nodded. "Okay, send her a text. Something boring and parent-like."

"How about this? Where the hell are you? You were supposed to be home hours ago!" Maerk said as he typed.

"Don't forget, 'your mother is worried sick.'" Liz flicked on her trace app and keyed in Dareen's ID. The reporting data for her daughter's comtab was turned off, of course—anyone could track you by that—but the family's IDs allowed her to trace a location if a message from another family member was accepted by the device.

"She's right here!" Liz pushed open the lobby door. "Dareen—" she broke off. The lobby was empty. "It says she's here!" She turned to Maerk, pointing at her screen.

"Her comtab *is* right there." Maerk pointed at a shabby table perched on uneven legs by a worn armchair.

TONY PUSHED OPEN the lobby door and stopped so suddenly Quinn slammed into him. "Liz! Maerk! What are you doing here?"

"We came for Dareen," Maerk answered.

"Is she here?" Tony asked.

Liz, standing by the lopsided table, shook her head. "We found her comtab." She pointed to the device.

"If it's here, she must be close," Maerk said. "Right?"

"Lucas said she was here half an hour ago," Tony said. "Did she leave a message on the comtab? Or maybe she's using the facilities?"

Liz looked up at the ceiling in disbelief. "What teenaged girl leaves her comtab while she uses the facilities?" She picked up the device. A tiny piece of paper fluttered to the ground. Liz stooped to pick it up. Her face went white.

"What is it?" Tony demanded.

"Liz, are you okay?" Maerk asked at the same moment.

Liz held out the slip of paper to her nephew. "They have Dareen."

"Who do?" Maerk asked.

Tony held up the scrap. "I don't know, but they must know who we are."

―――

QUINN PACED across the living room. They were back in the safehouse, the kids asleep upstairs. "I knew we couldn't trust her!"

"I'm not ready to condemn Francine...yet," Tony said. "She was helping us."

"Yeah, and then she stumbled on an easy target and decided to go back to her family bearing gifts." Liz jumped in, nodding at Quinn, in perfect agreement. "How could she pass it up? They've hated us for years. Having one of our children as a hostage would be irresistible, especially since you said her cover was blown here." Her hands clenched and unclenched, and she muttered, "When I catch her..."

"Her cover wasn't blown," Tony said. "She's out of a job, since we took the kids. She said she was ready to move on, but she wasn't ready to go back to her family. She made it very clear."

Liz shook her head in disbelief. "Only you would believe that story, Tony. Most of us aren't interested in leaving the family."

Quinn dropped onto the couch. This was obviously an old—and bitter—argument. Maerk sat beside her, muttering. Quinn raised an eyebrow at him.

"She's right—most of them aren't interested in leaving the family," he said in a low voice as Tony and Liz continued to argue. "But this might be the straw…"

"I'm sure they'd be sorry to lose you," Quinn murmured. Maerk had given them a rundown on Dareen's antics—and Lou's role in them—on the way to the safehouse.

"They'd be literally devastated to lose us. Lou can't run the ship without the four of us. She'd have to hire outsiders, and that's expensive. Dangerous even. But she's gone too far this time." He looked up at his ex-wife, nodding to himself. "I might have to remind her."

"What did the note say?" Quinn asked.

Maerk gave her a blank look. "Note?"

"The scrap of paper that was left with Dareen's comtab?"

"Oh, yeah." Maerk dug in his pocket and pulled out the tiny scribble. "It says 'we have her. We'll contact you'." He handed it to Quinn.

She glanced at the paper. "Do you have her comtab?"

He pulled it out and handed it to Quinn. "I don't know her password, so we can't get into it."

Quinn tapped the screen. "What's her favorite band?"

Maerk's face scrunched. "Uh, the Parcity Flavor? I think that's what they're called. But she wouldn't be stupid enough to use something that easy."

"Get your comtab," Quinn said. "Look up the lyrics to their most popular song. We're looking for a phrase that's easy to remember, something catchy and meaningful to a nineteen-year-old girl."

"How am I supposed to know that?" Maerk muttered. "Oh, wait. How about this: they don understan me."

Quinn typed in the misspelled words. The screen flickered and the message, "Hey, Dar!" appeared.

"Nice!" Maerk said. "Now what?"

"I'm not sure it helps much." Quinn hitched one shoulder. "We can see where she was before they dropped the comtab. I was kind of hoping she might have gotten a chance to leave us a message. Some way we could track her."

Maerk slapped his forehead. "I'm such an idiot! We can track her using that damn invisibility cloak." He tapped on his comtab, pulling up the app End had created to track the device's signature. "Tony!"

At Maerk's shout, Tony and Liz stopped arguing, their heads snapping around to glare at Maerk. He held up his comtab, ignoring their angry expressions. "Is it safe to call the ship from here?"

"I have a signal router." Tony crossed the room. He rummaged in a cupboard and flipped a switch, then groped the underside of the coffee table and pulled out a cable. "Plug that into your comtab. It'll encrypt the signal and route it through Hadriana City."

"It's already encrypted." Maerk fiddled with the cable.

Tony shrugged. "Double the fun."

After a moment, End's voice came over the speaker. "Did you find her?"

"No," Maerk said shortly. "There have been some, er, complications. Can you track that device? I must not be close enough to get a signal."

"Hold one." The line went silent, then End returned. "It's not on right now. Give me a second, and I'll pinpoint where it was when she turned it off." Another pause. "Sending you coordinates. Based on the movement in the minutes preceding the deactivation, she was in a car. I might be able to get an ID on it, if it's an auto-drive."

Liz sat on the coffee table and put a hand over the comtab. "Surely they wouldn't have been stupid enough to use a traceable car?"

Tony scrubbed a hand through his hair. "If it was Francine—and I'm not saying it was! She wouldn't have had access to a 'family' car.

She might have a personal car, which she may have scrubbed. Then again, she might not, since she was trying to go legit."

"Got it," End said. "Sending you the tracking ID. I think the safehouse has software to do a trace. I'll keep an eye on the device transmissions and let you know if it goes active again."

"We probably won't have a secure connection." Tony leaned in to speak. "Just text a message to your mom—say 'she's home.' And send the coordinates to my drop box." He straightened and went into the kitchen with his backpack.

"Affirmative," End said. "Where do you think she's going?"

"I wish we knew," Liz said. "Can you also scan for recent activity hereabouts?"

"Recent activity?" End asked. "You mean other families? Is someone else on Hadriana?"

"That's what we need to know," Liz said. "Send anything you uncover to Tony's drop. Be good. We hope to be home soon."

They could almost hear his eye-roll. "Yes, Mother." He signed off.

"Looks like she was headed out of the city when they turned the device off." Maerk held up his comtab.

"Is that—" Quinn grabbed the device and swiped. "She was headed toward Gretmar's place."

"What? No." Liz snatched the comtab from Quinn. "That makes no sense. There's no history of cooperation between the Zielinskys and the LaRaines."

"Is that something you track?" Quinn asked.

"Not specifically," Liz replied. "We keep tabs on LaRaine's activity, since we have connections to the staff. Or did." She glanced at Tony. "And we did more research when Tony asked us to help with your kids. As the family's business manager, I try to keep an eye on the competition, so I usually know who's operating where."

"This whole 'family' thing is really—" Quinn broke off, trying to figure out what she wanted to say. "The Marconis are a myth. At least in the Federation. I mean, when something weird happens, it's blamed on you guys. Stock market drop? The Marconis must be up to something. Citrus prices up due to a freak ice storm? Marconis must have developed a freeze ray. No one believes you're real. And I've never heard of the Zielinskys."

"We don't have time for a history lesson," Liz said.

"Besides, it's 'need to know' only," Maerk said in a stage whisper. "What's the plan?"

"I've got the car's ID." Tony stood in the kitchen door holding his stuffed bag. "I've got supplies, weapons, anything I can think of. Liz, Maerk, you're with me. Quinn, you stay here with your kids. I'll call when we get Dareen, and you can meet us at the pickup site." He tossed a comtab to her. "Use this to keep in touch. It's local only, which makes it harder to trace."

"Where's the pickup site?" Quinn asked.

Tony looked around the house. "Let's do it here. We'll need a new safehouse, anyway."

"Assuming we ever set foot on this planet again," Liz muttered.

CHAPTER 26

DAREEN RUBBED HER EYES. They were dry and crusty, and her body felt stiff. She yawned a couple times, hoping to get some tears flowing, while she figured out what had happened. The past was fuzzy, at best.

Her current location gave her no clues. She was in a tiny, dark room. The ceiling was too low for her to stand upright. The floor and walls were hard. A few steps led up to a small door she would have to crouch low to get through. Light leaked around the edges. She crawled up the steps and rattled the door. Locked, of course.

With a groan, she sank onto the bottom step. She remembered almost running into a woman outside Malinia's apartment. Then everything got fuzzy. The woman had seen her—she must have been inside the cloaking bubble. Dareen's hand crept to her bicep. There had been a sting—she must have been drugged. They'd ridden in a car, and Dareen had emptied her pockets at the woman's command. Obviously, the drug made her compliant. She'd happily climbed down into this stupid hole. Perfect.

What in the hell had she been thinking? Why had she even been at that apartment? She vaguely recalled telling her brother she was going to take the cloaking device to Tony. But why? Gramma hadn't—She rubbed her temples. She'd been acting like an idiot all day.

But she was feeling better now, so it was time to make a plan and take action.

But what? Dareen tapped her fingers on the step, looking around the cell. There was nothing on the floor, no cracks in the walls. Wait a minute— What was that? She moved to the back of the cell, intent on a patch of wall. In the dim light, it almost looked like a door.

TONY PULLED the car to the curb. "This is where End lost the signal. I'm going to start a sweep, looking for the vehicle's ID. If we keep going, we'll end up at the back gate of the LaRaine Estate, behind the potato fields."

"What's beyond that?" Liz asked.

"Nothin'," Tony said. "The estate extends for a zillion klicks that way. The road dead-ends at the gate."

"So, they had to be connected to LaRaine," Liz said.

"They could just be using her property," Maerk said. "A place that huge—who knows what could be going on. Who's your contact here?"

"Mary Ricardi," Tony said. "But she tried to double-cross us. Twice, so far."

"Did she know about Dareen?" Liz demanded. "Maybe she's going to try to trade Dareen for Quinn's kids."

Tony scratched his head. "I don't think so, but I'm not sure anymore. I thought I'd convinced Ricardi to stick with us, but LaRaine must have offered her even more credits. If she was smart, she got the witch to pay in advance. Or maybe LaRaine has another hold over her. Either way, she threw me over for her boss. But I didn't mention Dareen, or even how we'd be getting off-planet."

"It's gotta be that Zielinsky woman," Liz snarled. "When you left her at the apartment, she stumbled on Dareen and took the chance to grab her. Probably sold her to Ricardi."

"We haven't received any communication from Ricardi," Tony said. "If she wanted to trade Dareen for the kids, she'd have contacted me by now. And what are the odds that Francine ran into Dareen? Even if she did, she had no way of knowing who Dareen is. Your theory sounds like something out of an adventure novel."

"Truth is stranger than fiction," Maerk said, but the others ignored him. "Does it matter who grabbed her? We know someone did. Let's just go in, guns blazing, and grab our kid."

Liz smiled at her ex-husband. "You are super sexy when you go all bad-ass dad."

Tony rolled his eyes. "Can we focus, please? I've got a lock on the car, and it's parked in LaRaine's back garage. We know she has beefed up her security—although since we grabbed the kids, Reggie might have them out searching the town instead of securing the property."

"Do you still have access to their security system?" Liz asked.

"I'll connect as soon as we get close enough," Tony replied. While they'd been talking, the car had driven them up to the rear gate of the property. Tony had programmed it to stop a few meters short of the surveillance area. Now he took the time to back it off the road. "We can't hide it, but it shouldn't be too noticeable here."

"Why don't you send it back to the safehouse, and Quinn can take the kids to the shuttle?" Liz suggested after they'd climbed out.

Tony smacked his forehead. "I've been operating solo for too long. Great idea." While Liz and Maerk shrugged on their backpacks, he entered the commands and sent the message to Quinn. "Let's do a comm test." He inserted an earbud. "Check."

"Crystal clear," Liz's voice said in his ear, drowning out the buzzing of the local insects.

"Do you two have integrated systems?" he asked in surprise.

Maerk tapped his jaw. "No, but we have the new micro mics. Inserted under the skin. You can't see 'em at all."

Tony connected his external mic. "What about night vision lenses?"

"Hell, no." Liz pulled a pair of goggles over her head. "Those things are still too glitchy. Maybe when the tech matures. Ready?"

"Let's go."

They climbed over the stone wall and jumped down into the estate. There were no bushes or cameras here—just klick after klick of dusty fields. The dry, acrid dust tickled his nose. Tony wasn't sure if the potatoes had already been harvested or if they were still growing beneath his feet, but it didn't matter. "Watch your step. This is rough terrain."

"I've been doing this longer than you have, Tony," Liz said, with an edge to her voice. "I'm not a newbie like your friend, Quinn."

Tony held up a hand. "Sorry. Garage is that way."

They jogged across the fields, finding a reasonably flat path between piled rows of dirt. "Was this the closest you could get us?" Maerk gasped, holding his side. "I'm getting too old for this."

Liz grinned, her breathing unlabored. "More exercise, less pizza."

Tony dropped to the dirt. "Bogie, dead ahead." A man walked away from the garage, the burning end of his old-fashioned cigar glowing brightly in Tony's night vision goggles. The man took a few puffs, then wandered toward the big house.

Liz lifted her head out of the dust to watch. "Not a very good guard."

"Lucky for us," Maerk said.

"I think that was the maintenance guy, not a guard." Tony rose to a crouch. "Too big a paunch for a guard. Let's go."

They raced across the dirt and stopped by the garage. None of the moons had risen yet, helping to hide them from non-augmented eyes.

But not from cameras. Tony pulled his comtab from his belt pouch. "There are cams on the front of this building, and the far side."

"But none here?" Liz asked.

"One. Took care of it when we stopped," he said. "Inserting a recorded loop into the front cams...now. Alarms disabled. Let's check the garage."

Maerk pulled a cable from his pocket and plugged his comtab into the access-panel by the side door. He swiped and tapped, and the lock clicked. "Lazy." He shook his head sadly. "Don't even bother changing the admin password."

They crept through the garage but found nothing.

"The main house it is," Tony said. "Too bad you don't still have a kid-locator on her."

"We removed that when she turned sixteen," Maerk said. "When she started doing some work for the family. That thing was too easy to hack."

Liz laughed. "Besides, she had learned to spoof the original by the time she was twelve. We had to upgrade to a higher-test version."

Leaving the garage, they ran across the property to the gate in the back fence. The huge house loomed, dark except for a faint light in the kitchen.

Tony pointed. "We should see who's doing what in there. Ricardi might be involved after all."

"What, she's the only one who uses the kitchen?" Maerk asked.

Tony rolled his eyes. "That's why I said we should look. To see who's in there." He double-checked the cameras, then opened the gate. The three of them sprinted across the back yard toward the glowing windows.

"Can you see anything?" Liz asked Maerk.

"I'm not quite tall enough," he replied. "You wanna get up on my shoulders?"

"What is this, amateur hour?" Tony pulled a tiny device out of his pocket and set it on his shoulder. Flicking a few buttons on his comtab brought the tiny rotors to life, and the bug-like drone rose into the air, its noise hidden by the local insects' incessant buzz.

The screen of his comtab revealed the drone's view. The kitchen windows were open to the mild night air, and a nightlight provided the only illumination. No one moved inside the room.

"Too bad they have screens on these windows," Tony muttered.

Maerk grinned and pulled out a knife. He reached over his head and slid the sharp blade into the bottom of the window screen. He jerked the blade across then down, opening a small triangle in the fabric. "That big enough?"

Tony maneuvered the drone through the gap and into the kitchen. It buzzed along, skimming over the polished stone countertops and high-end appliances. No one lurked in the dim space, and the doors to other parts of the house were firmly closed.

"Hey!" a voice called. "Who is that?"

CHAPTER 27

DAREEN SQUINTED through the ornate grate that had been hidden behind the tiny door. From floor level, she couldn't be sure, but she thought a miniature drone had buzzed into the kitchen. "Uncle Tony!" she called again, softly. "Is that you?"

The drone buzzed into view and down to eye level. She waved through the grate, hoping the camera could see her in the dark cell. "It's me, Dareen!"

The drone buzzed up and down a few centimeters, as if nodding, then hovered.

"Are you coming to get me?" she asked when nothing else happened. "Hello?"

The drone buzzed away.

⸺

TONY FOLLOWED Liz to the closest door. Before he could stop her, she lifted her booted foot and slammed it into the door next to the handle. Wood splintered satisfyingly as the door broke away from the locking mechanism on the second kick.

"I have picks," Tony said. "You probably gave away our location."

"I needed to *do* something." Liz shoved the door inward and stomped into the garage.

"At least let me check for alarms before you do that next time," Tony said.

She glanced back at him. "Sorry, you're right. I'm letting my emotions override my good sense. But at this point, I'm not worried about stealth. We know where she is. Let's get her." She opened the door. A little hall ended in a door with light shining underneath. Liz moved toward it, her blaster in her hand.

"Actually, she's this way." Tony turned to the mechanical room. "Secret cell, hidden entrance…"

Liz glared and pointed. "Go."

The three hurried to the door, stopping on either side of it.

"Can I kick this one down?" Maerk asked.

"Try the knob first," Tony replied. "I don't think there's a lock."

Maerk flung the door open, and Tony and Liz popped their heads around the jambs on either side. Darkness greeted them, but their night vision goggles revealed cleaning supplies and neatly stacked boxes. It looked the same as the last time Tony had been here.

"The cell is over there." Tony pointed. "That shelf pulls away from the wall. I'll keep watch." He turned to peer down the hall.

Maerk shoved the boxes aside, toppling stacks with brutal efficiency.

"Try to keep it down! You two are like a wrecking crew!" Tony whispered over the comms from the door.

The scrape of the bookshelf on the floor as Maerk dragged it away from the wall was lost under Dareen's fierce whisper.

"Incoming! Four bogies in the kitchen!"

"*Futz!*" Tony slammed the door shut and looked for something to block it.

"Can we go out the window?" Liz looked up at the high, narrow opening.

"They'll be out there too, if they're smart." As he spoke, Mark shoved one of the heavier boxes in front of the door. "And I'm not sure I would fit."

"Then we'll blast our way out!" Liz waved her weapon.

"No!" Tony held up a hand. He pointed his blaster at the doorknob. "Stand back, I'm going to try melting the latch. It won't hold them for long." He fired a blast stream into the metal, turning the handle to a drooping mess.

Through the thin wood, Ricardi's voice called, "I know you're in there, Tony. You aren't getting out."

"You crossed the wrong family," Liz screamed. "You'll regret this to your dying day, you old hag!"

"Elizet Marconi?" Ricardi asked, her voice shocked. "Is that you?"

"Of course it's me," Liz cried. "You kidnapped my daughter. Did you think I'd just sit up in orbit playing tiddlywinks?"

"That girl is your daughter? I thought she was Tony's."

"What difference does that make?" Tony demanded. "You still double-crossed the family." He pointed toward the space between the heater and the wall. Over the comms, he whispered, "Go through there. I'll keep her talking and catch up."

"I—I thought Tony was working outside the family," Ricardi's voice turned wheedling. "I would never betray the family."

"Save it for someone who cares," Liz yelled over her shoulder, while urging her daughter through the narrow gap. "You next, Maerk," she whispered.

"Not sure I'm going to fit through here." He jammed his shoulder into the space.

"Hang on." Liz played a light over the boxy unit. "I think there's a latch down here." She stooped and fiddled with something on the floor. "Push this way."

The two grabbed the edge of the heating unit and shoved away from the wall. With a screech of rusty wheels, the unit rotated slowly about twenty degrees. The heavy wooden door came into view.

"*Futz.*" Tony stared at the gaping hole, rubbing his sternum. "Wish I'd known that earlier today. Twist the ring to open the door."

"What are you doing in there?" Ricardi demanded.

"None of your damn business!" Liz yelled back. She turned to her ex-husband. "Go!"

Tony shoved a few more boxes in front of the internal door and raced to the gap. The others had disappeared down the stairs. He paused for a moment, watching. Something thudded into the door, shaking the wall. When they got through the door and discovered their quarry missing, Ricardi would tear this room apart. She might already know about the passageway. If she did, she'd have someone watching the other end.

He ran across the room and opened one of the high windows. If Ricardi didn't know about the passage, that might slow their pursuers. He set a stepladder next to the window, then pushed it over, as if they'd toppled it after squeezing through the window.

He darted into the space behind the heater, grabbed the edge of the metal unit, and heaved. With another ear-piercing shriek, the appliance rotated back into place. He jiggled the unit to re-engage the latch, then dropped to the floor and fired at the underside. With luck, the latch would be welded shut. Then he followed the others down the steps.

QUINN SHOOK LUCAS'S SHOULDER. "Wake up. We need to leave."

Lucas rolled over, burying his head under the pillow. "Five more minutes, Mom."

"Lucas Reginald LaRaine, get out of that bed now," Quinn commanded in her best drill sergeant voice. Then she wrinkled her nose. "We need to change your name."

The boy groaned and pulled the blanket over his head.

Quinn looked up at the ceiling. "When do they learn to follow orders?" she whispered to the cosmos. No one answered.

With a snap of her wrist, she yanked the blankets off the bed.

"Hey," Lucas cried.

She grabbed the pillow off his head and tossed it aside. "Up, now. We need to go."

He snapped upright, his eyes wide with fear. "Evacuate?"

"No!" Quinn breathed deeply, fighting the panic that word induced. "No evacuation. But we need to meet Tony at the shuttle for extraction."

"Ooh, like a secret mission?" Lucas bounced out of the bed. He grabbed the clothes he'd tossed on the floor and shoved them into the duffle bag lying nearby.

"You might want to put those on," Quinn said with a chuckle. "Unless you want to be extracted in your pajamas." She crossed the hall to the second bedroom.

Ellianne lay asleep on the bed, her head hanging off the side. Quinn had hated to wake Lucas—they'd only been asleep for a few hours. But it was time to get off this rock, and she could only carry one. He could sleep in space.

Leaving Ellianne on the bed, she repacked the pink suitcase. Then she wrapped the little girl in a blanket and lifted the child to her shoulder. Ellianne snuggled in, her warm arms wrapping around her mother's neck. Quinn breathed in the little-girl sweetness, cradling her close. Tears pricked her eyes as she thought about how close she'd come to never experiencing this again.

"I'm ready!" Lucas announced from the doorway.

Quinn blinked rapidly and settled Ellianne more firmly in her arms. "Grab the caat, will you?"

Lucas grunted. "Sassy doesn't like me."

"Probably because you call her Sassy."

Lucas scooped up the sleeping animal. It squirmed out of his arms and stalked out of the bedroom. "Hey!"

The caat strolled down the stairs ahead of them and waited by the kitchen door.

"Does she know where we're going?" Lucas asked.

"How could she?" Quinn gave the animal a narrow-eyed look. She opened the car door, and the caat leapt in, crawling into the back seat. Quinn folded the seat forward and deposited her daughter in the rear, strapping her in. The caat curled up beside the child.

"You can sit in the passenger seat. I need to grab some more stuff. Stay with your sister. Leave your door open, so the car doesn't think we're ready to go. I'm not sure how Tony has it set up. Punch that red button on the dash if the car starts to move without me."

Lucas flipped a jaunty salute. "Yes, ma'am!"

She tossed the bags in the trunk, added the box of supplies she'd assembled after the others left, and climbed into the driver's seat. "Let's go." She waited for Lucas to close his door, then tapped the screen. A map to a small shuttle strip on the edge of town popped up on the display, preset by Tony. The garage door rolled open, and the car pulled out, lights off, and turned into the street.

The drive to the shuttle field passed quickly. Very few cars moved on the streets at this early hour. Even the LaRaine Estate looked quiet as they passed. Quinn's lips twitched at the twisted wreck of the gate blocking most of the driveway. The car purred by, accelerating as it reached open road.

They raced down the highway for a few klicks, then the car exited and pulled up to another gate. A light on the dash flashed red, and Quinn tapped the "authorize payment" button. The gate rattled open, and the car rolled inside. Lights sprang on, illuminating the apron and revealing three shuttles parked there.

"Which one is ours?" Lucas asked.

"Good question," Quinn said. "I don't suppose the car is set to recognize the family shuttle, do you?"

Lucas shrugged. "Wouldn't that give away too much information if the car was captured by an enemy force?"

"Enemy force?" Quinn laughed. Then she stopped. He wasn't far off. It had become exceedingly clear that the Marconis had enemies and allies on this planet. "Let's drive down the line and I'll see if I recognize the shuttle. I'm pretty sure it's the same one we came down on."

"Do you remember the name?" Lucas pointed to the closest shuttle. The name *Thanks, Dad* glowed in huge, flowing pink script on the nose. "That's probably not it."

"That does look a little fancier than Dareen's," Quinn agreed with a grin. She shook her head at the gold stripes and elaborate nose art. "And the next one looks brand new. Reentry does a number on the paint job, no matter how fancy." She rolled her eyes as they cruised past the second ship, shining white under the lights. It had a brilliant red banner painted across the back that read, "This *is* my other shuttle."

"So, it's gotta be that one." Lucas pointed at the farthest craft. Dark streaks stretched from the nose to the stubby wings at the rear. It looked weathered, but serviceable and bore a number, but no name.

Quinn nodded. "I think you're right." She reached into her pocket and pulled out the comtab Tony had given her. "See if you can get it open." She handed the device to Lucas. "I'll get your sister."

The shuttle's rear airlock popped open in response to the device, and Quinn carried Ellianne up the ramp into the cargo hold. The fittings for the drone hung above her head, empty. A waist-high cabinet at the back stood open, also empty. Sashelle strolled into the cargo hold and across the floor. With a graceful leap, she landed on top of the cupboard. A screen embedded in the top lit up as the caat walked across it. A red warning flashed on the small screen: Bike recalled.

"What did she do?" Quinn switched her daughter to her other shoulder so she could look at the screen.

"Looks like she recalled a bike," Lucas said.

"Thanks." Quinn rolled her eyes. "I don't know what I'd do without you."

Lucas grinned.

"I think there's a bed up there." Quinn hoisted Elliane higher on her shoulder. "Get the door. Your sister weighs a ton."

Lucas hurried ahead and slid open a door on the left. A pair of narrow bunks hung in a cubby between the cockpit and cargo hold, across from the airlock. This shuttle was configured for short trips from the ship in orbit to a planet, but smart captains kept emergency quarters and supplies in all their vessels. Quinn sent a mental note of thanks to Lou for her forethought and tucked Ellianne in.

She turned to unload the car but stopped in the doorway. Better safe than sorry. Reaching across the sleeping child, she unclipped the safety harness from its stowed position and latched it across her daughter. Then she and Lucas moved their gear from the car into the cargo space. After one last check of the car, she closed the ramp.

"Where's the caat?" Lucas asked as Quinn locked the hatch.

"Crap!" Quinn searched the hold, looking into the box of supplies and behind the pink suitcase. "Did she go back out?"

"Why would she do that?"

"Elli's going to be devastated." Quinn peered out the portal in the door but couldn't see anything moving under the bright flight-line lamps. As she watched, the motion-activated lights flickered out. She stood by the port a few more minutes, hoping to see a glint of Sashelle's eyes. "Where did Ellianne get that thing, anyway?"

"Grandmother took us to visit the formal gardens in New Astorian. The caat walked up to Elli and started rubbing against her legs. Dad tried to chase her away, but she followed us everywhere. He even called the security people, but they said they don't have jurisdiction over stray caats. Then she followed us home."

"New Astorian is fifty klicks from the estate. How did she follow you home?" Quinn turned to see if he was pulling her leg.

Lucas shook his head. "I have no idea. But the next morning, she was sleeping on Elli's bed. Maybe Elli hid her in the car."

"Huh. I guess we shouldn't worry too much about her getting lost, then. She'll find another little girl. I hope Elli gets over losing her, though."

The lights outside the shuttle flared on again. Quinn ran back to the hatch but couldn't see anything. "Tony hasn't called, has he?" She nodded at the comtab in Lucas's hand.

The boy tapped the device and shook his head. "Nothing here. What's that?" He pointed through the portal.

Three vehicles labeled UFPS Security Forces rolled through the gate.

CHAPTER 28

TONY DID his latch-melting trick on the inside of the stairway door. "Hold up," he called through the comms. "We need a plan." He hurried down the steps to join Liz, Maerk, and Dareen.

At the bottom, Maerk frowned at the tunnel leading away into the gloom. "Saint Benedict protect us." At Tony's raised eyebrow, he added, "Patron saint of spelunkers."

Tony bit his lip to hide a grin, then he cleared his throat. "Quinn knew about this passage, so we have to assume others do as well. They may have someone guarding the exit."

"Or they're sending someone now," Liz said. "We should hurry!"

Maerk grabbed her shoulder before she entered the dirt tunnel. "We should make a plan first. Where does this tunnel come out?"

Tony described the trapdoor behind the rocks and the cave. "Reggie seemed really surprised to see us. But that was hours ago. He could have sent someone to check it out and set a guard. It's what I'd do."

"I think we've already established that Reggie doesn't necessarily do the thing that makes the most sense," Liz said. "I say we go down there and surprise them."

"It's not really a surprise if they're expecting us," Maerk said.

"We can use this." Dareen reached into her boot.

They all turned to look. The girl held a small box in the palm of her hand. "What is that?" Tony asked.

"It's the cloaking device." Dareen grinned.

"You still have it?" Consternation covered Liz's face.

Dareen's grin widened. "When the old hag caught me, I had just put it into my boot. She took my comtab—I'm not sure she even realized I had the cloaking thing. I mean, when I opened the stairwell door, she was right there—inside the invisibility bubble. And I guess her eyes are bad enough that she didn't notice the distortion. I turned it off when she wasn't looking." While the drug had made her compliant, it hadn't made her stupid.

"We thought she was after the device, but maybe she just happened on you and decided—"

"Lou said this thing is dangerous." Liz snatched the box out of Dareen's palm.

"Really?" Dareen asked. "It hasn't hurt me."

"You don't know what it's done to you," Liz snapped. "It affects your decision-making. Why did you come down here without knowing anything about Tony's mission or where he'd be?"

"I came down to…" Dareen's voice trailed off and her eyes got wide. Her brows drew down and she tried again. "Tony needed…uh, I was helping?"

Maerk nodded. "That thing is dangerous."

"But it might be our ticket out of this tunnel." Tony pointed at the box. "Let's keep it in reserve. I'll scout ahead." He hurried down the tunnel.

The musty air tickled his nose, and he pinched it to hold back a sneeze. Earth and stone should muffle sounds, but he didn't want to take any chances. Dirt gave way to the rock tunnel. His comtab cast enough light so he could avoid loose rubble under his feet, but the battery was dying. At the far end of the tunnel, the trapdoor was shut.

Tony pulled a small can out of his backpack and sprayed lubricant into the lock and along the hinged edge of the door. He waited a few seconds, then turned the ring. It rotated easily, the bolt sliding quietly into the mechanism.

He raised the door a couple centimeters and slipped his drone through the narrow crack. With a swipe and a flick, he activated the device and sent the drone buzzing into the air. It turned a full circle, the night vision camera revealing nothing but stone and dirt. Tony pushed the door fully open and sent the drone into the cavern.

Nothing.

He sent a secure message to Liz and climbed out of the tunnel. Taking a moment to suck water from his canteen, he leaned against the boulder between the tunnel and the main cavern as the drone flew into the meadow outside the cave.

Still nothing. That didn't mean they were in the clear, though.

QUINN STARED out the window at the strobing red and blue lights. Federation security agents—they must be looking for her! "Lucas," she hissed.

"What?" Lucas's eyes were as wide as her own.

"See if you can wake Elli. Quietly." The eight-year-old was notoriously hard to wake and tended to scream when startled out of a deep sleep.

"I can carry her." Lucas puffed up his chest. "It would be quieter."

Quinn's lip twitched. "You're probably right. Make a little nest in that cupboard." She pointed to the bike storage cupboard at the front of the cargo hold. "Get Elli in there and be ready to hide with her. Take some water and food, in case you have to stay put for a while."

"That's the first place they'll look," Lucas said. "We need a better hiding place."

"I'll lead them away. They won't bother searching the ship if they see me running away. You two can escape with Tony."

"We're not leaving without you!" Lucas said hotly. "Besides, how do you know they aren't looking for me and Elli? I'm sure Grandmother sent them after us."

Quinn answered, her eyes on the cars again. "Maybe. Probably not. If I can distract them—"

"If they catch you, they'll take you back to prison," Lucas said. "Won't they?"

She couldn't meet his eyes. Chances were good they'd kill her outright rather than trying to capture her. But if she could get them away from the shuttle, maybe they'd follow her and leave the kids alone.

With a squeal of tires, Tony's car surged forward, racing toward the gate. Quinn had forgotten it was still sitting next to the shuttle. "What is it doing?"

Lucas bared his teeth in a feral grin and waved the comtab. "I sent it back to the estate. At emergency speed." As he spoke, the car skidded around the security vehicles grouped near the entrance and slammed through the gate. Metal and wood exploded in all directions. Two of the lighted cars lurched into reverse, burning rubber as they turned, then chased after the fleeing vehicle.

"Two down, one to go," Lucas crowed. "How do we get rid of the last one?" The comtab beeped. "Message," the boy said, holding the device out to Quinn.

```
Need extraction. Can I call car?
```

"Crap," Quinn muttered. She texted back:

```
                    Feds chasing car. Drone?
```

```
Drone. Can we land at shuttle?
```

```
                    Not yet. Working on it.
```

"They'll meet us here," Quinn told her son. "But we need to get rid of that last vehicle."

"I wonder if this shuttle has a rocket launcher." Lucas looked around the cargo bay.

Quinn laughed. "You've been watching too many vids. Normal people don't carry rocket launchers." Of course, the Marconis were hardly normal. "On second thought, let's check the cockpit."

Quinn slid into the pilot's seat and activated the control panel. Clicking on a manifest icon brought up a blank page—no cargo for this flight. She swiped through the maintenance logs and found the basic provisions. Food, canned air, spare filters, the usual. Then she pulled up the external cameras.

"Keep an eye on that car, will you?" She slid the camera view across the screen to the co-pilot's position.

"Still sitting there." Lucas dropped into the other seat. "Are they waiting for us to come out?"

"Probably waiting for their backup to return." Quinn swiped through a few more screens. The comtab sitting atop the console flickered and died. "That was odd." She swiped back, one screen at a time. On the second swipe, the comtab lit up again. Quinn grabbed it. She shook her head. "Tony thinks of everything." Holding the comtab over the screen, she pressed her palm against the shuttle's access-panel.

"Awesome!" Lucas crowed, staring at the new screens popping open on Quinn's panel. "Look, a rocket launcher! Em-cannon! Even a flamethrower!" His finger stabbed at the screen.

Quinn batted the boy's hand away. "Don't touch that! We need a plan before we start taking out Federation agents." Her blood ran cold at the thought. She wasn't built for taking out anyone. Not in cold blood.

Movement on Lucas's screen drew her eyes. "What is that?"

"Dareen's bike!" Lucas laughed. "Sashelle recalled the bike, remember?"

The bike swerved around the Federation Security car blocking the destroyed gate. It sped across the tarmac and slalomed between the parked shuttles. The security car launched away from the gate and chased after the bike, zipping down the apron behind the parked ships. The bike looped around their shuttle and sped back the way it had come.

"Is someone on the bike?" Quinn squinted at the screen. "It should have stopped here."

"Maybe it's Dareen?" Lucas suggested as the bike disappeared behind *Thanks, Dad* a second time. With a squeal of brakes and a cloud of burning tires, the car skidded around to follow. Lucas panned the camera, zooming in on the vehicles as they sped across the flight line toward the far fence. "Nope, no rider."

Bang! Bang! Bang! Blows echoed through the shuttle.

"What the hell?" Quinn swiped the camera window to her side of the screen and flicked through the views, stopping on the external airlock. "I don't believe it." She sat back in the seat, shaking her head. "It's Francine."

CHAPTER 29

AS QUINN STARED at Francine on the camera feed, her son jumped out of his seat. "I'll let her in!"

"Wait!" Quinn cried. "I don't trust her!"

"She drew off that last car," Lucas said. "She's got to be on our side."

"You stay here." Quinn got up from the pilot's chair. She pointed at the co-pilot's seat. "Keep an eye on that car. I'll let her in. And don't t touch the rocket launchers."

She stalked to the airlock, trying to make up her mind. Did she let the woman in? Send her away? Stun her and tie her up in the cargo hold? She pulled out the weapon Tony had given her. Thanks to her military training, she knew how to use it. She checked the charge and set it to non-lethal. She didn't want to kill anyone—except maybe Reggie.

No, not even Reggie. Although she might not be very sad if someone else did it.

At the inner hatch of the airlock, she paused. Tony had trusted Francine. But Dareen had been captured shortly after Francine disappeared. Maybe his trust was misguided. Maybe Francine was working with the Zielinskys. Or LaRaine. She groaned. Tony had been right on everything else. She'd trust him on this, too.

She hit the release and opened the inner airlock hatch. Francine smiled at her. Quinn stared. "How'd you get in?"

"I thought you hit the release." Francine reached down to scratch the ears of the caat winding around her legs.

"Sashelle!" Quinn's eyes widened. "Did she come in with you?"

"Nope." Francine strolled into the tiny hall. "Maybe she let me in."

"She wasn't— How—"

The caat followed the other woman out of the airlock. She flicked her tail dismissively and stalked across to the tiny bunk space, leaping up beside the sleeping girl.

Quinn looked at Francine. "Why are you here?"

"Same reason as before," Francine answered. "I want to get off this rock before LaRaine has me tracked down and thrown in the dungeon."

"Then why did you run off at the apartment complex?"

"I didn't run off!" Francine lifted her nose. "You deserted me! I was looking for *your* son."

"But you took Dareen!"

Francine frowned. "Who?"

"Tony's cousin. You grabbed her."

"No, I didn't." Francine leaned a shoulder against the bulkhead as if she hadn't a care in the world.

"The note said it was you," Quinn insisted.

"The note?" Francine shook her head. "Believe me, if I grab someone, I don't leave a note."

Quinn opened her mouth to argue, then stopped. The note hadn't identified Francine—they'd assumed it was her. Rather, *she* had assumed it was Francine. "You're right. It could have been anyone. But you were on her bike."

"Yeah, that was an adventure!" Francine laughed. "After you left,

I found that bike in the parking lot. The plates were registered to LaRaine, so I took it."

"How—"

Francine cut her off with a bland look. "I'm a Zielinsky. I have ways of checking vehicle plates. Anyway, I was riding the thing back to the estate, and it suddenly took off. When the Feds zipped past me, I figured I might need to make a quick escape. So, I overrode the recall and programmed in the red herring. When I got here and saw the last car, I activated the red herring and jumped off."

"The 'red herring?'"

"It's a pre-set route designed to take pursuers on a wild goose chase."

"Oh," Quinn said, still not sure if she should trust her. "I'm sorry we deserted you."

Francine shrugged one shoulder. "I survived."

Quinn stared at the other woman. How did she still look so elegant after all they'd been through tonight? No dust, no dirt, no whiff of sweat. And how had she ridden that bike with a pencil skirt?

"What?" Francine asked.

Quinn shook her head. "Nothing."

"Mom!" Lucas called from the cockpit. "We've got incoming!"

TONY, Liz, Maerk, and Dareen huddled in the back of the cave, close enough to the boulders that they could scramble over if they needed to hide. Maerk held Tony's comtab, watching the view from the tiny drone lazily circling the meadow outside. The incessant whir of insects filtered in, bouncing weirdly in the cave.

"I won't call the pick up drone until we have a safe landing place," Liz said. "It's low on power."

"That reminds me—" Tony dug through his bag then handed a battery pack to Maerk.

"Maybe we should go to the safehouse," Dareen suggested.

Maerk shook his head, glancing up from the screen. "It might be compromised. Does the family have another one here?" He fitted a cable into the device and plugged it into the battery. The screen brightened.

Liz scowled. "We don't do that much business on Hadriana. I don't trust our other contacts enough. If the Feds are after us, they'll cave."

"The safehouse is still safer than here," Tony said. "The problem is, it's too far to walk, and the car isn't available. We could call a cab?"

"Now that the Feds are involved, they probably have a net over the whole area," Maerk said. "Any vehicle that comes within a klick of the estate would be tracked. Does it seem odd to anyone else—" He broke off.

"What?" Liz asked.

"Quinn is a fugitive from a high-security prison." Maerk rubbed the back of his neck. "She escaped from death row, and they knew her family was here. Why weren't they waiting for you at the estate?"

"I thought it was because of LaRaine's hold on the locals," Tony said. He paced a few steps and turned back. "But I was expecting—you're right. It was too easy. At least until now."

"Do you think they were trying to plant her on us?" Liz asked. "Maybe this whole thing was just a way of getting a Federation stooge into the family!"

"Don't be ridiculous," Tony snapped. "Quinn isn't a Federation agent. I've known her for years."

"*She* didn't know *you* were an agent," Dareen said. "Works both ways."

"No," Tony said. "She wouldn't bring her kids into—"

"We don't know what the Federation might do," Maerk said. "Their views on human life are different from ours."

"No," Tony said again. "Quinn might have escaped from Centralus Prison, but she's small potatoes. They know she's innocent and probably harmless. No point in expending resources on someone so easy to nab. They counted on LaRaine's thugs to grab her, and now that they've seen how incompetent they are, they've sent in the experts."

"Anyone who's seen that video isn't going to think she's harmless," Maerk said.

"What video?" Tony asked.

Liz barked a short laugh. "Went viral. Hang on." She pulled out her comtab and scrolled through the screens. She glanced at Tony. "Don't worry, it's not connected to the net. I downloaded it a few days ago." She tilted the device so Tony could see the screen.

The video showed a ragged-looking woman in an incongruously cheerful cardigan. Her face was hidden by shaggy, brown hair. She knelt on the back of a man flat on the ground, his arms twisted behind his back. The woman leaned close to the man's head. Her hard whisper sent chills up Tony's spine. "You don't care who I am? Well, I'll tell you anyway. I'm one of the innocents that the Federation convicted because the real traitors are too hard to catch." She bounced her knee into his back, and the video restarted.

Tony snorted. "That was the pilot of the helo she stole. This must have happened before I got to the roof."

"She looks pretty competent for an innocent victim," Liz said.

"She looks like a desperate mother." Tony locked eyes with his aunt. "You'd do the same for Dareen or End."

Liz looked away. "Yeah, but I'm not a harmless victim, either."

Dareen's eyes glowed. "I knew Quinn was a badass."

"What are you suggesting, Liz?" Tony demanded. "Should we leave her here? Abandon her? They'll execute her if they catch her. Even if you're right. Because that's how the Federation does things. Agents are cheap, and they don't want to tip their hand."

Liz blew out a heavy sigh. "No, I don't want to abandon her. I like her. Let's get her back to the Commonwealth, and let—"

"I've got bogies," Maerk said, tilting Tony's comtab to show the screen. He pointed. "One here, maybe a second over here. They appear to be watching. Waiting."

"Those will be Feds," Tony said. "LaRaine's flunkies would storm in. Let's get moving. We'll use Dareen's stealth cloak to get past them and have the drone pick us up on the road. It's about a klick that way. Well-maintained path. I'm running in circles tonight."

"Why don't we use the cloak to sneak up on them and take 'em out?" Liz suggested.

"We don't know how many there are, or how they're communicating." Tony shook his head. "For all we know, they've got drones watching, too. They'd see their agents fall. Plus, that thing makes you behave irrationally—bad enough if we're sneaking through, but really bad on a takedown. What's the range on that thing, Dareen?"

The girl wrinkled her nose. "The stealth bubble is about a meter."

"That's too small for all four of us," Liz said. "We'll need to take turns. Maerk and I will go first, then I'll come back and get Dareen. Tony, you're last." She locked eyes with Tony, then flicked a glance at her daughter.

"That leaves you under the influence for a long time," Tony said.

"I'm the most rational of us," Liz said. "It will have the least effect on me."

"Right." Maerk scoffed.

Tony held up a hand to stop the bickering. "We don't really have a choice. Let's get it done. Fast."

"We all know what that thing can do to us." Maerk nodded at the device Liz pulled from her pocket. "So, stick to the plan. No improvising."

Dareen shivered. "You don't have to tell me twice. Or maybe you do."

Tony took his comtab back from Maerk and slapped him on the shoulder. "See you in a few. Wait near the road. There's a convenient bush to hide behind."

Maerk grinned and shook his head. "Very thoughtful." He linked his arm through his ex-wife's, and they winked out of view.

"It's creepy from the outside," Dareen whispered.

Tony nodded, focusing on his comtab. He flew the little drone to a tree and sent it crawling along the trunk. A Federation operative came into view. "Got ya." The drone crawled closer, and Tony turned up the audio. Insect noise echoed in his earpiece. "Where's your friend?"

"Can you see Mom and Dad?" Dareen peered over his shoulder.

"Not in this view. If they were using heat tech, we'd be screwed, but it appears they've underestimated us again." Tony flicked a couple of icons. "See, there they are." Two red ghosts, huddled together, appeared on the screen, near the edge of the meadow. They walked, quickly but carefully, past the agent and continued on the path, unnoticed.

Tony flew the drone to another tree on the far side of the open space and scanned. "There you are. Oh, and another friend there. Very good—didn't see you at all."

"Are you talking to them?" Dareen asked.

Tony shrugged. "Hazard of working alone." He flew the drone upward, hovering in the center of the grassy clearing. "Crap, there's a fourth! They're going all out. We need to stop talking."

Dareen nodded, her eyes wide.

Tony patted a boulder and gestured for Dareen to sit. He handed her the comtab. Text glowed on the screen.

```
Stay here and keep an eye on them.
If anyone moves closer, ping my
audio. I'm going to check the
trapdoor, in case they're coming up
behind us.
```

Dareen glanced up at him, and her eyes went wider. "Too late! Duck!"

CHAPTER 30

QUINN SWIPED THE VIEWSCREEN, enlarging the picture from the rear cam. A heavily damaged red Citralus XL sports car rattled through the gate. "Crap! That's Reggie! How'd he get his car back? And how'd he know where to find us?"

Francine ignored the questions. "We should get out of here. Lucas, let me sit there."

"Do you know how to fly this thing?" Quinn asked as they changed places. Lucas perched on the jump seat behind Quinn.

"No." Francine swiped the screen. "I've done some atmo flying, but nothing like this. You?"

Quinn covered her face with her hands. "Simulator, a million years ago. And twenty minutes with Dareen on the way down... Gah, was it only this morning?"

Pounding echoed through the ship. On camera, Reggie stood before the airlock, hammering with a metal-topped cane. "Quinn, I know you're in there! Open up immediately!"

"Look, it's Grandmother." Lucas pointed over Quinn's shoulder.

Gretmar LaRaine, matriarch of the LaRaine family and de facto ruler of the planet, struggled out of the damaged car. She wore a sleek rose suit and perfectly shined heels. Her carefully dyed hair shone golden under the harsh flight-line lights. The click of her heels on the tarmac snapped through the speakers as she approached the shuttle. "Quindolyn Templeton LaRaine, I demand you come out here this instant."

"Not for a million credits," Quinn snarled, flicking switches and tapping icons. "And that's not my name! We're out of here!" The shuttle engines hummed.

"Shut down this bird at once!" Reggie called. "You must answer for your crimes!"

Quinn twisted the joystick and pushed the throttle. The shuttle started moving, easing out of the parking slot.

Reggie jogged beside it, still hammering on the airlock. "Look what you did to my car!"

Francine frowned. *"That's* what he's worried about?"

"That car is his baby," Lucas said. "He likes it better than any of us."

The envious undercurrent cut Quinn to the core. "I can take care of that." She swiped the screen and stabbed an icon. With a rattle and a quiet pop, something ejected from the nose of the shuttle. A tiny rocket ignited and whooshed over the shuttle, dazzling their eyes with a massive, bright red arc. It slammed into the Citralus and exploded into a ball of flame. The pressure wave flattened Gretmar and Reggie on the tarmac.

Lucas whooped.

With an evil grin, Quinn pushed the throttle a little more, opening the gap between the shuttle and their pursuers.

"Mighta been a little overkill." The corners of Francine's mouth twitched. "But I like it."

Quinn looked at the video, stretching the view to zoom in on the twisted lump of metal and smoldering plastic. "It was the smallest rocket we had."

Reggie had pushed up to his hands and knees. He was still yelling, but the microphones couldn't pick up his words at that distance. Gretmar rolled slowly to her feet and dusted off her now-filthy suit. Her glare sent an instinctive surge of terror through Quinn's chest. "Let's get out of here."

"Can I use that weapons screen?" Francine reached out. "I think we should disable those other shuttles in case— Yup, here come the Feds." Two FSF cars rolled through the gate.

"Disable them?" Quinn asked. "Why? How?"

"Disable them because those FSF officers might have a shuttle pilot with them, and we don't want them following us." Francine flicked the screen. "As to how... That's what an em-cannon does."

"Em-cannon? You're going to fire an electromagnetic pulse at those two civilian shuttles? They're brand new!" Quinn stared at the other woman.

"Fried electrical system is easier to fix than what you did." Francine jerked her thumb toward the rear of the craft and the melted jumble of sports car beyond.

"But Reggie deserved that," Quinn said. "I don't even know the people who own those shuttles."

Francine shook her head and pressed the screen. "You're a fugitive. You can't afford to be nice to people just because you don't know them." The shuttle shuddered and ejected another rocket. It looped around and pierced the nose of the brand-new craft with a quiet thunk. A second rocket zipped away and thocked into *Thanks, Dad*.

"Nothing happened." Quinn peered through the front windows as the shuttle rumbled down the flight line.

"Not yet." Francine stabbed the screen again. A small flare flashed at the nose of each shuttle, followed by a soft whomp. "Not flashy, but useful."

"That was it?" Lucas asked, disappointed.

"'Fraid so," Francine replied. "Sometimes the best weapons are the most subtle. We fried all electrical systems on those shuttles."

"What's going to stop them from doing the same to us?" Quinn asked.

Francine opened her mouth, then snapped it shut. "If they have an em-cannon, we're in trouble. 'Course, they probably would have used it by now. Let's get this bird in the air."

"In the air?" Quinn squawked. "You can't be serious! I can drive this thing around the flight line all day, but I told you I've only ever flown a simulator."

"Doesn't matter. All the *futz* is on the line," Francine said. "We need to leave this rock, and you're the closest thing we've got to a pilot right now. I don't fancy waiting for Tony to show up."

Quinn stared at her, mouth open.

"Mom, those Federation cars are coming." Lucas pointed at the screen.

Quinn's eyes dropped to the viewscreen. "Francine, take them out before they block the runway. Lucas, strap in."

"On it, Mom!" The boy popped a sloppy salute.

Quinn ignored him, focusing on the viewscreens. She barely registered the shudder and pop of two more em-cannon shots. She worked her way through the checklists as fast as possible, then spotted a small link marked "emergency departure." One tap, and check marks appeared in the empty boxes in quick succession. The words "auto launch?" appeared onscreen. "Yes, please," she whispered and tapped the red button.

Nothing happened.

Quinn glanced at the screen again. The button had been replaced with the words "Are you sure?" above a red button labeled "yes, let's go" and a green one that said "don't do it, Gramma will kill you."

Quinn whispered, "Sorry, Lou," and slammed her hand down on the red button.

⸻

AT DAREEN'S SHOUT, Tony ducked and spun, yanking his weapon out of the holster on his hip. Gravel scattered behind him as Dareen dove behind a boulder. At least, he hoped that was what she did. He couldn't turn to check.

Ricardi stood before him, her cane raised and pointed in his direction.

"Drop it," he commanded.

The cane lowered but didn't drop.

"I said, drop the cane!" Tony ground out. He'd had enough of the flip-flopping old woman. "I'll give you to the count of one. Wa—"

Before he could get the word finished, the cane clattered to the stone floor. "I was just going to tap you on the shoulder."

Tony's eyes narrowed. "Yeah, right. Hands on top of your head and step away from that boulder."

"My balance isn't that good," the woman said. "This rock is the only thing keeping me upright."

"Tough *futz*, granny," Dareen snarled.

Tony pinched his lips together to hide his smile. Dareen playing tough guy was pretty amusing. "Who's with you?"

"I came alone."

"Dareen, watch her. I'm going to check." He waited until Dareen stood beside him, her stunner pointed at Ricardi. Then he made a wide loop around the woman, shining his comtab light behind the boulders. The trapdoor was closed, the latch still melted shut.

"How'd you get here?" Tony stepped back to look at her while keeping the tunnel entrance in view.

"There's another passage back that way." Hands still on her head, Ricardi pointed with her elbow. "This place is riddled with 'em. That one goes directly to my apartment."

"What do you want?" Tony asked.

"I want to cut a deal," Ricardi said. "You were right. I should never have considered taking LaRaine's deal."

"You should have thought about that before kidnapping Dareen."

"Yeah," Dareen threw in.

Tony leveled a quick look at the girl, and her shoulders slumped.

"I didn't want to kidnap her," Ricardi said. "But I knew you'd never agree to talk to me after what I did before. I needed leverage. And she was there. I was afraid she'd get picked up by the Feds."

"Right, I'm sure you had her best interests at heart." Tony stepped behind the old woman and pulled one of her hands off her head. He slid a quik-lok restraint out of his pocket and tightened it on the old woman's wrist to secure her hands behind her back then pushed her to a seat on a boulder. "Dareen, watch her. Stay well back and shoot if she moves."

"You got it, boss." Darren moved to the side of the cavern so she could cover both the woman and the entrance.

Tony nodded at his cousin and climbed over the boulders. In a shadowy corner beyond the trapdoor, a narrow cleft led to another rock-lined tunnel. The floor was smooth as if well used. He shone his light through the opening, but nothing appeared to be moving in the gloom.

"We need to get out of here," Tony muttered to Dareen when he returned to the cavern. "There's no door. More people could arrive any second."

"What do we do with her?" Dareen asked.

Tony shrugged. "Leave her here. Someone will find her eventually."

"No!" Ricardi struggled up from the boulder. "We need to talk. I want to keep working with the family! I need the money."

"What was it you said, Dareen?" Tony asked in a conversational tone. He turned back to Ricardi and in unison they said, "Tough *futz*, granny."

"You!" Liz's voice echoed off the rocks as she appeared in the middle of the cavern. "I'll tear you—"

Tony grabbed his aunt, clamping a hand over her mouth. "Liz, shut up! Someone will hear—"

"Too late," Dareen said again, swinging around to face the entrance to the cave.

CHAPTER 31

"FEDERATION SECURITY!" The man at the cave entrance swung his weapon from Tony to Dareen. "Freeze!"

With a shriek, Liz ripped away from Tony's grip and slammed into Ricardi, knocking the old woman off the boulder. Liz dove on top of her, slamming her forehead into Ricardi's nose.

"I said freeze!" the officer screamed, his gun pivoting toward Liz.

Dareen shot him.

The stun beam scattered against his chest armor. He whipped around to fire at Dareen and collapsed in a heap.

"I decided I was done with all this sneaking around." Maerk kicked the agent gently as he ambled in. When the man didn't respond, Maerk leaned down and pulled the tranquilizer dart out of the agent's neck. "Good batch of tranqs." He waved the dart at Tony in approval.

"Uh, thanks?" Tony said. "How many did you take out?" He grabbed Liz's arm and dragged her off Ricardi.

"Counting this one? Three," Maerk said. "There was one more, but he ran off."

"We need to move. NOW!" Tony yelled. "Go, go, go!" With each shout, he pushed one of them toward the cavern entrance. "Call the drone, Liz!"

At the entrance, Tony held up a hand to stop the group. "Hold! Dareen, what's the drone say?"

"Oh, crap." The girl fumbled in her pocket, finally pulling out the comtab. "I see three bodies... Hang on." She swiped. "Unconscious. A fourth person over there, about a hundred meters." She waved to the right. "He might be calling in."

"I'm sure he is," Tony said through gritted teeth. "Liz get the drone to the road *now*. Dareen, send the bug ahead to check for bogies. Maerk, take down that last guy."

Maerk loaded his dart-thrower and ran out of the cave, ducking low. Liz swiped at her comtab. Dareen's fingers flew over the mini-drone's controls. They waited, seconds stretching out into hours. Tony wished he knew which of Maerk's saints to pray to.

"Number four down," Maerk's voice said through the comms.

"Inbound," Liz said. "Eight minutes."

"Clear," Dareen called. "No one between here and the extraction point."

Tony glanced around the cave. On the far side, Ricardi had struggled to a sitting position, her shoulders hunched up around her neck. Blood poured down her chin. Across the space, the Federal agent lay face-down in the dust. Tony shook his head. Not one of his cleaner missions. He looked at his family and sighed. "Stay on the path. Fast as you can go. Stick to the plan. Let's move."

THE SHUTTLE SURGED FORWARD, slamming Quinn back in her seat. Francine grimaced, and Lucas grunted. The craft tore down the runway, gathering speed. Halfway along, a line of Federal agents scattered as the ship bore down on them. Quinn choked back a giggle, watching them scramble off the runway.

The seat rattled beneath her, and the view on the screen shook.

She clenched her teeth to keep from chipping one or biting her tongue. Suddenly, the rattling stopped as they lifted off. They whooshed over the twisted wreck of Reggie's car, where Quinn spotted Gretmar standing off to the side. Even from this distance and speed, she could feel the woman's glare.

"Launch sequence complete," a voice said. "Altitude is five hundred meters and climbing. Orbit will be achieved in ten minutes, twenty-three seconds."

"We don't want orbit," Quinn said. "We need to meet Tony and the others. How are we going to do that?" The screen showed an illustration of the flight path, accompanied by changing numbers as they continued to climb. A line of icons lined the right side of the screen. Holding her finger over the first one brought up a little bubble that read "setup."

She slid her hand down the screen. "How about in-flight adjustments?"

"Don't look at me," Francine said. "I told you, light aircraft only. Gliders, turboprops. I don't do space."

"Where's that comtab?" Quinn looked around the cockpit. "We need to get Tony on the line."

"Here!" Lucas held up the device.

Quinn stretched her arm back toward her son, barely snagging the comtab he offered. She rubbed her shoulder absently as she keyed in a message. A sudden vibration startled her, and she nearly dropped it. She fumbled the device and then poked the screen and grinned. "Hey, Tony, am I glad to hear from you!"

"Quinn, we're in the drone. Are we clear to land?" Tony demanded.

"No. I, uh, we're, hang on." Quinn looked at the screen.

"Over New Astorian." Francine pointed at a map.

"We're currently at two-five-thousand over New Astorian and climbing. Heading zero-two-four." Quinn grinned with pride over her official-sounding response.

"You're where?!" Tony demanded. "Did you launch the shuttle?"

"We had no choice," Quinn said. "There were Federal Agents. And Gretmar."

"Are you being pursued?" Tony asked sharply.

"No, we disabled the other shuttles on the apron."

"You disabled them?" There was as short silence. "How?"

"Em-cannon," Francine said.

"Who is that?" Tony said.

"Francine." Quinn grimaced at her co-pilot. "She's my weps."

"Are you telling me a Zielinsky is messing with the weapons system on my shuttle?" Liz's voice came shrilly through the speaker. "What the hell?"

"I had no choice!" Quinn's voice sounded whiny even in her own ears. What the hell, indeed. She cleared her throat and tried again, her voice stronger. "We were surrounded and needed to take off. Since I'm the only one with ANY shuttle experience, I took command. We can talk about this later. Right now, we need to figure out what to do next."

"We also needed to depart, so we're aloft in the drone." Liz's voice was cold and even. "Power is low, and we couldn't wait for sunrise to recharge, so you need to meet us somewhere. Are there any rural runways on this planet? Someplace we won't have Feds breathing down our necks."

Quinn gritted her teeth. Like it was her fault the Feds were after them! Well, it kind of was, but it wasn't as if she'd done something illegal! Except disable two cars and two shuttles, the little voice in the back of her head said. And blow up Reggie's car. A laugh bubbled up. She'd started out an innocent victim, but she'd definitely taken to a life of crime like...like a Krimson spy. She bit down on another laugh and a snort escaped.

"Sorry," she muttered.

"Dareen says we can use the airfield where she picked up the, uh, where she did a pickup yesterday." Liz's voice went silent for a moment. "It's in the desert. Let me put in the coordin— Never mind, we won't make it that far."

There was silence for a moment. Then Liz's voice again.

"Perfect. We need you to do a low-orbit scoop."

"What?!" Quinn cried. "Yeah, sure. After I do a fly-by of the Centralus Prison, okay?"

"Come on, Quinn," Liz said. "You're doing great. The programming will take care of most of the details. In fact, we don't really need you to do anything except start the sequence." Muffled background noises made it difficult to hear her voice.

"What's going on?" Quinn asked. "Let me talk to Tony."

"Tony is...busy," Liz said. "He's helping Maerk with, um, some calculations."

Quinn hit the mute button and turned to Francine. "Does she sound odd to you?"

Francine shrugged. "How would I know? I've never met the woman."

Quinn made a face, then unmuted the comms. "Can Tony take a break from his calculating long enough to talk to me?"

"Sorry, it's kind of complicated," Liz said. "That's why it's taking two of them to get it done. Dareen's here—you wanna talk to her?"

"Hey, Quinn!" Dareen said.

"No, I don't need to talk to Dareen," Quinn replied. "No offense, Dareen. I just want to confirm something with Tony."

"He says you should do the scoop," Dareen said. "He's nodding his head, emphatically. Seriously, he looks like a bobblehead. But we need to act fast!"

"Fine," Quinn said. "What do I need to do?"

"There's a program in the computer," Liz said. "You just have to activate it, and the shuttle will take care of the rest. Maerk is sending the coordinates now."

"If your shuttles can do all this stuff on their own," Quinn asked, "why do you even need a pilot?"

"The pilot is there in case anything goes wrong," Liz said. "But nothing will, so it'll be fine."

"Famous last words," Francine whispered.

"You are not helping," Quinn growled.

Francine grinned.

"You realize if I screw this up, we're all dead, even you?" Quinn asked. "You don't have a magic flying carpet."

Francine blew out a sigh, hard enough to make her hair fly away from her forehead. "Yeah, I know. What do we need to do?"

CHAPTER 32

"SHE'S ACTIVATED THE SCOOP." Liz stared at the drone's control panel. "You can let him up."

Maerk took his hand off Tony's mouth and rolled off his back.

"What the hell is wrong with you three?!" Tony shouted.

"There's nothing wrong with us," Liz said. "You're the one who's being a pansy."

"You just told a novice pilot to initiate an extremely complex maneuver!" Tony roared. "You're going to get us all killed."

"Power is low." Liz gestured at the screen.

"We could have landed!" Tony cried. "There was plenty of juice to get us to that desert runway. Or that remote spot beyond the LaRaine Estate. There's no reason to undertake an extremely risky operation like this!"

"Landing a shuttle is risky, too," Liz said. "She could just as easily crash it that way."

"The autopilot is pretty good at landing." Dareen rubbed her forehead. "Maybe Tony is right."

Liz swung around to glare at her daughter.

"She has a good point," Maerk started. When Liz's head snapped in his direction, he cowered. "Uh, but Liz's plan is good."

"Give me the comtab." Tony extended his hand.

"Too late to change the plan." Liz held the device out of Tony's reach. "Intercept is in forty seconds."

"I'm not going to call Quinn," Tony said. "At this point, it's safer to let the scoop proceed."

Liz handed the device to Tony. "What are you going to do, then?"

Tony ignored Liz. He swiped through a couple screens and spoke. "Kert, Tony. That device scrambles everyone's brains. If we don't make it back, you need to know that. Everyone who has used it is acting erratically. It sounds like Lou might have turned it on once, too."

"Hey!" Liz shouted. "What the heck?"

Maerk pulled out his stunner and aimed it at Tony. "Sit down and shut up."

A GRATING buzzer rattled through the cabin. "What does that mean?" Quinn hollered. The pilot's viewscreen flashed red, and words appeared on it: "Drone altitude inadequate. Abort?"

She slapped the mute button. "Liz, it says your altitude is inadequate!"

"I know," Tony said. "The power is really low. With four of us on board, the rotors aren't getting us high enough."

"Tony! I was starting to think you weren't there," Quinn said.

Tony laughed harshly. "Me, too."

"What do we do?" Quinn asked.

"Nothing you can do," Tony replied flatly. "Set the shuttle to return to the ship."

"Find a safe place to wait, and we'll come get you."

Muffled sounds issued from the speakers, then another voice spoke. "Quinn, this is Liz. We don't have enough power to land. We've got parachutes, but we're over the city, so if we land safely, we'll be captured before Lou can get to us."

"What?" Lead formed in Quinn's belly, anchoring her to the seat like a high-G launch. "Okay, we'll have to mount another prison break."

Francine reached across and muted the mic. "Do you know what the stats are on unpowered drone landings? They're terrible. Chutes almost never deploy properly. If we can't get them, they aren't going to make it to prison."

"What?" Buzzing filled Quinn's ears. Tony and his family were going to die because of her? "No! We can fix this. Tell me how to fix it."

"There's nothing—" Tony's voice broke off, followed by more muffled noises.

"What are they doing over there?" Quinn asked.

Francine shrugged. "My guess is there's a way to save them, but it will be dangerous to the shuttle, and Tony's trying to convince them not to try it."

Quinn slapped her hand down on the armrest. "Stop it! All of you. Tell me how to fix this."

"It's a crazy maneuver for a novice pilot," Tony said. "If one of us were over there..."

"I don't care! You wouldn't be there if it weren't for us. We're going to get you out of this!"

Francine swallowed heavily, her face turning a little green. "On second thought, maybe they're right. Maybe we should let them land and send someone down to get them later. I might be able to make a deal with someone if we need to. My family has contacts on Hadriana, too."

"No," Quinn said. "We are not going to let them plummet to their deaths. You decided to join us, so now you're stuck here. Liz, tell me what to do."

"Are you sure?" Francine jerked her head toward the back of the shuttle.

Breath caught in Quinn's throat. Her children were on board. If she screwed this up, they'd all be dead. "How dangerous is this—I mean, to the shuttle?" Liz started to answer, but Quinn spoke over her. "Not that my life is more important than yours, but my kids are here! If it was just me, I'd do it, no questions asked."

"You'll be fine," Liz said breezily. "The shuttle has all kinds of safety protocols built in. You won't crash."

Quinn glanced back at Lucas. The boy nodded. "You can do this, Mom. I know you can."

"Besides, Lou would kill us if we came back without her family." Quinn snorted. "All right, Liz, I've already cheated death once. I can do it again."

"Okay, Maerk has programmed the sequence. He's uploading it to the shuttle now. It will get you to the right altitude. Then you'll have to do the rest. You'll get in front of us, activate the scoop, and hold it steady until we're aboard. This is much lower than we usually do retrievals, so it's going to be rough. Just keep the shuttle steady."

"Roger." An icon appeared onscreen, and Quinn's finger hovered over it. "Ready?" She glanced at Francine and back at Lucas. They both nodded. "Go." Her finger mashed the screen.

The ship nosed down, dropping like a stone. They lifted out of their seats, the restraints cutting into shoulder and hip. Through the viewscreen, the land masses grew as they dropped lower. And lower.

"There it is!" Francine pointed through the viewscreen. The shuttle abruptly nosed up again, forcing them down in the seats.

Quinn breathed deep, trying to keep the nausea at bay. "All I can see is— Oh, there they are!"

The shuttle flattened out, but the ride didn't get any smoother. All around them, metal and plastic rattled. The comtab jittered across the top of the console. Quinn caught it as it tumbled off the edge.

"Quinn." Liz's voice cut through the noise. "You're right above us. Now you'll get in front of us and drop the scoop. Keep the shuttle steady. The auto-pilot should take care of it, but you might need to override the low-speed alerts."

"Okaaaay." Quinn drew the word out. She looked at Francine.

"Isn't that dangerous? I thought she said the safety protocols would keep us from crashing? If we override them..."

"Nothing to worry about!" Liz said with a cheerful laugh. "We do this all the time. You'll be fine."

Was that muffled swearing in the background?

The shuttle swooped over the drone then braked precipitously. Alerts flared. Klaxons blared. Quinn slapped the mute buttons as fast as her fingers would move. "Low-speed alert," she read. "Low-altitude alert. Proximity alert."

"Shuttle *michael tango ex-ray four niner one*," a new voice snapped out. "You are too low. Airspace over Hadriana City is restricted below three thousand meters. Climb and maintain four-two thousand."

"Air traffic control. I'll take this." Francine swiped a screen to her side of the console and slapped a button. "Acknowledged, Hadriana City. We're experiencing some difficulty with our engines. Attempting to climb."

"Sending coordinates for emergency landing sites," the voice said.

"Not necessary, Hadriana," Francine said, her voice calm and smooth. "Our engineer is making some adjustments. We'll be..."

Quinn tuned out the conversation, focusing on the screens before her. "Liz, the airspeed indicator is in the red! What do I do?"

"Hold course!" Liz called back. "We're almost there!"

A massive *thunk* shook the shuttle. "What was that?" Quinn cried.

"Just the scoop," Liz said.

"No, it wasn't," Tony's voice came through, thin and distant. "Abort, Quinn!"

"What? Tony?" Quinn yelled. "Tony!"

"Ignore that," Liz said. "Tony's been out of the loop too long. We've done some significant upgra—" The word cut off with a little yelp. Then she continued, as if nothing had happened. "He doesn't know what he's talking about. It's fine."

"Let me talk to him!" Quinn demanded.

"Almost there!" Liz said. "You can chat when we're aboard."

The ship jerked again. The comtab crashed to the floor.

"—a minor adjustment." Francine's voice cracked on 'minor.' "Almost there. Thank you for your patience, Hadriana."

"Shuttle *michael tango ex-ray four niner one!*" the controller yelled. "PULL U—"

Francine slapped the screen and cut him off mid-word. "Oh, shut up."

"We're dropping!" Quinn shouted.

"Keep it steady!" Francine cried. "Isn't that what she said?"

"Easier said than done!" Quinn pulled back on the stick. Another alarm blared. *Maintain scoop distance* flashed across the screen. "*Futz!*" Quinn froze, then edged the stick forward again. The warning disappeared, replaced by the flashing low-altitude banner again.

"Shuttle *michael tango ex-ray four niner one.*" Another new voice joined the chaos. "This is Federation Security. Proceed to heading—"

Both women slammed their hands on the mute button. "SHUT UP!"

"What?" the voice cried.

Quinn slapped the button again, cutting off the transmission.

Crack!

The shuttle swooped upward. The G-meter swung into the red and they were crushed into their chairs. "What's happening?" Quinn yelled. Or tried to yell. The air was forced out of her lungs. Her vision started to darken around the edges. Roaring in her ears drowned out everything else.

CHAPTER 33

FREEFALL. Her arms floated, weightless. Only the seat restraints kept her from drifting across the cabin.

Gravity returned, slamming her back into the seat. The comtab she'd dropped earlier crashed to the floor again, the face shattering. Quinn looked to her right. Francine hung in her harness, her face blank.

"What happened?" Quinn whispered.

"I think we made it," Lucas said.

Quinn's head whipped around. She's almost forgotten her son was there. "Yeah, but did they?"

Lucas pointed forward. Quinn's eyes followed his gesture to the console. A green banner across the top advertised, "Drone secure."

"Liz, you okay?" she called through the shuttle intercom. If they were secure inside the shuttle, they should be able to hear and respond.

"We're alive," Dareen said.

"All four of you?" Quinn demanded.

"All four of us," Tony said tiredly.

Heaving a sigh of relief, she swiped the screen, searching for the shuttle status.

"Shuttle *michael tango ex-ray four niner one*, this is the *Peregrine*," Lou's voice said. "What the hell kind of stunt are you pulling?"

Quinn scrambled for the comms and hit the respond button. "This is shuttle *michael tango ex-ray four niner one*. No stunts, ma'am. We'd like to *ronday-voodoo*. Mission complete."

———

QUINN SAT on the worn couch. Ellianne's curls brushed across her arm, rasping her jump-sensitive skin. She glanced at Tony, huddled in the other corner. He groaned, cradling his head in his hands. As soon as the shuttle had docked, Lou had raced for the jump point, ignoring the queues and complaints from Hadriana Prime. Tony had only managed to chug two beers before they jumped. Quinn didn't know where they were now, but as long as it wasn't Federation territory, she didn't really care.

"Pain patch," Lou dropped a flimsy square in Quinn's lap. Bright red letters advertised "extra strength."

"Is that going to be enough?" Quinn ripped the package open.

"No," Lou replied. "He'll be sick for a couple days. But we need him now."

Quinn leaned over and applied the patch to Tony's neck. She smoothed it on as carefully as she could, trying not to jostle him in any way.

"Young man, take your sister to your cabin, please," Lou said to Lucas, who was sitting across the room. "The adults need to chat."

Lucas looked at his mother. Quinn nodded. He sighed but gathered up his comtab and stood. Ellianne gave Quinn a quick hug and bounced up. "Can we play Tin-tar?" She took her brother's hand.

"Sure." Lucas heaved an exaggerated sigh and shot a narrow-eyed glare at Lou as they left.

Lou watched the kids depart, the caat leisurely following, then took the armchair at the end of the low table. She stared across the worn plastic at Quinn and Tony. "I want to hear your version of events."

Quinn glanced at Tony. He gave her a "go for it" gesture and leaned his head against the back of the couch, eyes closed.

"You know about Dareen?" Quinn asked, stalling for time.

"Yes, she, Liz, and Maerk gave me their report as soon as we jumped."

"So, you know she ran into Lucas in Hadriana City?" At Lou's nod, Quinn gave her a rundown on the events of the previous night. "Once we got back to the safehouse, they went looking for Dareen. I stayed with the kids until Tony sent the car to take me to the shuttle port. Then we launched, scooped up the drone, and came back to the ship."

Lou drummed her fingers on the table. "You launched, scooped the drone, and came home," she repeated. "I seem to have heard something about rocket launchers, Federation agents, and low-altitude maneuvers."

Quinn nodded. "Like I said, we launched, scooped the drone, and—"

"Came home," Lou overrode her. "What's your assessment of the, er, decision-making process that occurred on the drone?"

"I—I wasn't there, so I'm not sure my input has any value." Quinn darted a glance at Tony.

His lips quirked.

"Spoken like a true Federation officer." Lou harrumphed. "Do your best to stay out of trouble."

"Hey." Quinn launched to her feet. "I didn't do anything wrong. I got myself and my children off that rock, and I rescued your floundering drone. Do you have a problem with that?"

Lou snorted a laugh. "No, I do not. You did well. And I'm impressed you classify destroying two shuttles and three cars as 'nothing wrong.' That's Marconi-level chutzpah." She put her hands flat on the table and leaned toward Quinn. "But right now, I am trying to assess the degree of impairment experienced by three of my crew. If you could give me your honest assessment, that would be helpful."

Deflated, Quinn dropped back to the couch. "I think that device is dangerous. Liz was totally irrational at times. They did something to Tony—I don't know if they knocked him out or tied him up or what, but they wouldn't let me talk to him. And that drone is tiny enough… If he was conscious, I should have been able to hear him over the comtab." She looked at Tony.

He dipped his chin in the tiniest of nods. "Liz was irrational, and Maerk and Dareen were egging her on. At one point, Maerk put his hand over my mouth so Quinn wouldn't hear me disagreeing with their decision."

"What decision was that?" Lou asked.

"To do the drone scoop!" Tony jerked upright then froze, wincing in pain. He took a deep breath and slumped back into the couch. "You know as well as I do that a novice shuttle pilot should never attempt a drone scoop. And then with the altitude problem… We shouldn't have done any of that. I tried to convince Liz to skim across the fields and land in the hills west of the estate, but she insisted there was enough power to get to the runway. Then when we couldn't land there, due to, uh, Quinn's visitors—" He glanced at Quinn and her lips twitched in response. "We could have laid low and waited for the drone to recharge." He massaged the back of his neck. "Failing that, we could have retreated to another part of the planet. This whole thing was a disastrous mess."

"But you got back," Lou said.

"We got back," Tony agreed. "Barely."

Lou tapped a repeating sequence on the table. After a moment, Quinn realized she was using Morse code, the ancient dot-and-dash system. She concentrated, digging through ancient memories.

T.

Z.

F.

U. T. Z. F. U. T. Z…

Quinn bit back a laugh.

Lou glared.

Quinn glanced at Lou's fingers, still drumming, and back at her face.

Lou's fingers froze and she gave the younger woman a wry grin. "So, what's your plan?"

"My plan?" Quinn glanced at Tony. She had no plan. She had no idea what would come next. She looked back to Lou and shrugged.

"My plan," Tony said, his voice low and gravelly. He cleared his throat. "My plan was to take Quinn and the kids to the Commonwealth Refugee Center."

Quinn stared at Tony. "Refugee center?" Her voice squeaked. She'd seen refugee centers, both in person and in the media. They were uniformly bleak, barren, hopeless. Illness ran rampant, food was terrible—when it was available at all. Gangs controlled everything.

Tony touched her hand. "It's not what you're imagining. Refugees in the Commonwealth—especially political refugees—are treated much better than in the Federation. You'll be given a place to live, and a stipend to live on. The schools are good, and they'll offer retraining so you can get a job. They might ask you to do some PR work—you know, tell people how much better the Commonwealth is than the Federation."

"I don't know," Quinn said. "I may be a traitor, but I'm not actually a traitor. I mean, I only did what I had to do to get away. I— The Federation is still my home. I don't think I can aid and abet the enemy."

Tony cocked his head, then nodded. "I get it. They won't make you do anything you don't want to do. But you'll be safe. And alive."

It sounded better than what Quinn had been thinking, but it still sounded lonely. "Wha— What are *you* going to do?"

"He'll stay with us, of course," Lou said. "That was the deal when we agreed to help him."

Quinn stared at the woman. "You blackmailed your grandson?"

"I negotiated a deal," Lou said. "He wanted help. We wanted him back. Win-win. If anyone was extorting, it was him. He threatened to blow our cover if we didn't help you."

Quinn looked at Tony. "Really? You shouldn't have done that."

Tony shrugged, then winced. "She didn't believe me, and I wouldn't have done it anyway. But a deal is a deal. I agreed to work for the family. I don't have a job anymore, so it's fair enough."

"I thought you retired," Quinn said. "Doesn't that give you enough income to live on?"

"Sure. But I'm too young to retire. It would be boring. I'm used to excitement."

"Like cooking the Federation books on Fort Sumpter?"

"Exactly," Tony agreed.

"Great." Lou stood. "We'll drop Quinn and the kids at N'Avon and be on our way. We're in the outer planets right now. It'll take a couple days to reach N'Avon. I wanted to give you enough time to recover before planet-fall, Tony. You should go to bed."

"Wait," Quinn said as Lou headed for the door. "Where's Francine? And what about Liz and Darren and Maerk? They need medical attention or therapy or something."

"What about them?" Lou asked. "We'll stop in N'Avon to have some scans done. Make sure that piece of *crepic* didn't do any permanent damage."

"You're going to turn that thing over to the Commonwealth, right?" Tony asked. "I know someone..."

Lou's eyelids drooped, hooding her eyes. "Yeah, we'll take care of it."

"Lou, you'll give it to me to turn in," Tony said, iron in his voice. "You got a dose of that thing, too. Someone who didn't needs to be making the decisions."

"Fine," Lou huffed.

"Where's Francine?" Quinn asked again.

"She's in the brig," Lou said. "I haven't figured out what to do with her yet."

CHAPTER 34

FRANCINE SAT ON HER BED, her legs crossed, her hands folded in her lap. She tried to meditate, but it was so boring. She didn't look up as the door slid open.

"I brought you some breakfast," Quinn said. "May I come in?"

"Be my guest." Francine gestured expansively. "My castle is your castle."

Quinn set the tray on the table at the end of the bed. "This isn't too bad as cells go."

Francine smiled a little. "I guess you'd know. This is my first time."

"This is a standard crew cabin. It could be a lot worse." Quinn perched on the single chair by the table. "Eat while it's hot. Kert makes excellent biscuits."

Francine looked at the tray then picked up the biscuit. She broke a corner off and looked around the tiny room. "I can't believe the Marconis live like this."

"Is the Zielinsky ship better?"

"Gods, no," Francine said with a shudder. "Why do you think I left?"

"I don't have a clue." Quinn leaned back in her chair. "That's probably why I didn't trust you." She paused, looking at the younger woman. "I'm sorry. You saved my bacon out there. Thank you."

"I live to serve." Francine rolled her eyes. She ate the chunk of biscuit. "This is good!"

"Told you." Quinn leaned forward. "But, really, thank you."

"You're welcome. Don't tell anyone I was helpful. Don't want to ruin my reputation." Francine picked up the biscuit. "And don't tell anyone I ate this. I can feel the kilos piling on just looking at it."

They sat in silence while Francine polished off the biscuit. And the eggs and bacon.

Someone knocked on the door, followed immediately by the panel sliding open.

"Good thing I wasn't in my negligee," Francine said dryly.

Lou stomped into the cabin. "I'm letting you go. When we get to N'Avon."

Francine's eyes narrowed a fraction. "Why? I can't believe the family posted ransom that quickly."

Lou shrugged. "I didn't contact them."

"Really?" Francine leaned back against the wall and crossed her arms over her chest. "Why not?"

The old woman pinned Francine with her gaze. "Because now you owe me. And I *will* call in that favor. When I do, you'll do what I need."

Her eyes narrowed to tiny slits, Francine stared back, ice meeting steel. "Or what?"

Lou looked away with a shrug. "Or I contact the Zielinskys and tell them where you are."

"I think I'd rather stay in the cell," Francine muttered. "Fine, I owe you. If you can find me. I don't intend that to be easy."

Lou smirked. "I'm sure you don't." She turned to Quinn. "You, too."

"What?" Quinn squeaked.

"Tony may have bankrolled this operation, but you put my family in far more danger than we bargained for." Lou pointed a bony finger at Quinn. "You owe me."

Quinn gulped. "Uh..."

"When I ask you for help, you provide it, no questions asked."

"Now hang on," Quinn said. "I have kids! I can't provide help at the drop of a hat! And I'm not a crim— I mean, I'm a law-abiding citizen! I can't help you with anything, uh, unsavory."

"Unsavory?" Lou raised her eyebrows in mock disbelief. "Like helping a death-row inmate escape? Yeah, you wouldn't want to do that."

"I— Sorry." Quinn rubbed her temples. "Look, I'll help if I can, but my kids have to come first."

"Don't worry, we wouldn't get in the way of family." Lou smiled. It did not make Quinn feel better.

TONY, Quinn, Lucas, and Ellianne stood in the foyer of a huge government building on N'Avon. They'd passed through the security check at the front entrance, although the caat had drawn some surprised looks. Now, Sashelle sat in a box at their feet, licking her paw and ignoring everything around her. The soles of dozens of dress shoes clacked across the marble floor as their owners hurried to meetings.

Tony shivered. "Don't miss this at all."

"Did you work here?" Quinn asked. "I thought you were 'in the field' all the time?"

"All government buildings are the same," he said. "Big, cold, impersonal. Think about StratCom. Or the justice building in Romara. I worked in that accounting office for two years."

"The people seemed friendly." Quinn's lips twitched. "That Evelyn Seraseek was quite happy to see you."

Tony laughed. "Yeah, Evvie always did have a soft spot for me. It's my good looks and sparkling personality."

"No doubt," Quinn said. "I'll miss you, Tony."

Tony's smile faded. "I'll miss you, too. I'll try to visit when I can. We get back here fairly frequently. And you memorized my drop box code, right?"

Quinn nodded.

"If you need me, leave a message," Tony said. "If it's urgent, say 'We had a visitor last week. I wish you could have met them.' I'll get here as fast as I can."

Quinn tapped her temple. "Got it all cemented in here. But hopefully, there won't be any emergencies. I just want a quiet, normal life."

"The Commonwealth will take care of that," Tony said. "I've turned in that device and filed a report with my department. They've arranged for your intake interview. It'll be someone who knows about Fort Sumpter, and the role you played there."

"What role?" Quinn asked. "I followed directions—did what you said. You saved us."

Tony shook his head. "No, you took charge when we needed you to. Without you, I don't think I could have wrangled that herd of cats to do anything." He glanced at Sashelle. "No offense."

Quinn chuckled as she waved off his praise.

"Seriously," he continued. "I wouldn't be here if it weren't for you."

"I believe that," Quinn replied. "Without me, you'd still be on active duty."

Tony shrugged. "Who's to say that would be better? As Maerk likes to say, 'We are where we need to be.' I have no doubt we both have great things coming."

A tall, thin man with antique glasses perched on his nose strode across the hall. "Tony! Good to see you! And you must be Quinn."

"This is Walten Bourqnight," Tony said. "He'll take care of everything. Walten, this is Quinn, and her kids, Lucas and Ellianne." The caat meowed loudly. "And Sashelle, Eliminator of Vermin, of course."

"Of course," Walten said, as if he were introduced to caats every day. He leaned down to scratch Sashelle's head. The caat tolerated the attention with silent indifference. Quinn's shoulders relaxed a fraction. This guy seemed okay. Maybe this would work out.

Walten straightened and shook hands with Quinn and both kids. He and Tony did a manly half-hug. "Did you catch the game?"

"Not this time," Tony replied. "I was a bit busy. I'll have to catch the highlights later."

Quinn narrowed her eyes at the men. Was that some kind of code? What could they be saying to each other? She shook her head. She was being ridiculous. Tony knew lots of government employees— they weren't all spies.

Tony's comtab beeped, and he turned to Quinn. "I have to go." He looked into her eyes. "You will be amazing."

Quinn threw her arms around Tony, pressing her cheek against his. "Thank you," she whispered. "Come back. Soon." She released him and wiped her eyes.

"You can count on it!" Tony said. With a jaunty salute to Lucas and a quick hug for Ellianne, he was gone.

EPILOGUE
THREE MONTHS LATER

QUINN STEPPED into her quiet apartment. The kids were still at school, so she had it to herself for a few minutes. If she didn't count Sashelle, which she didn't. The Eliminator rarely acknowledged her presence. Today, she lay stretched across the back of the couch. Her ears didn't even twitch when Quinn said, "Hello, Sassy."

Quinn dropped her bag on the table and connected her comtab to the apartment network before heading to the kitchen for a snack. When she came back, an icon flashed on the screen. Two messages.

The first one a reminder from the dentist—she had an appointment the next day. She shook her head. No matter how many times she tried, they insisted on sending those messages to the apartment system, not her comtab. Bureaucracy.

The second message was from an unknown number. She clicked it, and a familiar voice came through the speakers. Her heart stopped, and a rushing filled her ears. Her finger was slick on the screen—it took two tries to replay the brief message.

"Hi, Quinn. We had a visitor last week. I wish you could have met them."

FIND out where Quinn and Tony go from here in *Krimson Spark*.

AUTHOR NOTES

July 28, 2023

Thank you for reading the first book in the Krimson Empire. I first wrote this book in fall, 2019, and it was published in 2020. Right now, we're in the last days of the Kickstarter campaign to relaunch the book.

It's been fun to revisit this story. At the same time that I've been re-editing, I've been writing the prequel (as a campaign stretch goal.) The timelines are ten years apart—in the prequel, Tony was a brand new secret agent, and Quinn was still on active duty, so their relationship was reversed. Quinn was the expert, and Tony the noob, trying to figure out how he fit into his terrifying new landscape.

I'd like to take a moment to thank my original publisher, Craig Martelle. He believed in this project when it was just *The Trophany*, and he published the entire series under his imprint when I had very few fans. He gave it a much larger audience than I could have at that time, and I will always be grateful.

I'm also grateful he was willing to return the rights to me now, so I can weave the Krimson Empire into the larger Huniverse and introduce it to even more people.

AUTHOR NOTES

Thanks so much to my amazing Kickstarter backers. I've listed your names on the next page. Without you, this relaunch would have been so much harder!

I'll be republishing the entire series soon, distributing it through all of the retailers. I also plan to make the books available for sale on my website. If you know anyone who'd like a copy of the series, please send them to juliahuni.com. And if you enjoy hopeful science fiction with heart and humor, check out my other series.

You can find me all over the inter webs.

Email: julia@juliahuni.com
Amazon https://www.amazon.com/stores/author/B07FMNHLK3
Bookbub https://www.bookbub.com/authors/julia-huni
Facebook https://www.facebook.com/Julia.Huni.Author/
Instagram https://www.instagram.com/Julia.Huni.Author/

If you'd like to keep up to date on what's going on with my writing, sign up here. Plus, you can download a short story about Sashelle.

Thanks to my fabulous Kickstarter supporters:

Alice Hickcox
AM Scott
Andy fytczyk
Angelica Quiggle
B. Plaga
Barb Collishaw
Brenton Held
Bridget Horn
Buzz
C. Gockel

AUTHOR NOTES

Carl Blakemore
Carl Walter
Carol Van Natta
Cate Dean
Chicomedallas123
Christian Meyer
Clark 'the dragon' Willis
Clive Green
Craig Shapcott
Daniel Nicholls
Danielle Menon
Dave Arrington
David Haskins
Debbie Adler
Diana Dupre
Don Bartenstein
Donna J. Berkley
E. C. Eklund
Edgar Middel
Elizabeth Chaldekas
Erudessa Gentian
fred oelrich
Gary Olsen
GhostCat
Ginger Booth
Giovanni Colina
Greg Levick
Heiko Koenig
Hope Terrell
Ian Bannon
Isaac 'Will It Work' Dansicker
Jack Green
Jacquelin Baumann
Jade Paterson

AUTHOR NOTES

James Parks
James Vink
Jane
Jeff
Jim Gotaas
John Idlor
John Listorti
John Wollenbecker
K. R. Stone
Karl Hakimian
Kate Harvey
Kate Sheeran Swed
Katy Board
Kevin Black
Klint Demetrio
Laura Rainbow Dragon
Laura Waggoner
Laury Hutt
Liliana E.
Luke Italiano
M. E. Grauel
Mandy
Marc Sangalli
Marie Devey
Mark Parish
Martin
Mel
Michael Carter
Michael Ditlefsen
Michael L. Whitt
Michelle Ackerman
Michelle Hughes
Mick Buckley
Mike W.

AUTHOR NOTES

Moe Naguib
Niall Gordon
Nik W
Norm Coots
Patrick Dempsey
Patrick Hay
Paul
Pauline Baird Jones
Peggy Hall
Peter Foote
Peter J.
Peter Warnock
Ranel Stephenson Capron
Regina Dowling
Rich Trieu
Robert D. Stewart
Robert Parker
Rodney Johnson
Roger M
Rosheen Halstead
Ross Bernheim
Sarah Heile
Sheryl A Knowles
Stephen Ballentine
Steve Huth
Steven Whysong
Susan Nakaba
Sven Lugar
Ted
(The other) Ted
Ted M. Young
Terry Twyford
The Creative Fund by BackerKit
Thomas Monaghan

AUTHOR NOTES

Timothy Greenshields
Tom Kam
Trent
Tricia Babinski
Valerie Fetsch
Vic Tapscott
walshjk
wayne
werelord
Wesley Dawes
William Andrew Campbell (WAC)
Wolf Pack Entertainment
Yvette

ALSO BY JULIA HUNI

Krimson Empire
Krimson Run
Krimson Spark
Krimson Surge
Krimson Flare

Colonial Explorer Corps
The Earth Concurrence
The Grissom Contention
The Saha Declination
The Darenti Paradox

Recycled World
Recycled World
Reduced World

Space Janitor
The Vacuum of Space
The Dust of Kaku
The Trouble with Tinsel
Glitter in the Stars
Sweeping S'Ride
Orbital Operations (a prequel)

Galactic Junk Drawer

(contains Orbital Operations
The Trouble with Tinsel
and Christmas on Kaku)

Tales of a Former Space Janitor
The Rings of Grissom
Planetary Spin Cycle
Waxing the Moon of Lewei
Changing the Speed of Light Bulbs

Friends of a Former Space Janitor
Dark Quasar Rising

Julia also writes sweet, Earth-bound romantic comedy that won't steam your glasses under the name Lia Huni.